Praise for

'The best-written ... ... an Hill, *Good Housekeeping*

'A exemplary crime novel' *Literary Review*

'   ard to praise highly enough' *The Sunday Times*

'   s of excellent character sketches . . . and the dialogue is lively
      convincing' *Independent*

'   ham has the gift of delivering well-rounded eccentrics,
      her with plenty of horror spiked by humour, all twirling into
      uggering *danse macabre*' *The Sunday Times*

'A wonderfully rich collection of characters . . . altogether a most
impressive performance' *Birmingham Post*

'Ev yone gets what they deserve in this high-class mystery'
Sunday Telegraph

'Wickedly acid, yet sympathetic' *Publishers Weekly*

'Excellent mystery, skilfully handled' *Manchester Evening News*

'One to savour' Val McDermid

'Her books are not just great whodunits but great novels in their
own right' Julie Burchill

'Tens n builds, bitchery flares, resentment seethes . . . lots of
atm   here, colourful characters and fair clues' *Mail on Sunday*

'A m tery of which Agatha Christie would have been proud . . .
A beautifully written crime novel' *The Times*

'Characterisation first rate, plotting likewise . . . Written with
enormous relish. A very superior whodunnit' *Literary Review*

'Swift, tense and highly alarming' *TLS*

'The classic English detective story brought right up to date'
Sunday Telegraph

'Enlivened by a very sardonic wit and turn of phrase, the
narrative drive never falters' *Birmingham Post*

'From the moment the book opens it is gripping and horribly real
because Ms Graham draws her characters so well, sets her scenes
so perfectly' *Woman's Own*

'An uncommonly appealing mystery . . . a real winner' *Publishers
Weekly*

'Guaranteed to keep you guessing until the very end' *Woman*

'A witty, well-plotted, absolute joy of a book' *Yorkshire Post*

'Switch off the television and settle down for an entertaining read'
Sunday Telegraph

'A pleasure to read: well-written, intelligent and enlivened with
flashes of dry humour' *Evening Standard*

'The mystery is intriguing, the wit shafts through like sunlight . . .
do not miss this book' *Family Circle*

'A treat . . . haunting stuff' *Woman's Realm*

For my friend
Shirley Gee

Caroline Graham was born in Warwickshire and educated at Nuneaton High School for Girls, and later the Open University. She was awarded an MA in Theatre Studies at Birmingham University, and has written several plays for both radio and theatre, as well as the hugely popular and critically acclaimed Detective Chief Inspector Barnaby novels, which were also adapted for television in the series *Midsomer Murders*.

Detective Chief Inspector Barnaby novels
by Caroline Graham:

Other novels by Caroline Graham:

THE ENVY OF THE STRANGER

CAROLINE GRAHAM

headline

First published in 1984 by
Century Publishing Co. Ltd

First published in revised edition in 1991 by
HEADLINE PUBLISHING GROUP

First published in this paperback edition in 2009 by
HEADLINE PUBLISHING GROUP

2

Cataloguing in Publication Data is available from the British Library

ISBN 978 0 7553 5547 1

Typeset in Sabon by Avon DataSet Ltd,
Bidford-on-Avon, Warwickshire

Printed and bound in Great Britain by Clays Ltd, St Ives plc

Headline's policy is to use papers that are natural, renewable and
recyclable products and made from wood grown in sustainable forests.
The logging and manufacturing processes are expected to conform to
the environmental regulations of the country of origin.

HEADLINE PUBLISHING GROUP
An Hachette UK Company
338 Euston Road
London NW1 3BH

www.headline.co.uk
www.hachette.co.uk

Envy's a sharper spur than pay

Fables: The Elephant and the Bookseller
John Gay

Prologue

He hadn't thought it would be like this. He had thought about killing of course (he had thought about little else since she had entered his life) but in his imagination and dark dreams it had all happened rather differently.

The knife was the same; the one he had in his hand now, slicing and stabbing and driving home. The one he had used during the long rehearsals when he had paced about plotting and planning and practising the death strokes. The movements had been easy then, the blade quick and bright.

Inevitably he had rehearsed the emotions too: as he feinted and lunged he experienced them in embryo; like an actor halfway towards grasping the climax of a scene, his heart and talent not yet fully engaged.

During these bouts of shadow play he was always supremely in control. Excited and lustful of course, elated naturally, but there was never any sense in which he felt that he was not utterly suited to the role of executioner.

But now it had all gone terribly wrong. Suddenly it was upon him and not at all in the way he had expected. For a start the scene was different. Although he had rehearsed in his own room he had always pictured the actual killing taking place somewhere else against a background undefined, but perhaps faintly exotic.

His emotions too were different. They could perhaps have originally been named lust, excitement and elation but nothing could have prepared him for the dazzling change in his mind and body once the first incision had been made. It was as if the act threw a switch somewhere in the depths of his psyche and the voltage leapt. The energy then released could not be compared with that which daily got him through his exercises and normal routine. It was a black, boiling tidal wave, lifting him as it rose, urging him to a greater frenzy so that when it ebbed, leaving him stranded on the crimson bed, he looked up and around him and could not believe his eyes.

But most of all she was different. The way she had just turned up. Almost presenting herself to him, forcing his hand. And her body was different. He had kept his knife sharp, honed to a shining razor edge and had pictured it sliding into her as if through butter. But feinting and lunging through the air was one thing, flesh and blood were something else. Things got in the way: cartilage and gristle and hard, white bone. He never knew which blow killed her. It seemed to take so many.

He crouched, motionless, still humped over her body. Miraculously all was quiet. No one banged on the ceiling to complain, no one climbed the stairs to rap on the door. Trembling now he got up, washed his hands, crammed a few things in a bag, put on his jacket. Gradually as the real world returned so did his sense of the rightness of things. He had only done what had to be done. And if the Fates

2

were with him surely that was just another indication that what he had done was right. He crossed to the door, not looking back. All that was behind him now.

Until the next time.

Chapter One

It had taken him a long while to collect the photographs. At first he had not been at all selective. Any well-known face would do. He had even pinned up people famous just for being famous. People like Jerry Hall. But quite soon that proved to be eminently unsatisfactory. For one thing they were so elusive. You never even saw Jerry Hall. She was not on television or in the movies. And never on the radio. Occasionally there would be a picture of her at a particular night club or disco with a group of people who weren't famous at all. So Jerry had to go.

It gave him a certain amount of pleasure, taking them down from the wall. The ones who hadn't quite made it. He would tear the faces across very slowly once or twice and sometimes set fire to the pieces in a saucer, watching a quarter of a smile, a springy curl aligned with a glinting pupil, turn toast brown, then black, then flaky grey.

It might be some time before the blank space was filled. There was no hurry. He was gradually getting all three walls exactly as he wanted them. The fourth was nearly all door except for some shelves containing his collection of very special books. In one way the wall facing the window was the most satisfactory. Certainly the most glittering. An odeon of stars. He was proud of 'odeon'. He had come across the word in an American magazine and it had seemed the perfect collective noun for his glitterati. He now used it frequently, having long forgotten the source. Unknown words had a quite potent charm for him and he always carried a small notebook 'for jotting purposes'. Many of the photographs were signed, some with dedications. 'Best Wishes Burt Reynolds'. 'With Very Best Wishes Faye Dunaway'. And mentioning his name. His real name, not the name he was christened with which was ludicrously unsuitable. The last time he had admitted someone to his room the visitor had looked at the photograph of Robert Redford ('To Fenn – All Good Wishes') and said the signature was just stamped on. There was no point in arguing. He knew that a concerned person like Robert Redford, renowned for his concern over declining species, would not dream of being so dishonest. The girl never knew why he made her cry afterwards.

The second wall had a definitely lower voltage. Stage and television actors, mainly from this side of the Atlantic. They could not help having a dimmer glow. Hollywood was uniquely Hollywood. Ian McKellan was there, showing in the bony planes of his face and smouldering dark eyes a febrile energy, only just contained. Fenn admired people like that; he knew how they felt. There were actors from *EastEnders* and *Neighbours* and Ian McShane from *Lovejoy*. Nothing from the lighter side. He never watched the comedies. The odd times he'd tried, he'd switched off in a state of extreme irritation. They always seemed to be about failure. Seedy old men bumbling about, plans coming to nothing. Stupid women in the fashion world dressed up like scarecrows and always drunk.

The third wall was covered with personalities. In other words people with no special gifts or talents but who, unlike himself, had had all the breaks. People like Esther Rantzen and Chris Tarrant and Anne Diamond. In the very centre of the wall was an empty space about a foot square.

One of the advantages of living in London was that you actually got to see famous people in the flesh. Once he had been walking down St James's Street and had seen Kenny Everett go into a chemist's. He had immediately followed and they had stood side by side at the counter. When the assistant approached, although she did not look at him he had spoken up promptly saying: 'I think this gentleman was first,' for all the world as if he did not know who the man next to him was. Kenny had looked at him, frowning a little as if wondering if they had met before then said: 'Thanks.' Another time he had been in the lift at Harrods with Janet Street Porter.

But of course film stars were something else. They lived behind high walls guarded by electronic eyes and uniformed men with Dobermans. And spent their days trailing coppery limbs through aquamarine water or lying by the pool toying with a frosted glass, a pile of unread scripts to hand. At night they gathered in flocks, like brilliantly plumaged birds, sipping champagne and gazing out through vast picture windows at the Beverly Hills landscape, imprisoned by their fame and beauty like gods in Valhalla. And that was how it should be. It made him sick when one of his fanzines did a feature on how ordinary some star or other really was. Showed them icing a cake or digging the garden.

He could never keep their picture on the wall after that. After they'd lowered themselves.

The space on the third wall was for himself. He had got the photograph but would not put it up, would not even hold it against the empty square just to see, until he had made it. It wouldn't be right and besides he was superstitious. He was a hundred per cent sure there was a place for him in the galaxy but there was no point in tempting fate. The pictures had been done by a guy in Great Portland Street specialising in theatrical photography. He had come by the address in a rather roundabout way.

To go back a bit, he had first decided to become famous as a writer. He had heard on the radio that many celebrated authors carried notebooks everywhere and, as he already did the same, this seemed almost an omen: a signpost as to where his future lay. But the notations in his book, however earnestly he studied them, yielded up neither the plot for a novel nor a film scenario and he reluctantly came to the conclusion that the well-known writers must have been looking at and listening to quite different people in much more interesting parts of the world.

Acting too had led him up a blind alley. He had sent away for brochures from various drama schools, decided Central and RADA were the only two worth bothering with, then discovered his parents wouldn't pay the fees. His father had always been unsympathetic (he called it standing firm) but his mother had usually managed to get round the old miser. This time she hadn't been able to do a thing and the next day, in spite of her whining and hanging round his waist like a sack of coal, he had left home and never returned. Both schools, he discovered, offered scholarships

– but the problem of finding suitable pieces for an audition and the money to pay someone to coach him had proved all too much. Added to this he had met an actor called Brett in the Salisbury, who had been a Gold Medallist at RADA and was now doing Father Christmas at Selfridges, which he called 'resting'. And five years after graduating the guy was still doing voice exercises every morning and spending every spare penny on mime and dance classes. Brett told him over half of the profession were out of work on any given day and that you couldn't work without an Equity card and getting one was incredibly difficult. Then he had suggested Fenn might try modelling and given him the Great Portland Street address.

At first the photographer had been very enthusiastic. He had placed his sitter carefully in front of black velvet drapes and bustled about with several lamps crying: 'Those cheek-bones are a joy to light, dear.' But as the session progressed he seemed less pleased. He tried to dissuade Fenn from staring straight into the camera, turning his face this way and that, talking all the time.

'We are serious today. What's the problem? Girlfriend hanging on to the goodies? Can't believe that. We're quite the Adonis. Perhaps it's the ozone layer – I know some of you young people get your knickers in a twist about that . . . No? Must be the weather then. Or have we just dropped out of our little bunk buttered side down? Got to have a bit of a smile on at least one of these. Modelling and theatre people like to see all the expressions the artiste can rustle up and the wider the range dear, the more likely there is to be one that catches their eye. So far you've been just a tiny bit monotone, if you get my meaning? What I say to all my clients is, think lovely. It's the light behind the eyes that matters – much more than all the lights I'm using. Think of someone who really matters to you . . . oh come on, you must be able to think of one person. How about family . . . ? My what a darkening of the brow – sorry I spoke. Friends then – hasn't that special person come along yet?'

He crouched behind the Pentax and sighed. Thick as a navvy's bum and twice as unaccommodating. The boy said: 'You were highly recommended to me. By a well-known actor.'

'I believe you, dear,' the photographer lied pensively, pulling on his Tyrolean braces. 'There's been a lot of well-known faces through my cubicles. We still haven't had that smile. Come on – force it for Lawrence. Mmmm . . . that's a mite wolfish. Not auditioning for Hammer yet you know.' Oh God, another frown and a sulky pout about to break forth unless he was much mistaken. Well, he'd done his best. You couldn't bring out what wasn't there. Then he said something he always said at the end of a session. The thought had occurred to him years ago and no longer seemed in the slightest degree revelatory but he repeated it anyway. 'Of course in the good professional pictures the sitter looks as if he's made it already.' He glanced up and stopped in his tracks. The boy was transformed. So might a refugee have looked on being given a visa for the promised land. And only two shots to go. He took them quickly, easily. Just as before there had seemed to be no way of coaxing light and life into the boy's face, now there seemed to be no way of containing it. His eyes shone so brilliantly they seemed to be full of tears, the blood coursed under his skin leaving a warm rose stain, even his amazing bronze hair seemed more alive. Burnished, lifting around his head in a crackling nimbus of light. There was no uncertainty in his smile; nor the slightest hint of vulnerability. Lawrence had photographed the smiles of hundreds of young hopefuls, watched whilst they agonised over the twelve proofs, knowing that the one which went into *Spotlight* could make or break. And there had always been, no matter how cocky or handsome the face, a measure of fragility in or behind the mouth. But not here. Lawrence looked up and met the full force of the smile again. He decided he preferred the frown. 'That's it,' he called.

Now Fenn knelt in his room with a stack of pictures in front of him. The poncey photographer had tried to dissuade him from his final choice. The one where he was looking straight into the camera. Had said it was a bit limiting. Luckily Fenn guessed what he was up to. He'd sussed out nonentities before. Jealous bastards who'd stop you getting on if they could. Like that guy in the Salisbury. He must have known Lawrence whatsisname was crap. Perhaps they worked together and the actor got a rake-off. Well – this time next year it would be different. This time next year it would be Bailey or Lichfield. He spread out the photographs. Even though he couldn't escape a slight feeling of disappointment the multiplicity of images heartened him, seeming to give validity to his dreams. He picked them up and fanned them out with his hand then stacked them again, bent them slightly backwards and whirred them through with his thumb as though they were a deck of cards. That was much better. His face danced by, white and silver and black, cinematically alive. He had

11

rejected the idea of coloured photographs, feeling that, however skilfully done, they would appear banal, straining after effect. And he had been right.

He heard Mr Christoforou – his landlord and proprietor of the Oasis fish and chip shop – yell: 'Post.' He waited a moment, then opened his door and went down the stairs. His nostrils pinched together at the whiff of stale chip fat. On the fourth step lay a letter, the scarlet BBC in the top left-hand corner jumping out at him. This would be the television interview.

He had obtained a copy of the magazine *Contacts* and immediately scored through all the regional and freelance companies. He had no intention of leaving London or of letting himself be used by some cowboy outfit just to get his face on the map. He decided to make some tea and not open the letter till it was ready. His sink, cooker and electric kettle were concealed behind a screen in the corner of the room. There was also a cupboard with a tiny pile of domestic equipment. One cup and saucer, two tumblers, a plate, a saucepan, a frying pan. There were two tumblers because he had had the idea, when first setting up on his own, that you had to offer a girl a glass of wine or some sort of drink. Part of the foreplay, as his books called it. But it hadn't worked out quite like that. Either they couldn't wait or, no matter how much you gave them, all they did was whinge and find reasons why they couldn't. 'In which case,' as he had said to one of them, quite reasonably he thought, 'why come back here in the first place?'

Apart from the screen there was a narrow bed with an old-fashioned oak headboard, a table, a hardbacked chair, a chest of drawers with two handles missing, and a black and white television. Currently the drawers held several watches, leather wallets and jewellery newly liberated from Bond Street and not yet disposed of. He was getting low on cash and would have to shift them soon. Everything was scrupulously clean. Light was from a naked bulb. He had tried a paper shade but it only gathered dust. He was not displeased with the room. It was only temporary. An anteroom. Just a step away from where the drama, which would add meaning to his life, was about to start. Rather like an actor's dressing room where he would go over his lines, apply his make-up and get into his costume all the while listening to the play unfolding on the Tannoy.

So Fenn waited, preparing himself for fame. He knew how important that was. The press was full of stories about young people, some even younger than himself, who had been thrust into the limelight and been unable to cope with the wealth and adulation that had followed. Famous people breathed a rarer air, the purity of which could make you ill if you weren't acclimatised. It was like reaching a high mountain peak without doing the climb. It made your nose bleed and sometimes your veins as well. That wouldn't happen to him. He wasn't easily swayed. People's dislike or liking left him equally cold. Fear was something else. At school some of his peers had been afraid of him and he had liked that. People would do anything for you if they were afraid.

He poured boiling water into his little brown teapot, replaced the lid and sat down looking at the letter on the table and wondering how many people would have had his self-control. Most would have run down the stairs, snatched up the envelope and torn into it. He had decided against applying for any particular position, feeling sure that once he was working in the television centre it was only a matter of time before he was noticed. Obviously there would be some sort of basic training; there were no doubt technical tricks to be learned, but really it all came down to personality in the end. Looks and personality. Mentally he selected his clothes for the interview. Terylene trousers in light brown, nice and tight. His beige jacket with the latest lapels, a mohair mix, lovely and soft. His cream tie with a shine like silk, picking up the jacket colour in a scroll motif, and his shirt fawn (opaque nylon) with a self stripe. (One of the older salesmen in Cecil Gee's had told him that there was nothing more elegant than varying shades of the same colour.)

He poured the tea, added Carnation milk and half a dessertspoon of sugar and sat with it at the table. He opened the envelope, slitting it carefully with his knife. First he withdrew his photograph, then the letter which wasn't very long. It spoke of experience and education; of background and degrees. It declined to grant him an interview. He frowned then began to read it again, very slowly and carefully, as if the first rapid perusal had missed some vital clue. He checked the name and address, thinking perhaps another person's letter had been sent to him by mistake. But all was quite in order. And it was his photograph. He picked it up and sat, feeling as if he had been kicked in the stomach. The sweat on his face was cold. He let out his breath in a long shuddering sigh. He should have known it would be a closed shop. You had to be in with the right people, then you got everything handed to you on a plate. He read the letter again. A degree for Christ's sake. A degree to sit in front of a camera and spout a load of drivel or introduce *Top of the Pops*. A degree in what? Geography? English? Maths? History? He ran through every subject he could think of and was surprised to see, when he had finished, the letter reduced to a little pile of paper shreds and the knife quivering in his hand. He swept the paper neatly into a pile and dropped it, a fluttering snowdrift, into his plastic bucket under the sink.

He felt better then. Able to look at things more reasonably. He remembered reading somewhere that television was the religion of the masses, so they must get thousands of letters. His had just got lost in the pile. It had probably not been seen at all by anyone of consequence. Someone right at the bottom of the ladder, an assistant to an assistant, had answered it. Straight from university; got into television by the skin of his teeth and now making sure no one else gets a look in. Probably overweight and unattractive. Fenn now thought he had made a mistake enclosing a photograph. He realised he was still holding the knife and pressed the catch. The blade vanished and he replaced the knife in his pocket. His tea was stone cold. He poured it away, washed the cup and returned to sit at the table and work out his next move.

There was no point in writing to all the other companies. The heads of department, the power people, would never get to see his letter. He saw that clearly now. There would always be someone in the lower echelon blocking the way. He must use other methods. He had to be careful. It was important not to antagonise people (people who mattered that was); on the other hand if they were never going to hear of him through normal channels, other means of attracting their attention must be found. Not for the first time he cursed his parents. Other people with not a fraction of his looks and style were right at the top of the heap just by being born in the right family. Famous names drifted in and out of their childhoods, reading bedtime stories, becoming godparents, ready with just the right introduction when the time came. And he knew no one. But then, the thought surfaced slowly, had he ever tried? Just because you weren't born in the right circles didn't mean you couldn't break in by other means. You had to box clever. Be psychological. Famous people had needs didn't they? They wanted to be admired, told they were wonderful, looked young, were loved by thousands, otherwise why did they struggle to become famous in the first place?

And he could do all those things. For as long as it was necessary to worm his way in. Once he'd got his foot in the studio door there'd be no problem.

He got up and went over to his personality wall. Male or female? He was attractive to both. Men had tried to pick him up as often as girls. An older man might be a good bet but it would have to be one without a son, and how the hell would Fenn find that out? Then again you never knew which of the people on the box were gay. They didn't let on, like artists and writers. The real top dogs might be a bit difficult to get to; on the other hand smaller fry would not only have less influence but still be scrambling up the ladder themselves. It was important, so important, to get it right.

He moved across to the other side of the room. From there the problem of selection seemed less formidable. Each separate square in close-up reminded him of his lack of success; rebuked him almost. Now they seemed to bleed slightly into each other, making each face as unimportant as the next. He realised then that there was no right way of choosing. All of the people were unknown to him. How could he weigh one against the other? He might as well close his eyes and stab with a pin. He remembered his mother being allowed one selection in the weekly pools coupon and how she had always squeezed her eyes up and pointed with a knitting needle. He had thought then how stupid she was but now he saw the appeal of such an action: of handing yourself over to the Fates. And why should they not be kind? Wasn't it his turn? Hadn't he waited long enough? And the beauty of it was, he wouldn't be responsible. Whatever happened no one could turn round and say: 'Why did you choose me?'

He drew the knife out of his pocket and pressed the catch. Suddenly his hand seemed much longer. An extra talon, winking silver, sprang out, catching the light. He loved the feel of the handle. It was so friendly, always warm and smooth. He knew the precise weight of the knife and could have balanced it on a hair from his head. He drew back his arm, transferred the bulk of his weight to his back foot and stood, poised for a second. Then he closed his eyes. And threw.

'Can we go and see the frozen teddies today? In Marks and Spencer's.'

'No. You have to go to the dentist this morning.'

'Tomorrow then?'

'On Saturday. We'll go on Saturday.'

Kathy started furiously chewing her lower lip. Roz reached across the breakfast-table clutter and touched her hand. 'It's only three days, darling.'

She tried to remember how long three days seemed when you were seven.

Kathy's brother stopped eating for a brief moment. He had so far demolished sausages, tomatoes, an egg, lots of toast, marmalade, two tangerines, cereal and almost a pint of fruit juice.

'Can I have some coffee, Mum?'

'I don't see why not. You've sampled everything else.'

He went over to the cafetière. 'Do you want another cup?'

'Please.'

He poured very carefully into large, Italian earthenware cups. Cold sunlight seeped through the basement window, touching his thick, straight fair hair. He was tall for nearly thirteen and thin, the prodigious amounts of food that he consumed apparently sacrificed to some unappeasable intestinal god. She noticed the tender hollow at the base of his neck, as sweet and delicate as when he was small, and wondered when this changed. And if, when it did, it was a sign that one had finally grown up.

'Do you want some coffee, Dad?'

The Times, Leo's protective breakfast screen, rustled slightly. He made a sound, noncommittal, half grunt, half murmur.

'What do you think he means?'

'I think he means . . .' and Roz mimicked the sound to perfection. She and Guy snorted with laughter. Kathy smiled a bit uncertainly. She had learned, by watching the others, that it was all right to laugh at Daddy, yet did not quite have the confidence to do so herself. *The Times* vibrated, getting ready to speak. Guy whispered: 'Page the

18

oracle.' Roz shook her head at him. They both drank their coffee.

Leo said: 'I wish you could discover a breakfast cereal that doesn't spit every time you pour liquid on it.'

'We have searched everywhere, O mighty one!' Pause. No response. 'Boots and Sainsbury's. Safeway and Tesco's. Even the little Greek shop on—'

'All right Guy, all right. Eat your breakfast.'

'I've eaten my breakfast.'

'Already. You don't usually give up so easily. You've only been sitting there half an hour. I hope you're not sickening for something.' Leo lowered his paper and Roz wondered for the hundredth time why anyone so kind should have been given such forbidding features. When she had first met him she had thought of the Demon King in pantomime. Black brows, almost joining at the bridge of his nose, dark, dark eyes. A beautifully shaped mouth which turned down a little at the corners, making his face look sad, almost sour in repose. But he was smiling now and looking several years younger than thirty-eight.

'Mummy – do I have to go to the dentist?'

Guy said: 'Mervyn's mother has promised him a complete set of false teeth for his fifteenth birthday.'

'Nonsense.' Leo folded *The Times*. 'Go and get your coat. And finish your egg, Kathy.'

'Can I give it to Madgewick?'

'He won't eat it, darling. You know what he's like. He had an egg yesterday.' Roz told herself her youngest child's lack of appetite was only a phase and the fact that the phase had already lasted for nearly two years was nothing to worry about.

'Actually Madgewick says he'd like some chicken today.'

'No he doesn't.' Guy was scathing. 'Cats have an extremely limited vocabulary. You must learn to curb your imagination.'

'Why don't they have false teeth? They never clean them. Why don't cats have to go to the dentist's?' Kathy glared accusingly at Madgewick's basket next to the Aga. He opened one eye and gave her a slumbrous, indifferent glance.

Guy had found him in a dustbin outside a dress shop (Madgewick Modes), more dead than alive, in a filthy condition and with a broken leg and tail. Rescued, cleaned, cared for and mended at great expense, he had repaid them not with gratitude but with displays of quite astonishing condescension and grandeur. He had a tortoiseshell patch over one eye and one white ear, a black and white torso, ginger leggings and a striped tail. Cast to perfection by Nature to play the Fool, he played the King with absolute conviction and, if he evoked respect and admiration rather than love, did not seem to mind.

Leo got up. 'I'll take Guy as you're going to the dentist's.'

'Oh darling, would you?' Roz and Leo touched cheeks briefly. Kisses for courses she thought, remembering his private, night-time kisses. Fifteen years of night-time kisses and there were still lingering traces of the churning excitement which had once consumed her as she had waited for him outside the gates of the Middlesex Hospital.

As a houseman he had always looked tired. They would go to the nearby Spaghetti House, eating the cheapest thing on the menu, trying to make it last but not letting it get cold. Leo was frequently distressed and would talk throughout the meal about what was troubling him. Sometimes it was the attitude of his fellow housemen; men no older than himself who seemed callous and already hardened. More often it was a dying patient: 'They look at you, Roz, as if there was something you could do. As if you could stop it. Reverse things. As if you were God. I don't know what to say.' Loving him, she was intensely sympathetic yet always had difficulty in giving her complete attention to his words. Looking at the hopeless parting in his dark hair, watching his narrow, strong fingers gesturing, gripping his fork, sometimes reaching out for her hand, would leave her so weak with longing that there seemed to be no energy left for anything else. For six weeks he had worked on the children's ward where some of the patients were terminally ill and she had thought then that he would give up. Every time they met he looked whiter and older and more exhausted. But she had known by then that they would marry and have their own children, and found it hard to understand why this did not comfort him.

She looked at him now, tall in an elegant pin-striped suit, smelling discreetly expensive. He carried an extra twenty pounds or so, but easily. His shoulders looked a little bulkier, his waist a fraction thicker, but that was all. Guy came down the basement steps from the hall, wearing an anorak and carrying a sports bag. As Leo picked up his briefcase Roz reached out impulsively: 'Leo—'

'Mm?' He was distracted, already at the hospital, but he paused and looked at her expectantly. Roz felt awkward. Neither of them went in for 'do you remember' conversations, probably because they were so happy in the present. The children were waiting too. 'Will you be late?'

'Don't think so, I'll ring. Come on, Gargantua.' He and Guy started up the stairs. Usually at three-thirty Guy walked to Kathy's school and Roz collected both of them there. She could hear him talking to his father.

'Why can't we have a Porsche, Dad?'

'The way you eat you're lucky we're not all on pushbikes.'

'Mervyn's dad's got a Porsche.'

'Mervyn's dad's a crook.'

'He's not – he's not! He's an entrepreneur.'

The front door opened and closed, replacing lozenges of coloured light on the hall carpet. 'Finish your toast, darling. I won't be a minute.' Roz ran up the stairs and into the long sitting room on the ground floor. The Citroën was parked opposite on a resident's permit. She watched Leo check the road and cross, his arm around his son's bony shoulders. He unlocked the car on the pavement side and Guy hurled his bag and then himself inside. Leo got into the driving seat. Neither looked back. Why should they? She didn't usually stand and wave and didn't know why she had chosen to do so this morning. She spent a moment trying to discover the reason. Why she should suddenly, after years of quiet content, have such a piercing sense of her own happiness. She was not introspective by nature and in any case her daily life, crammed as it was with work and family responsibilities, left little time for reflection. She took so much for granted. Leo's constancy, the health and well-being of her children, her own health and stamina, financial security. What if any of these things disappeared? The fabric of other people's lives was ripped apart every day, why should she be immune? Her previous content now seemed to be nothing more than stupid complacency. She reached out and touched the glossy, white wood of the window frame.

'Mummy?' She looked at the grandfather clock. Fifteen minutes to get to the dentist. The day took over, thankfully demanding all her attention.

'*Mummee* . . .'

'I'm coming, darling.' She hurried from the room.

Fenn walked across to the fourth wall. At first he was conscious of the keenest feeling of disappointment. The knife was vibrating, the point lodged between two glossy lips. There was no mistaking the directness of the hit; it would be cheating to pretend otherwise. He grasped the handle and withdrew the knife, then crouched down until his face was level with the photograph.

She had very beautiful eyes with long lashes, false without a doubt. And her mouth, even with the slight tear now across her front teeth, seemed just about to smile. Of course she had plenty to smile about with her luck and her money. Funny that radio had not occurred to him before, yet now the choice had been taken out of his hands – the more he thought about it the more sensible it seemed. Disappointment faded as he dwelt on the more positive aspects of this enforced change in his plans. Fewer people would be scrambling after jobs in radio, that went without saying, and once established it would be easy enough to make the transition to the small screen. Look at Wogan and Jimmy Savile, to name but two. He might start by being a DJ – any fool could put records on and yak – or he could interview people, which might need a bit of training but there were probably courses the station would send him on.

He brought his face very close to the lovely woman in the photograph and smiled. He smiled at the contrast between her unawareness and his knowledge. He savoured the fact that he knew her life was about to change and she didn't, like a new and rare taste on the tongue. He wanted to rush out, get on the Tube and travel over to City Radio. To go up to her office and sit down and tell her about himself and how she had been chosen to help him; but of course he wouldn't. These people liked everything done through the proper channels, even though they'd often slipped in through the back door themselves. And after all what were a few more days?

He removed the picture from the wall (it didn't seem right now for her to be left with the others) and carried it to the table. Then he went out and bought a new Pentel and some smart blue paper and matching envelopes. He already had notepaper and pens but felt that these were spoiled in some way, unlucky, having been used for letters which had not brought about the desired response.

He sat at the table, propped up the photograph and opened his new pad. He felt a simple appeal would be best. They could go into his future plans when they met. He wrote his address with immense care, making sure each line was precisely beneath the previous one and finishing with the date. It suddenly seemed crucial that he didn't botch this first attempt. The virgin sheet was crisp and smooth. He was aware that he was holding the pen far too tightly and relaxed his grip. With the other hand he picked up her photograph.

He really liked that mouth. There was something almost

defenceless about the line of the parted lips. All to the good. A hardbitten career bitch might prove, provisionally, a tough nut to crack. He brought the face so close that it was almost out of focus, and felt a familiar and exciting disturbance. He wouldn't be at all surprised if, when they met, she didn't feel the same. Yes. He nodded and laughed, looking across at his bookshelf. If the chemistry was right he'd be able to show her a thing or two. Really open her eyes. But he was wasting time. He tightened his grip on the pen again and started to write.

'Dear Roz . . .'

Sonia Marshall switched off the dicta-machine as Roz entered the office, swung around in her chair and folded her hands, in a tranquil manner, in her lap. She knew how much highly strung, creative personnel appreciated an area of calm in their place of work.

'Good morning Mrs Gilmour. Isn't it a lovely day?' Roz had given up asking Sonia to use her Christian name. 'I adore those jeans. Aren't they new?'

Roz was wearing (apart from the jeans) a cream silk shirt, pale grey cashmere cardigan tied around her waist, some cornelian beads and chestnut boots. Her long dark hair, piled rather hurriedly on top of her head and secured with an ivory comb, was already falling down.

'No. Got them in the Armani sale last year.' She seized the guillotine and attacked the mountain of post on her desk. She tried to encourage Sonia to work in the reporters' room, whilst being well aware that the reporters were encouraging Sonia to work in her room. At the moment the reporters were winning.

'I love this time of year don't you? There's something so crisp about late autumn days isn't there? I just can't wait to bite into them. I leap out of bed in the morning . . .'

In the morning eh? Gosh, thought Roz, then told herself not to be mean. She could make quite a lot of noise with the guillotine if she tried, slamming the blade down hard. After a moment she saw Sonia swing back to her machine, stretch out her bony wrists with their charmless bracelets of angry eczema, and start typing. She still talked though. Phrases of ineffable sweetness, punctuated by the thud of the guillotine, filled the room. It wouldn't be so bad, thought Roz, if she hadn't known that her secretary disliked her.

Sonia was ambitious but kept quiet about her plans. She regarded her present position as a mere stepping stone in her career, but while she occupied it was determined to do the job thoroughly. She was quite without perception or humour and not very intelligent, and would have been surprised and distressed to know how nakedly she revealed her hopes for the future. Roz, seeing the pitiful armoury with which Sonia was equipped to scale the dizzy heights of admin, viewed her with a mixture of pity and irritation. This morning irritation was winning. She interrupted a throbbing description of the previous evening's sunset.

'Most of these can have standard replies, Sonia. I've put the number under the clip. I'll do the rest at home and bring the tape in on Friday.'

'Shall I sign the standard replies as usual, Mrs Gilmour?'

'Yes. That's OK.'

There was an awkward silence. Letters were a tricky area. A few weeks ago Roz, who was accustomed to signing a stack of replies at a time without reading them, had

26

noticed a paragraph which looked unfamiliar. She had checked the letter, then gone through the rest of the pile. Nearly all of them had been amended and contained brisk little homilies to the writers suggesting that perhaps their troubles were largely of their own making, and that they should pull themselves together and go in for self-help a bit more. Like a great many sentimental people Sonia was markedly short of the milk of human kindness. There had been a not very pleasant confrontation: Sonia tearfully insisting that at her interview she had been told that secretaries were encouraged to work on their own initiative and Roz saying that although she was always happy to listen to Sonia's ideas (not true), if she dictated a letter she expected to have it typed with a reasonable degree of accuracy.

She stuffed about nine letters into her briefcase, leaving three piles on her desk secured by bulldog clips. The letters on pile one were from people believing she was an Open Sesame to a career in radio; on pile two from people who believed she could get them any sort of job anywhere where all other avenues had failed; and pile three were fairly straightforward consumer problems where the next step for the correspondent was to contact the local CAB or nearest consumer group.

'The London Library rang just before you came in. They have the book you wanted.'

'Oh marvellous.' Roz was working on a biography of the tenor Michael Kelly and had been held up for a week or so waiting for *The Libertine Librettist* by April Fitzlyon.

'How is he coming along? Your Mr Kelly?' Sonia cooed. Her voice was all concern. She sounded as if she was bending over a pram. Roz resisted the temptation to reply: one more tooth through and he's put on nearly two pounds.

'Fine. Er . . . why don't you stay and work in here when I'm gone? It'll be quieter than the reporters' room. You'll probably get on a lot better.' Duffy and his crowd would appreciate that. Maybe they'd do the same for her when their room was empty, as it was quite a lot of the time.

'Oh no – thank you. I love a bit of company. I can't understand these people who seal themselves away from their fellow humans. I mean . . . what are we here for if not to help each other?'

'Well, it's up to you.'

When Roz had left Sonia crossed to the window and stood, invisible, behind the slatted blinds. She watched the black Golf back out of the line of parked cars, leaving a large white RG clearly visible on the ground. Still she waited. Roz had been known to get halfway to the gates, then pull into the side, slam on the brakes and race back to the office for something she'd forgotten. She really needed a personal assistant. Sonia had tried to fulfil that role but without success. All her little reminder notes had been brushed aside. Dashing after Roz with things she had forgotten only provoked irritation. She had even found a personalised number plate, R G 100, in the *Standard*, had rung up, got all the details and put a note in Roz's tray. When she read it Roz just hooted with laughter and said she'd know where to go if she ever got ideas above her station.

The Golf had disappeared. Sonia crossed to Roz's desk and lowered herself into the swivel chair. She opened the diary. This year Roz had kept the one from EMI and disposed of the other twenty. All the record companies and some of the agents sent stuff at Christmas, which was difficult to understand as Roz wasn't even a DJ. Typically the week was blank. Roz had a scruffy notebook in her handbag in which she kept appointments, and there were always a couple of envelopes floating around in the office with things she had to do scrawled all over them. Sonia tightened her lips and sighed. She'd done her best. Who could do more?

She sat up straighter behind the bank of telephones and picked up Roz's chunky No Nonsense fountain pen. She drew the pile of job-hunting letters towards her and the corresponding pile of standard replies. There was a space in these after 'Dear' to insert the supplicant's name. Some of their signatures were indecipherable, but the first one she picked up had signed his name in a very flamboyant fashion and then printed it carefully underneath as well. Sonia smiled, a little patronisingly, and started to fill in the reply.

'You stupid—!' Count to ten, thought Roz, drawing a deep breath. A portly man had stepped straight out in front of her, hailing a taxi on her right. She braked immediately and he stepped around the car, banging the bonnet with his briefcase.

'You don't own the road, you know.'

Better make it a hundred. He heaved himself into the taxi. Don't answer back, Roz told herself, childish jibes like 'shove off fatty' trembling on her lips. She wound the window down and stuck her head out. All she could see were two vast pumpkin-like shapes tightly covered in shiny blue serge. She started to giggle. The pumpkins vanished and the face reappeared, glaring at her as the taxi moved away. Roz let in the clutch and followed. She hated driving in town and was only doing it today because of Kathy's visit to the dentist. Going to the London Library had added to the complications of the journey home. She drove down High Holborn, up St Giles High Street and on to Tottenham Court Road.

She decided to drive home through the park. There were still a few leaves left on the trees but the early November sky was grey and cold. She passed the metal skeleton of the aviary, with its taut web of fine steel, and glimpsed the giraffes delicately lumbering across their paddock and sneering, in a silly sweet way, at people looking over the gate. It was about time she and Leo brought the children to the zoo again while it was still here. Perhaps they could come on Sunday.

Down Prince Albert Road and across Primrose Hill. As she entered her home ground Roz began to feel more relaxed. She and Leo had always lived in North London. They had started their married life in a couple of rooms on the top floor of a terraced house in Mansfield Road. It was ten minutes' walk from the Royal Free where Leo was working. When on call he sometimes came home instead of sleeping at the hospital. There was a pay phone in the hall shared with the downstairs flat. They had one or two pieces of furniture from her mother and had picked up the rest from a junk shop in Gospel Oak. Leo's parents, who disapproved of the marriage on grounds that were forever unexplained, had given them a ridiculously pompous canteen of cutlery from Harrods: a twelve-piece setting with an elaborate design rioting all over the handles. Roz used it every day, getting a lot of ironical pleasure from arranging it around their chipped, odd pieces of crockery and flinging it into the old enamel sink afterwards. She would scrub the pieces then with Vim and a cheap scourer but they remained smugly unscratched and solidly respectable. There was a buckled cooking utensil rather like a paella dish with a handle which Leo called simply 'the pan'. They toasted cheese in the pan and cooked sprats, made griddle cakes and heated-up sausages and beans. They used it for mashed potatoes and stewed fruit and in the summer tossed salad in it. They had even, when Roz had thrown the teapot at Leo one night, made tea in it. She wondered where it was now and if two lovers had come across it in a second-hand shop and were bearing it back to a shabby room with a Baby Belling next to the draining board and a chest of drawers, one of which always stuck. 'God Roz, what is the matter with you?' she murmured. 'It must have fallen to pieces years ago.' She remembered Leo saying: 'Put on the pan said greedy Nan.'

They had eaten when they could. Between shifts at the hospital, before his early morning call. She remembered waking at a quarter to three one morning, to find him sitting on the side of the bed with two mugs of mulligatawny and a pile of corned-beef sandwiches. Their happiness had an intensity usually only associated with impending doom; their quarrels were infrequent and brief, though noisy while they lasted. Afterwards, when they had made love, the reasons for the quarrel seemed unbelievably silly. Sometimes Roz couldn't remember the reason at all. They never quarrelled now. Why should they? They both had everything they wanted. Enough success to reward them for the lean years but not so much that their family life was disturbed. Enough money to live comfortably but not so much that they felt guilty. And enough sleep. At last. She remembered going to the cinema round the corner from their flat at South End Green. A rare treat. The film was *Chariots of Fire*. All around them Roz could see girls resting their heads, in the time-honoured manner, on the shoulders of their lovers. Within seconds Leo's head was on her shoulder, moments later he was fast asleep. She adjusted her coat to make him as comfortable as she could, took his hand and watched the film alone.

At that time she had been reading French History at University College and was in her final year. She had got an upper second and if, unmarried and with a less cluttered life, she could have got a first, it would have struck her then (as indeed it did now) as a pretty poor exchange.

Camden High Street: nearly home. Almost immediately after graduating she had picked up some work doing research for a flat-bound historian in The Albany. An ideal occupation for someone at home with a small baby. He had been impressed and recommended her to his nephew who was working on a TV documentary on the Boer War and needed someone to go through the picture libraries. She was quick, perspicacious and thorough; the nephew recommended her to someone else and the next two years passed in a pleasant, if not very stimulating, manner. Then Leo had qualified and come into a legacy almost simultaneously.

A maiden aunt living in Kent, whom he had not seen since he was a child, had died and left him half her money. The other half she had bequeathed to a donkey sanctuary. The humour of this was not lost on either Leo or Roz and they spent a mad half-hour deciding, if they owned the sanctuary, how they would spend the money. Their list was comprehensive if unorthodox, ranging from donkey boots (wellies if wet) and waterproof hats to porridge with cream, false teeth for the elderly and soothing music for donkeys who had come from disturbed homes. The words palliasse, donkey jacket or 'The Donkey Serenade' had reduced them to near hysterics and Guy in his cot, uncomprehending, had chortled as well. They still laughed of course, Roz thought a little defensively, parking a few yards from her home, but not so frequently and certainly not over such silly things. Everyone had to grow up some time.

She locked the car and stood for a moment on the pavement, looking down the street. Even twelve years ago their house had seemed expensive. They had put all Leo's money down as a deposit and had still had to take out quite a sizable mortgage. Today, even though he was now a consultant and she had her work at City Radio, buying into Gloucester Crescent would be out of the question. A few weeks ago a house, just a few doors down from their own, had been sold for two hundred thousand pounds.

She walked around the corner to the Greek shop and bought a kebab takeaway. Chunks of delicious marinated lamb scented with oregano in a pouch of soft pitta topped up with onions, lettuce and tomatoes and sprinkled with lovely Greek olive oil, green and fragrant, redolent of baking earth and brazen, heartless sun.

As she let herself into the house she knew immediately it was empty and felt relieved. Sometimes she didn't mind Mrs Jollit and the everyday story of Finsbury folk; today was not one of those days. She had the book she had been waiting for and she wanted to start work. She went down to the kitchen. All the debris from the communal Gilmour breakfast thrash had miraculously vanished. The floor gleamed, everything was spotless, neat and tidy. She took a large glass goblet from a wooden cupboard by the window and some Perrier from the fridge, cut a large chunk of lemon, squeezed a few drops over her salad and put the lemon in the glass together with several ice cubes. She poured over the Perrier, tore a sheet off a paper-towel roll and put everything on a tray. Then she filled the kettle and switched it on. She glanced at the old schoolroom clock. Fifteen minutes, then to work. Just time for a browse through the *Guardian*. She bit into the juicy meat. Madgewick jumped heavily on to her lap, purring, sniffing at her lunch.

'You're a pig Madgewick. And you wouldn't like it – it's got onion in.' He gave her a haughty look, stopped purring and jumped down again.

The Perrier was clean and fresh in her mouth. She ate very little during the day and never touched alcohol until the evening. This was partly to keep her weight under the zip-straining level of nine stone and partly because she simply functioned better when slightly hungry. Her mind felt less cluttered, her body light and empty. She finished the food and got up to make her coffee. She used a single M & S filter as she was by herself, then unbuckled her large canvas bag.

This was a fisherman's bag, waterproof and capacious, with lots of sections. She tipped out a stack of tapes. Like anyone with their own radio show – although hers contained next to no music – Roz was bombarded with demo discs from groups and soloists. Ninety-nine out of a hundred were dreadful: unmusical imitations of whatever was currently going over big in the charts. The hundredth never seemed to arrive on her desk. They were returned with a brief note and a list of the top half-dozen record companies. Guy heard them all.

'Just in case, Mum. You never know, there might be another Nirvana.'

As far as Roz was concerned one Nirvana was one too many. She added the top of the milk to her coffee, tucked her book under her arm and left the kitchen.

As she mounted the stairs Roz started to experience the beginnings of a metamorphosis that never failed to delight her. This change reached its apogee as she sat down at the desk in her study. It began with what felt like an almost physical shedding of her public personality. Each step on the thick pile carpet sloughed away, like the useless skin of a snake, a little more of Roz Gilmour, phone-in host, wife, mother of two; nanny, chef, chauffeur, head of comfort stations. By the time she reached the gleaming white door she was brimming with anticipation. She opened it and stepped in.

This was her room. Leo rarely came there. The children never. There was a vast walnut kneehole desk by the window with eight drawers and a green leather top with a gold edging in a Greek key design. On this was a large opalescent vase, an almost perfect sphere of Oriental simplicity. It was filled with dried honesty and beech leaves and some tattered silk poppies. She sat down, her back to the window, and took a long swallow of the coffee. She delayed opening her book for a few more moments while the room settled around her, like the magic cloak in a fairy tale, making her other self invisible.

Although it had been furnished over seven or eight years with bits and pieces bought or inherited and from quite different periods, the room had a serene and homogenous air. Some of the things (a fretwork Victorian mirror, a silver Edwardian photo frame) had been picked up in Camden Passage before it became ultra smart. She and Leo had wandered around, hand in hand, Guy resting in a sling against her heart, exclaiming with pleasure at their finds. Her mother had supplied a tall, narrow mahogany cupboard with diamond-shaped panes of glass which held all her books, and a squashy armchair.

It was a dark room – she had painted the walls bitter chocolate – but lightened by the lovely ivory cornices and a small Persian rug which she had bought in Liberty's on the day she had signed her first radio contract. It glowed before the empty fireplace like the embers of a fire; sienna and apricot, lemon and cream. There was a Sony music centre tucked away in a corner, the speakers facing each other across the room. When she had brought the curtains home in triumph from the Portobello market, Leo had looked at the crusty folds of old forties chenille and said they looked like elephant dung. But when carefully washed and rinsed, half a dozen times, the softest and most subtle patterns of rust and rose, and apple green, had been revealed. She had then paid something like ten times their value to have them lined.

She finished the coffee and put the cup aside, close to a framed photograph of her parents. The father she had never known looked proud and a little uncertain in his wing commander's uniform; her mother gazed adoringly up at him through masses of white veiling. She had been widowed five months later after an airforce accident over the Netherlands.

Roz placed her book directly in the centre of the desk. It was a life of Lorenzo da Ponte, Mozart's librettist and a friend of Michael Kelly. The biography on which she was working was important to Roz for many reasons. She was refreshed when entering the open and sane world of the Enlightenment to which Voltaire and Newton and Mozart brought such exquisite order; and it satisfied her natural talent for research. She sniffed out facts tenaciously and had a very sharp eye for connections, seeing in a letter or diary entry allusions which a less astute reader might have missed. She enjoyed putting flesh on long-dead characters, recreating their patterns of living, their clothes and artefacts in her mind's eye, until she could almost smell the eighteenth-century streets of Vienna and London.

The disparity between what people said of themselves in their various memoirs and letters and what their friends (and enemies) said of them posed problems which she enjoyed wrestling with, and the fact that a great deal of the material was in French kept her grasp of the language fresh and supple. The time she could spend was limited but this didn't seem to matter. She was doing something which she approached with high seriousness and which kept the academic muscle, developed by her years of study, in trim.

She had friends in the media, and one or two in advertising, who asked about her work when they met with a look – slightly wistful, slightly resentful – that Roz had learned to recognise. (No need to ask what work they meant.) They spoke of the novels they were going to write, the plays, the series of etchings that were only awaiting the clearing of the spare room or the youngest child entering primary school, to get set up. But as time went by and Roz's work progressed they spoke of their plans less and less, as if they were bereaved parents who could not bear to contemplate her healthy offspring.

She took a small travelling clock from the top left-hand drawer of her desk, set the alarm for three-fifteen and replaced it. Just before she started to read she contemplated for a moment the wonderfully harmonious perfection of her life. She felt like a juggler passing, with the skill born of long practice, bright oranges from hand to hand. As Michael Kelly or work at the studio fell into her cupped palm, so Leo and the children were flung out into the world of work and school, only to fall again into her waiting hand when the right time came.

She bent her head. Truly, she thought, the greatest happiness lies in doing work that involves the total forgetting of the self. Utterly content she placed her notepad next to her book, picked up her pencil and started to read.

Chapter Two

'And how will you be able to cope on this desert island, Fenn? Are you a practical man? Could you build a shelter?'

Fenn was never quite sure what to say at this point. He had the idea that admitting to being good at do-it-yourself might give the impression he was a bit moronic. On the other hand he didn't want the listeners to think he was one of those limp-wristed types who couldn't cope in an emergency. This was after all an opportunity for them to get to know a little about the real Fenn. The celebrity off his guard. He usually compromised by saying: 'Well Sue – I'll have a go. Can't vouch for the outcome.' Then following it up with a laugh to show there wouldn't really be much of a problem.

'And you're allowed to take one object – not of any practical use.'

This too had caused him a spot of heart-searching. He veered between taking something useless but very witty, like a pair of skis, or something which would tease the audience. Give them just a hint of the style in which he usually lived.

'You place me in quite a dilemma here. I don't like to think of early mornings without my pure mohair dressing gown.' Or coffee from Fortnum's? No – that wouldn't do. The BBC weren't allowed to advertise. A few bottles of my favourite red table wine? Yes, that sounded OK. Quite polished. He had already rejected champagne, feeling it a bit common.

'And a book? The Bible and Shakespeare are already on the island.'

'In that case, Sue, there really isn't the need for another, is there? He's a great, great writer. I rather feel if Shakespeare hasn't said it that means it isn't worth saying.' You had to be a bit more careful with the Bible. He was going to upset some of his fans whatever he said. 'As for the Bible . . . it's as much a part of our English heritage as our stately homes and gardens. I'm sure like all great works of art it means something different to every one of us.'

He was really pleased with this response to the book question. As far as he knew no one else had come up with anything like it. It would stamp him as a real original. Of course Sue would then press him to name another book and he had already decided to choose whatever was at the top of the bestsellers at the time. He wasn't much of a reader (apart from his special collection) and he could hardly – he snuffled with laughter at the thought – suggest one of those.

Music, too, was of no interest. He would take half his titles from the current top ten and half from the box of classical records in the library. He had copied four down the other day and planned to change them once a month. He assumed there were trends in classical music just as there were in pop and he wanted to keep up to date.

He rehearsed all the time for various situations which would be thrust upon him as soon as he were famous, but

Desert Island Discs was his favourite. It really showed you'd arrived. He never tired of going over and over his responses to Sue Lawley's questions. He had created parents, schools, friendships. There was a teacher who had seen his remarkable talents flowering in adolescence and had tried to adopt him. A wonderful collection of friends, 'the old gang', who begrudged him none of his success and whom he still saw occasionally for a night on the town.

It was almost time for the post. He amended the pop half of his record list and put it in his manila folder with all the other details of his new life. That's what's real he thought, as he pressed it to his breast savagely. What you create yourself. That's what's real. He had the strangest sense that inside the folder was, in some indefinable way, the very essence of himself. It was as if, simply by listing experiences and naming names he had transmuted, like an alchemist, the base metal of his personality to the purest gold. It seemed to him that, as people shrink and disappear into the pages of books in animated films, so had he, purged of the dross of failure and hopelessness, disappeared into the file until the warm glow of success would quicken him to life. Then he would rise and put on luxurious flesh and beautiful clothes, and an angel's voice, and come into his own at last.

He opened his door. The smell of frying oil no longer bothered him. He would not be there much longer. No post today. Four days since he had written. It wouldn't do to be impatient. She must have stacks of mail; a woman in her position. Perhaps her secretary was off sick and it was all piling up somewhere. He didn't want to be unreasonable. He looked at the calendar. Monday the seventeenth of November. He would give her till Thursday.

*

On Tuesday the phone-in was on 'Housing'. As always Roz was touched by the fact that so many people seemed to believe that she could work some sort of miracle and produce a home (or hospital bed or whatever) where the local authorities had failed. The calls had been predictable. Tales of years on the waiting list: others, less deserving, getting preferential treatment. People who were in the know. Or had relatives on the Council. And always resentment, understandable, over immigrants desperately seeking a better life. How quickly tolerance for the outcast, supposedly woven into the British character, disappeared when jobs and houses were in short supply. Roz sometimes wondered how long her own compassion, never seriously tested, would survive if she had no home or job.

The programme was nearly over. The Birdman had settled on the line and was in the middle of a little homily: '. . . study their nesting habits. Large areas should be made available – people sanctuaries as it were – these poor souls could be given material to build nests, just temporarily. Then when permanent homes become available they could be dismantled. Or reinforced and kept standing for other poor families.'

Roz had not known whether to laugh or be alarmed when the Birdman started to contribute regularly to her programme. But his firm conviction, that all of society's ills could be solved by studying, even copying, the behaviour of birds, caught the listeners' fancy and, on the rare occasions when he did not phone in, Roz got several letters asking if he was all right. He was courteous, quite brief and she never had to cut him off for bad temper and swearing.

'Rather like prefabs?'

'Exactly! You always know just what I mean, Miss Gilmour. No reason why we shouldn't use mud. It's plentiful and our friends the martins manage very well.'

'But what about when it rains?' Roz kept her voice serious only with an effort. She had just caught sight of Louise in the control room, tweet-tweeting through the glass.

'Well you have to mix it with straw of course.'

'Of course. I'm sorry – I didn't think.' On impulse she added: 'You've contributed to the programme so often and we don't yet know your name.'

She was longing for him to say Mr Swan or Mr Starling whilst knowing such a blissful pairing would be too good to be true.

'I don't care to give my name Miss Gilmour, if that's all right with you. I don't feel able, at this juncture, to take on a volume of correspondence.'

Oh how wondrous, thought Roz, and made the mistake of glancing at the sound panel again. Louise was now standing, her elegant shoulders and elbows lifted. She flapped them up and down, mouthing silent squawks.

The Birdman took flight. A woman from South East Twenty-Six started talking about her daughter who'd been on the Council list for six years and had been discriminated against 'because she had this slight personal problem'. Roz, along with several thousand listeners, was immediately intrigued but the second hand of the studio clock jerked forward, leaving them all for ever in the dark as to the precise nature of Anne Marie's shortcomings. Just as well, perhaps. Roz frequently had the impression that 'out there' was a seething cauldron of frustration and despair and was grateful for her insulated soundproofed box.

She signed off, gestured to Louise for music and announcements, and walked out of the studio and round to the control room. The next programme was on tape. Louise checked the level, started the reel and took off her headphones. She and Roz smiled at each other.

Louise said: 'What do you think his name is?' She rooted in her bag and unwrapped a Mars Bar.

'No idea. I'd rather not know really. Poor old soul.'

'He might not be old.'

'Oh – I'm sure he is. I think he has a council flat in East London with a little balcony. And he keeps himself very smart and clean and puts on a fresh collar every day.'

'And there'd always be a bit of washing in the bathroom.'

'Or on a string line on the balcony in warm weather. And he might have a rabbit in a hutch.'

'But never a bird in a cage.'

Louise looked a little like a bird herself, Roz thought. Her canary-yellow hair stood up in soft little spikes and her bones were as delicate as a sparrow's. She was wearing her usual conglomeration of clothes: black holey skirt, three tattered sweaters, spiked leather dog collar and a badge reading: Trash Head. She bit daintily into the Mars.

'How many is that today?'

'Five. No – tell a lie – six.'

'It's only twelve o'clock.'

'I had two for breakfast.'

'I thought you were cutting down.'

'I am cutting down. Yesterday I had three for breakfast.'

'Ughhh . . .'

44

'And I discovered,' Louise's eyes shone with the memory, 'if you melt one in a double boiler it makes smashing fudge sauce. You can pour it over everything. Like gravy.'

'You'll be sorry when you're forty.'

The trouble was Louise had a skin as translucent and gleaming as the inside of a conch shell and a nineteen-inch waist. An inch for every year. Why should she believe that another twenty years would transform her into a middle-aged matron? Roz remembered what it was like to be nineteen. Knowing not only that you would never, ever be forty but that you were immortal.

'Are you coming to the canteen for lunch, Roz?'

'No. I've got some shopping to do. Anyway, watching you chomping has quite put me off.'

'Ahhh . . . poor Duffy.'

Mike Duffield, announcer and sports reporter, had a penchant for Roz which had been acknowledged by everyone in the station for some time. Everyone but Roz, that was, who regarded his romantic raillery and hot, intense glances over the polystyrene coffee beakers as rather a joke. Sometimes she got fed up with it, sometimes she hardly noticed, she never took him seriously.

'He'll have to languish unrequited today. It doesn't seem to do him much harm. How's your love-life anyway?'

'Oh . . . you know. A bit samey . . .'

Samey it never was. Roz had commented once on the phenomenally rapid turnover in Louise's boyfriends only to be told:

'Well, it's like books isn't it? Once you've read them you don't want to start the same one all over again. You go out and find another.'

At nineteen Roz had been married for six months. She watched Louise check the controls with her deft and sensitive fingers and reflected how nice it would be if the girl was a bit more ambitious. She had a bright, outgoing personality, was intelligent and had tons of energy but seemed to live happily from day to day and have no ideas as to the shape of her future. Roz couldn't help contrasting her with Sonia who had plenty of ambition and nothing to fuel it with. As if picking up the thought Louise said:

'Have you seen Rebecca of Sunnybrooke Farm today?'

'No. And I'm going to nip off before I do. She's got plenty of work to be going on with.'

'I shouldn't go up to your office then. I heard Duffy telling her how much quieter it would be to work there instead of the newsroom.'

'The swine!' Roz couldn't help laughing. 'I'll clear off then.'

'See you.'

Louise was tearing the crackly brown shiny paper off her seventh bar as Roz pushed against the felt-lined door. Just around the corner of the corridor she brushed past Sonia and braced herself for a saccharine blast, but Sonia turned away as if she had not seen Roz at all. She was carrying a tray with a cup of coffee and looked rather flushed.

The letter had come. He had not stayed calm this time but had ripped it almost in half in his eagerness to get the envelope open. Now he sat, with the torn page dangling from his fingers, in stunned surprise. He looked at it again. She hadn't even bothered to reply to him personally. A printed sheet with his name inked in. Hoping he would 'forgive such an impersonal reply' and talking about her 'overwhelming volume of mail' which made it impossible to reply to everyone individually, much as she would like to.

Much as she would like to! What bloody rubbish! His hand tightened around the letter until the bones of his fingers seemed about to split the skin. Clever though. Very cunning the way she got over how important she was. Trying to kid you she couldn't move for fan mail. That every second of her life was full of important, interesting things. Very bloody clever.

He crossed over to his table and stared at her picture. His eyes filled with tears of rage and frustration. And there was nothing he could do now. The die was cast, as the saying went. When the knife had left his hand all freedom of choice had gone with it. Like a supplicant at the shrine of the Oracle he had knelt and waited to be told his fate; to be shown the way. And she was his way.

He sat down on the hardbacked chair. He made himself breathe more slowly, to relax his muscles. The fingers of his right hand were hooked like the talons of a bird. He straightened them out one by one. The letter slipped to the floor. He picked it up and smoothed it out. And then he noticed something.

He had been so overwhelmed by the rejection that he had not bothered to read it to the very end. Now he went through the final paragraph and saw the letter was not from Roz Gilmour at all. From her desk yes – but signed by someone else. The same thing had happened again. Just like at the BBC. Some secretary had taken it upon herself to intercept his letter and send off a reply. Roz hadn't seen it at all. He was overwhelmed with relief.

He studied the cramped little signature more closely. 'Sonia Marshall'.

Sonia Marshall had better watch out. Once he was installed at City Radio she'd find herself having to look for another job. He smoothed out the paper and copied Roz's name and the office number and address into his jottings book, then threw the letter into his grey metal waste basket. He drew his chair up to the table, took a clean piece of paper and sat frowning with concentration. What should his next step be? The really crucial thing was to contact Roz. He would try the studio first. If she wasn't there he'd ring her at home. Or should he write to her at home? Yes – that was the thing to do. She'd certainly get the letter OK then. And he could express himself more clearly in a letter. What with the pips going and trying to feed in ten pences. And she might be put off by him living in a place with a pay phone. Might think he wasn't quite of the right calibre. He checked his change. Three tens and a twenty. That should be enough. It was only a local call.

He picked up his jotter and ran down to the hall. Above the pay phone was a huge trade advertisement for Caribbean soft drinks. A vast black woman in a turban brandished pineapples like hand grenades against an inky sea. Her tombstone teeth were as white as the sand. Some had been inked in, some displayed telephone numbers. The shredded lino beneath his feet was almost gluey with dirt. He balanced his notebook on the top of the pay box, lodged a ten-pence piece on the slot and dialled. Pips. He pushed in the coin. 'City Radio'.

'Could I speak to Roz please?'

'I'm sorry?'

'Roz.' He posed a patient but jocular question. 'As in Gilmour?'

'Oh. I think Mrs Gilmour has left the building but I'll try her office for you.'

Mrs Gilmour. He hadn't thought of her as married. For some reason this displeased him. The phone buzzed several times.

'No. I'm sorry. You might try Friday after the programme. It finishes at—'

'I know when her programme finishes. Look – perhaps I should have explained. This is a personal call. Roz is a close friend of mine.'

'It's you who doesn't seem to understand, if you don't mind my saying so.' Now it was the girl's turn to be patient. 'Mrs Gilmour's not here. I can't conjure her up out of thin air.'

Damn the girl. He didn't know what to say. You never knew when these people were lying. On the other hand there was no point in antagonising anyone unnecessarily at this stage.

'Fine. OK . . . I'll . . . um . . . give her a ring at home.'

'All right. Thank you for calling. Good—'

'Wait a second . . .'

'Yes?'

'If you could just give me her number.'

'Her private number?'

'That's right.'

'But . . . don't you have that, Sir? I mean – being her close friend.'

The little bitch! 'What's your name?' That had got her. A silence. He heard a muffled sound. A bit like a sob. Then someone said something, inaudibly. There must be two of them. He was right. A second girl came on the line.

'Can I help you?'

'I think your colleague has probably explained the situation correctly. I'd like Mrs Gilmour's home number please.'

'I'm sorry. We're not allowed to give personal numbers to members of the public.'

'Oh.' He couldn't deny that was a bit of a setback. Better stick to the letter idea. 'Her address then. I'll pop a note in the post.'

'Or that either. If you write to *Roz's Roundabout* she'll get the letter.'

'I've mislaid my address book, you see. I promised Roz I'd ring today. She'll be furious if I don't.'

'Mrs Gilmour will be in the studio tomorrow. If you leave your name and phone number I'll personally see that she gets them.' Like hell she would. They'd end up where his letter had; with some stupid cow of a secretary. She added: 'I'd lose my job if I gave out this sort of information.'

He thought quickly. 'To tell you the truth I'm supposed to be going there for supper tonight and I can't make it.' That was good. Inventive. The ability to think on your feet. That's what separated the men from the boys. 'So obviously I'll have to let her know.'

'I see.' Pause. That had foxed her. 'In that case I'll be happy to ring her at home and pass the message on. Could I please have your name?'

The pips went. In the few seconds before he was cut off he could hear the pair of them making cretinous, gurgling sounds. He wanted to smash the receiver against the wall but replaced it gently, almost tenderly, on the rest. Control was very, very important. After all none of this was Roz's fault. The fact that he was being blocked at every turn was nothing to do with her. And eventually, he reminded himself, these girls would be doing the same for him. Protecting him from adoring fans. And he'd be grateful then. He might even remind them of today. They'd be embarrassed until they saw that he was laughing.

But, he thought as he climbed the stairs, all that didn't actually get him any further forward. Sitting at his table he briskly scored through: Contact Roz (office). Contact Roz (home). Then he sat for a long time, staring at the pad.

He seemed to be up against a brick wall. He had always thought of himself as the sort of person who was at his most effective in difficult situations. 'Adversity brings out the best in me,' he would say. In fact there was a card over his wash basin which put it brilliantly, better than he ever could: 'The impossible we do at once. Miracles take a little longer.'

He picked the letter out of the basket. He must try to read it in a more detached way. Taking everything so personally only gave him a headache. Perhaps going through it again might give him an idea. He smoothed out the paper. There was something written under the signature. 'Personal Secretary'. Between 'Sonia Marshall' and 'p.p. Roz Gilmour' she had written 'Personal Secretary'. Now there was a connection worth examining. You got to the secretary, you got to the boss. And that would be much easier. That would be a piece of cake. Not to say enjoyable. He read over the glib phrases again in the letter she had, so indifferently, sent to him. One long jeer really. Yes, he owed Sonia Marshall. But it was she who would be doing the paying.

Roz was very much aware of Sonia's ramrod back in the corner of the room. No talk of biting into crunchy, apple-like wintry days this morning. No cosy enquiries about Michael Kelly or Roz's home life. Just a cool 'Good morning Mrs Gilmour' in response to Roz's own greeting and then a continuous, impersonal rattling of the typewriter keys. It was most unusual but not unwelcome.

Roz was already late, having unfortunately not escaped before Mrs Jollit arrived for what she called her daily whiparound. Roz had only once or twice witnessed this whirlwind during which time she had remained, pinned to the wall as if by some centrifugal force, until the storm had passed. She had been reminded of the Disney cartoon 'The Sorcerer's Apprentice', when brooms and mops leapt to their business of their own accord. Mrs Jollit seemed not so much to handle as to magnetically attract cleaning equipment. She would blow out her cheeks with their scrawls of broken veins and suck in her breath with hisses of concentration as she worked.

This morning Mrs Jollit had cancer of the left knee. When, three years ago, she had first come to Roz she had confessed to a terrible pain in her shoulder and said she was sure it was cancer. Roz had been immediately sympathetic. Like many women she was inclined to fear the worst at the onset of any new pain or unexplained sensation, and had sent Mrs Jollit to her own doctor, paying for an X-ray, so that both their minds could be set at rest. The X-ray showed a perfectly healthy shoulder. Since then Mrs Jollit had had cancer of the lungs, heart, kidneys and spleen. Of the nerves and spine and liver and womb. So far the only crucial part of her body not to succumb was the brain and, as Leo said, any disease that could locate Mrs Jollit's brain would make medical history. Interspersed with the ongoing saga of her volatile innards were tales of Gavin, her youngest grandson, on whom the police, for incomprehensible reasons known only to themselves, had some sort of down. Her voice, on one note and oddly unemotional considering the apocalyptic nature of her revelations, followed Roz to the front door.

'I've died a thousand deaths this week already dear, believe you me.'

Roz glanced through her letters briskly. Half an hour passed. Only two were really complicated, involving a bit of research in the files and a phone call. She decided to make some coffee. Paradoxically, after wishing for months that Sonia would stop prattling so that she could think in peace, the girl's silence was beginning to irritate her.

'Would you like some, Sonia?'

'No thank you, Mrs Gilmour.' Rattle, rattle. Tap, tap.

'Please yourself.' Roz got out a cup and saucer, a box of filters and a carton of milk. She loathed the powdered stuff and had a tiny fridge in her office. It also held a white-wine box and a few glasses. She supposed that Sonia's hauteur was intended to bring forth a question. To find out what the matter was. Well, she was damned if she would be provoked. She would take advantage of the quiet to get on. Doubtless it wouldn't last long. The atmosphere was as thick as chicken soup.

'Is something the matter?'

'The matter, Mrs Gilmour?' Sonia attacked her keyboard with great force. Rattle, rattle, tap, tap, thump. 'Heavens no. What could be the matter?'

Roz made the coffee, got out her State Benefit Pension file and started to leaf through. She couldn't concentrate and looked across again at Sonia's back. Ripples of resentment were almost palpable, hovering around her shoulders like ectoplasm around a medium. Roz was just about to try again when Sonia spoke.

'I'm sorry I'm not in the reporters' room today, Mrs Gilmour. They're all out you see and Mr Winthrop's using the room to interview people.'

So that was it. Roz recalled running into Sonia after leaving the control room the other day. She remembered too that Sonia had been carrying a cup of coffee. She took her secretarial duties very seriously and was always overattentive. Roz had asked her more than once not to bother to bring down coffee at the end of a programme. She must have been outside the studio door, hurrying away as soon as she realised Roz was leaving.

Roz felt absolutely wretched. Overwhelmed with guilt. They had been laughing, she and Louise, Roz remembered it very clearly. Laughing over the fact that she and the reporters were trying to palm Sonia off on to each other. She looked across again at Sonia's thin shoulders and felt the keenest shaft of pity. What must it be like to be plain, without much nous in an intensely competitive world and to believe that only by being persistently and falsely bright and sunny would others tolerate having you around? And then to hear two women, already more than well equipped with everything you lacked, women who could afford to be endlessly, carelessly unkind and still win, laughing at you.

The silence lengthened. Roz's thoughts backed her into a corner. What could she say? Apologising would add insult to injury. Being nice or especially friendly would be (rightly) construed as insincere and motivated by guilt. Nothing she could say was going to make *her* feel better. She wondered if there was anything she could say or do that would make Sonia feel better. She closed the Pensions file, rested her head in her hands and thought.

It was not difficult to come up with things that would please. Sonia had been extolling her unused talents, more or less obliquely, ever since Roz had known her. Hints of what she could do, if only given the chance, were never in short supply. Most of these ideas were quite beyond her capabilities but one which surely wasn't was the *Saturday Show*. This consisted of music, interviews and phone-ins with a young studio audience, and went out live the first and third Saturday in every month. Although most of the staff were either technicians or front men there were always a few extra girls needed to welcome guests, flatter, make coffee, serve drinks in hospitality. These were known as the dolly mixtures and were recruited from the ranks of typists and receptionists in the building. There was no remuneration, it being assumed that the opportunity to inhale the same air as pop stars for a brief hour or so was payment enough. Competition was keen. Sonia had applied frequently but had never been chosen. Roz decided to speak to Toby Winthrop.

A couple of years ago, after the birth of their second child, Toby's wife Jill had succumbed to attacks of the most appalling depression. During the six months they had lasted, Roz had spent a lot of time with her. The women had become close friends. Toby was a brusque man and not given to speeches but Roz had been aware of his gratitude. She had it in the bank as it were; now was the time to draw it out.

She left the office and hurried down to the reporters' room. She found Toby, between interviews, surrounded by all the clutter of the newsroom. Chattering telex, silent typewriters, stained plastic cups, spilling ashtrays, plants quietly choking to death in the smoky air. She told him what she wanted.

'This is no time to thrust your macabre jests at me, Roz. I'm seeing subs all morning. That's enough to freeze a man's water without black jokes.'

'Please Toby. I'm serious. Why can't she? Just for the next couple of shows?'

She watched Toby's nose, which Louise had once likened to a raspberry sponge pudding, quivering and flexing itself. It was only marginally more carmine than the rest of his face but seemed to have a life of its own. Experienced staff regarded Toby's nose as an accurate barometer, predicting the degree of heat in the wrath to come. The rest of him, as always, looked like a ferociously used, still unmade, king-sized bed.

'How would you like it, eh? If you were a tender young male, having just survived a night of booze and banging your guitar, not to mention assorted women, eyelids glued back – just had your morning fix – to be faced with Patience Strong and that rusty-nail-over-a-blackboard smile? It can take the enamel off your teeth at ten paces, that smile.'

Roz was silent. It would not be tactful to point out that, as station head, Toby rarely saw Sonia's smile or suffered exposure to her greetings-card philosophy. Cavernous, roseate nostrils closed, grinding gingery tufts of hair. Toby's nose looked stern.

'It's like a basilisk simpering.'

Roz waited a little then said, gently: 'There's always at least six of them, Toby. Who on earth will notice her?'

'Notice her? *Notice her?* She'll stand out like a bloody turnip in a bride's bouquet.' But Toby's voice had gone off the boil. 'Who have we got on Saturday?'

'Dave Winch guesting. Some kids from the Holland Park Stage School and the Street Theatre from Brixton. And Viridiana.'

'Viridiana? Aren't they heavy metal?'

'I think so. It's not my style, as you know.'

'My son's into heavy metal. Relentlessly into I could say. I don't see why they shouldn't suffer for a change.'

'Oh thank you, Toby. It's very sweet of you.'

'But I am, darling. I'm terribly sweet. Just hopelessly misunderstood.'

It wasn't going to be as easy as he thought. Fenn sat, well down in his seat, at the end of the second row. Originally going to the *Saturday Show* had seemed like a spot-on idea. Mingling with the audience he would enter the building then, as they all gravitated towards the studio, slip away and find Roz Gilmour's office. He assumed they'd all have typed cards on the doors. Or perhaps little triangular blocks on the desks with the occupier's name painted on. But it hadn't worked out at all like that.

57

In the first place there had been a dozen people, wandering up and down, gimlet-eyed, policing the queue. He didn't think that was too strong a word. Then, once they'd got inside, he'd tried to sit on the back row near the Exit sign but had been guided (well, forced really) down to the front. Once everyone was seated he had got up to leave, telling the guy at the door he wanted to use the toilet. He'd been shown where it was then, when he came out, the bloke was still there, waiting to show him back to his seat. He sat down grudgingly and was soon swamped by waves of boredom. Before the show even started there was an overweight goon, covered in bronzer and with permed hair, who introduced himself as 'your friendly neighbourhood warm-up man'. Skipping up and down with a mike on a long lead, talking to members of the audience, cracking stale jokes. Sweat poured off him. He made fun of people and they laughed sycophantically, grateful to be noticed. Bum-lickers thought Fenn. He kept his face frozen, giving the comedian a despising look. The man kept his distance.

The show proper wasn't much of an improvement. Mediocrities introducing other mediocrities; screwing their transatlantic voices up to an hysterical pitch as if this would transform their guests into people worth listening to.

The reaction of the girls in the audience to Viridiana made him sick. They were practically wetting themselves with excitement. Then a drama group came on from the East End Street Theatre, faced with a bunch of kids from a proper stage school, and for a bit this looked promising. The Street Theatre were going on about connecting drama with real life and how they were voicing all the anger and the fears of the people, and the stage school came back saying the real theatre of the people was the telly and actors needed training and discipline and toughness. Then one of them said any fool could go leaping about the market place wearing a clown's nose and banging a tambourine and a black boy from the Street Theatre said he thought the other lot were a load of wankers. Fenn (and the rest) sat up, but within seconds Dave Winch had smoothed everything over so you couldn't see the join and the show dragged on.

Fenn didn't agree with having coloureds on the radio or television but he knew that media people had to pretend to be unprejudiced and he was quite prepared to go along with this. Just as long as he didn't have to touch one of them. The thought made his flesh creep. He looked at his watch. Another ten minutes.

The warring theatricals had disappeared and a young girl with tri-coloured plaits was being interviewed. She had just cut her first single which was already number seventeen in the charts. She was explaining that she wanted to expand into an all-round entertainer and was taking acting and dancing lessons, also Hatha Yoga to develop her top register. Fenn let his eyes and mind wander. He noticed the control box. A man was sitting alternately glancing out into the studio then down towards, presumably, some invisible instruments. Behind him a second man had a clipboard. They were both wearing headphones. A couple of girls hovered. He wondered if that's where he would start. In the control box. He saw himself at the end of a session, winding up the tape: 'That's it boys and girls – and thanks. Great show.'

All around him people were chatting now. Rising; putting on coats. The show was over. He got up too. Some of the audience were going up the steps to the exit, others down to the studio floor. Part of the chrome barrier had been pushed aside and people were approaching the compere and guests. The control box was empty now and everyone, technicians, musicians, performers and audience were milling around on the floor.

Fenn joined them. He didn't quite know why except that it meant he could stay in the building a little longer. He listened to the kids fawning on the pop group and gave them a look of disdain. The lead vocalist, Mel Cazalis, his tattooed barrel chest bursting through Japanese leather armour, was wearing girls like campaign medals. A small space appeared in the centre of his exuberant red beard. Sounds emerged.

'Yah . . . I guess . . . that is . . . fine . . . right . . . absolutely . . .'

Fenn circled, unnoticed, the periphery of the group. Gradually he felt his frustration and resentment drain away. He began to feel at home. Secure. He almost believed he was part of the elite already. The little core he could just glimpse through jostling shoulders and flaring hair.

There were tables at the back of the studio – roped off – with sandwiches and flowers and bottles of wine. Several girls were fiddling with the glasses and nervously moving vases about. They could have stepped straight out of one of his girlie mags. They had the same tumbling hair, glossy parted lips and blushing cheekbones. They even had the same teasing expression: part come and get me, part untouched by human hand. Some wore clothes buttoned up from thighs to jawline but tight as a second skin, others wore dresses so loose and revealing it was a miracle they stayed on at all. All of them kept glancing across at Mel Cazalis. Hot, preening glances. Then he saw another girl in a plain suit standing back in the shadows. She looked older than the others and wore an almost indifferent air. He thought perhaps she was in charge.

Where did they all come from? Surely the studio didn't hire tarts? No. They looked hopeful but not professionally so.

Members of the audience were being herded out. People from the show were making concerted moves towards the barrier. A gap was widening quickly between the two. He glanced at the ushers. They were halfway up the aisle, their attention on the two exit doors. Everyone was leaving in a very docile manner. The showbiz group was quite large, each man, guest and host alike, busy displaying himself to the best advantage. All talking, none listening. Fenn gradually hung back. He had no plan; he only knew that he was in the building and to be out in the street in a couple of minutes would be back to square one with a vengeance. He was amongst the last half dozen, still moving along the row of seats. He pretended to drop something on the floor, mumbled sorry as the rest of the row pushed by then, with a quick glance around, stepped across the gap and glued himself to the perimeter of the magic circle, adding his own incantatory phrases to the acolytes' chorus.

'The video was really hot shit.'

'Red-hot man.' That sounded alright. Best just to echo everything.

'Of course it'll have to be edited. That part with the baby's coffin – I mean – the Beeb'll never wear that.'

'Never in a million years.'

'I mean – they only just passed "Serene in Saratoga". And then we had to cut the hari-kari.'

'Right.'

Wine was being handed round. Fenn took a glass, barely touching it with his lips. He drank little at the best of times and today especially would need all his wits about him. He made his way to one of the trestle tables, aware that the tension was making him hungry. The plates were piled with multi-coloured brownish strips covered in little bumps of food. Olives, gherkins, pimentos.

'Mm. Nice.' He selected one and smiled at the girl, posed behind the table ready to refill a glass, offer a canapé, help a man unwind. It was one of the buttoned-up variety. She smiled back but in rather a dim way. He felt a flicker of anger, knowing she'd assessed him, wondered about his status and relegated him to the lower echelon, perhaps as a hanger-on. He would have girls like this for breakfast when he'd made it. Starting with her. The smile became suddenly a thousand watts brighter. The lead guitarist approached brandishing an empty glass that Fenn had seen filled about ten seconds before. Eyelashes like sooty feathers swept glowing cheeks. Her breasts strained against the brocade jacket. If breasts could turn inwards he thought they would have beckoned. She emptied the bottle into the musician's glass which was then still only half full. Turning she called: 'Sonia? Is there any more Sancerre?'

The girl in the dark suit came forward. Quickly Fenn turned away, stepping back into the crowd. From a safe distance he took a long look. He told himself not to get excited. There was more than one Sonia in the world and no doubt more than one working for City Radio. She was a dog and no mistake. But perhaps that would be to his advantage. Make it easier. She looked as if she would be thankful for any mercies, however small. He moved into another circle where one of the loose floaters was offering a tray of canapés. He took one; it tasted faintly fishy and faintly rubbery and stretched when he bit into it.

'I'm mad about your cd.' She gazed up at Cazalis. 'I've played it a hundred thousand times.' A pause, heavy with suggestion. 'Especially just before I go to sleep.'

'Yeah?' he slipped an arm around her and squeezed her breast.

'Before I go to sleep I . . .' He bent his head. Fenn walked to the next group followed by a burst of laughter. Here he found a clutch of far lesser lights and it was much easier to get the girl's attention.

'I say – isn't that Sonia Marshall over there? In the dark suit?'

She followed his gaze. 'That's right.'

Just to be a hundred per cent sure he added: 'Roz Gilmour's secretary?'

'Mm.' She turned away leaving Fenn to assimilate this latest stroke of good fortune. He tried to restrain his imagination, already leaping ahead, seeing in this wildly advantageous coincidence the answer to all his problems. He must play it very, very carefully. He walked over to the trestle.

'Do you mind if I offer these back?' He put his plate with two canapés down on the table. 'I'm afraid the food's always the same at these dos.' That was neat. Implying familiarity. 'I'm sure one mass caterer does the lot.' He paused, then a flash of inspiration: 'Probably Dunlop.'

Sonia looked at him but did not smile. She had been wondering, ever since she arrived two hours ago, why she had wanted for so long to come to the *Saturday Show*. She should have known what it would be like. She had stood in the cloakroom, barely acknowledged by any of the other girls, although she saw them every day of the week. She was wearing her black suit which she had thought so elegant, with a white broderie-anglaise blouse.

The suit had cost Sonia a small fortune in Brown's. She spent a large part of her salary on clothes but the effect was never quite right. She never looked anything like Louise who could part with a fiver down the Portobello and look as if she'd spent the day in Yves St Laurent. With Sonia it was just the reverse.

She caught a sudden cruel glimpse of herself as they all left for the tables. She looked like a crow in a nest of butterflies. This realisation had taken away the little confidence she had, and she had stayed in the shadows, wishing only that it were over and she could return to the security of pretence. Of believing that one day there would be a transformation scene. That one day everything would change. And now one of the guests had come, probably pitying her solitary state, to do his good deed for the day. His tone had been definitely patronising. The fact that he was very good-looking only added to her irritation.

'I wouldn't know. I rarely attend these "dos" as you call them. Helpers are usually recruited from the typing pool. It's just that one of the girls was taken ill at the last minute and I offered to help out.'

He saw through the words of course. Appreciated the defensive attitude. Somehow he had to ally himself with her.

At the moment he was quite obviously one of them. He decided to take a calculated risk. He banked on her own feelings of isolation and loneliness, and her idea of correct behaviour, to pull it off.

'I'm terribly sorry. I . . . I was feeling a bit lost. Girls like that . . .' he nodded behind him, 'so glossy and hard. I find them rather alarming. I'm afraid I've overstepped the mark.' Throat dry, he turned away.

'Oh! Don't go.' Sonia, gracious now that he had shown vulnerability, was smiling. 'It's I who should apologise. After all I am a hostess and so far I've hardly done a thing. Er . . . would you like some more hors d'oeuvres?'

He turned back. She had already forgotten his opening gambit, which indicated confusion. That was a good sign. The situation was tilting, very slightly, in his direction.

'Not really.' He smiled back. 'Thank you.'

'Some wine . . .' He had left his glass on another table. 'You don't seem to have any.'

He hesitated. 'Well . . . just half a glass . . . To be honest I rarely drink.'

'Me too. I mean . . . neither do I.'

This was far from true. Sometimes in her tiny flat, relieved of the need for displays of gaiety, Sonia would contemplate the length of the evening – and, once a week, the length of the weekend – and sink the best part of a bottle before going to bed. Now she poured half a glass for each of them, glad she had lowered a couple of tumblers before the programme started.

'Do you think perhaps we could sit down?'

Sonia looked round. There were hardly any chairs but the steps up to the announcer's dais were thickly carpeted and flanked by potted palms, giving a little privacy. 'How about over there?'

'Lovely.' He followed her across and they sat, side by side, holding their glasses. They assessed each other: Sonia furtively, Fenn with a calm and friendly gaze.

He wondered how old she was. Anything between twenty-eight and thirty-five. Her hair was lank and, although recently done in a very elaborate style, was already separating into clumps and going its own way. There was dandruff on her collar. Her eyes were dark brown and hard, like beech-nuts. Her lipstick was far too bright and she had made the mistake of drawing a wider outline over her own narrow lips and not blotting them out first, so that she appeared to have two mouths. She wore a black suit and a lacy blouse that covered, as far as he could see, a practically concave chest.

For her part Sonia was relieved that her first impression, that he was remarkably handsome, proved to be not quite the case. His eyes, set rather close together, were the most unusual colour. The pupils almost amber and slightly elongated. They reminded her of a goat's eyes. His nose descended in a straight line from between his brows as would the nosepiece of a Roman helmet. His bottom lip was over-full, a bit sulky, and the back of his neck was marked with several acne scars. Both his neck and hands were very red as if he scrubbed them frequently and fiercely. His nails were wonderfully clean and he gave off a sweet but antiseptic smell.

His clothes, she thought, were most peculiar for someone attached to the rock scene. Matching tie and shirt, Terylene trousers, even a handkerchief, rising to three even points, in his jacket pocket. Of course this might be the newest thing (like having ducks on the wall again), but she doubted it. He did not have the supremely confident air, far beyond bravura, of the genuinely avant garde. No. Clotheswise he'd missed the boat by miles.

Fenn had noticed as soon as he'd arrived that all the studio staff were wearing jeans or cords with plain sweaters, leather jackets and, in one case, a brilliant jersey in rainbow stripes. Now he saw Sonia giving him the once-over and accurately guessed at her conclusion. It pained him to admit how wrong he'd been but it had to be faced and, if possible, any damage repaired.

'You don't think I usually go around looking like this, I hope?' He picked up a fold of Terylene distastefully. If he could have held it at a distance he would.

'Um . . .' Sonia's rather dingy skin darkened as she saw he had read her thoughts. Not a delicate, cheekbone blush but an uneven mottling. Her nose seemed to lengthen in her embarrassment.

'I've been for an audition. It's that sort of part. You know . . . some awful little creep, miles out of date about everything.' That hurt but he had to make it convincing. 'I thought if I looked the part I'd have more chance.'

'Ohhh . . . you're an *actor*. But what are you doing here then?'

'Just filling in . . .' Fenn glanced over to the residue of the group, now almost stupefied with drink and festooned with female flesh, making their way towards the doors which led to the deserted offices. He waved. The second guitarist raised a fist like a York ham and mumbled something unintelligible.

67

'Kenton's a friend from drama school. He got me on the payroll to help with publicity.'

Sonia, now utterly floored, studied the hydrangeas. This was a mistake. Hardly concealed behind the large blue flowers Mel Cazalis now had his hand inside the pants of a sensationally voluptuous girl. Far from pushing it away she was smirking with pleasure as if she had trapped, between the silk and the skin, some rare prize. Realising her companion had followed her gaze Sonia hurriedly looked away. Fenn spoke:

'I can't stand all that. Dope, sex, booze . . . they're burned out already. What will they have to offer the right girl when she comes along?' He gave her a wry look. 'Sorry. I expect that sounds terribly old-fashioned.'

'I don't think you should apologise. It's nice to think some people still feel that way.'

'I don't think I could make love to a girl unless I was really serious . . .' He watched Sonia out of the corner of his eye, tugging down her cuffs, trying to cover the eczema. 'But all I'm doing is talking about me. Tell me about you. I don't even know your name.'

'Sonia. Sonia Marshall. And there's not a lot to tell. I'm just a secretary.' Damn! Why had she said that? And in any case it wasn't true. She was personal assistant to all sorts of interesting people.

'Oh come on Sonia. One's only got to look at you to see you're not just a secretary.'

'Well,' pleased at the chance to elaborate she added: 'Actually I work on *Roz's Roundabout*. Research. Follow-ups. Handling clients . . . you know.'

'But I love *Roz's Roundabout*. One of my favourite

programmes. You must tell me all about it. What's she really like?'

That didn't go down too well. He felt Sonia withdraw slightly. So she didn't like her boss. He stored the fact away for future reference. That could be very useful.

She shrugged. 'All right. Like a lot of famous people. Pretty ordinary when you get to know them.'

'And how did you come to start in radio?'

That was all it needed really, the occasional question and interested nod. For the next twenty minutes Sonia talked non-stop. By the time she had run down, nearly everyone had gone. As soon as she stopped she started to worry that she had talked too much; that she had bored him. But he was looking just as interested now as he had at the beginning.

He said: 'I was wondering.' Then he broke off, looking away from her. 'No . . . it doesn't matter . . . you'll think I'm silly . . .'

'No I won't. Go ahead . . .' She suddenly thought perhaps he was going to ask her out to lunch. Her stomach contracted. What would she say? How would she handle it? But his next words both reassured and disappointed her.

'I feel like some sort of stupid fan . . . what I wanted . . .' He stopped again, managing to look shy, hopeful and excited all at once. I wasn't far out he thought, describing myself as an actor. 'I'd so love to see where you work. Where the *Roundabout* really starts.' He added, watching her expression: 'I knew you'd think I was silly.'

'Of course I don't.' She rose to her feet, watching his face and those strange eyes light up. Refusing him would have been like denying a child a treat. 'It's on the fourth floor. Come on . . . we'll have to take the lift.'

He followed her behind the drapes and into the corridor. The lift was small. Fenn stood close to her, managing to imply, without a word, that he would have liked to be standing even closer. When they got out she turned left and immediately left again. Easy to remember. There was no card on the door.

His first feeling when they stepped inside was of intense disappointment. What a cluttered little hole. He had expected sumptuous carpets, a huge desk, perhaps a furry settee. But there was a shabby brown haircord on the floor, chipped grey filing cabinets, a couple of standard desks, stacks of reference books and a notice board with holiday postcards and scraps of information pinned to it. Just like any ordinary office.

Covering one wall was a huge blow-up of Roz (not the picture he had at home). She looked very beautiful. The wind had blown a strand of hair across her mouth. She was bending down to talk to a child and holding a microphone in her gloved hand. She was smiling and the child was laughing back. Pinned to the photograph, over her chin, was a curling cavalier beard made out of black paper.

'Shouldn't you take that off . . . before she comes in on Monday?'

'Oh that's been there for ages. Duffy in the newsroom put it on. When I tried to remove it she said no. Thought it was an improvement.'

They both stood and stared at the picture, separate unspoken resentments briefly uniting them. Sonia wondered how any woman could be so careless about her image that she could think a black beard was something to laugh about, and Fenn was wondering if Roz had, after all, instructed Sonia to write to him.

'Do you have a lot to do with the programme's mail?'

'Good heaven's yes. There's the odd letter of course that she'll take the trouble to answer but mostly she just passes everything over to me. All that compassion that flows over the air . . . if you work here you soon learn to take that with a pinch of salt.'

That was no more than Fenn expected. Anyone who was really concerned about down and outs and incompetents must be a right mug. But he had found out what he wanted to know. Sonia had sent the letter, right off her own little bat. Roz didn't even know he had written. The next approach would have to be much more direct. If Sonia was as well in as she implied, Roz's phone number should be in her address book.

'Happy now?' She was studying him archly, head on one side. For all the world, he thought, like a bloody budgie.

'Well . . . to tell you the truth it's a little bit disappointing. I expected something more glamorous.'

'I think coming behind the scenes in any of the media is a mistake.' Sonia spoke airily, secure on her home ground. 'It's the same in films and television you know. The places where the real work goes on are usually rather sordid.'

'I'm sure you're right.' Then, remembering his assumed profession Fenn added: 'It's the same backstage. Very tacky.'

As they turned to go he touched her arm. 'Sonia – I know this is Saturday which means you're almost certainly busy . . . and I know it's short notice but . . .' He blurted out the rest of the sentence in a rush: 'I wonder if you could possibly come out to dinner with me?'

She looked away. She could feel her cheeks turning red and her throat tightening. She bit back an eager acceptance. People took you at your own evaluation. She didn't want him to think that she had nothing planned. That she never had anything planned. On the other hand if she hesitated or took an even greater risk and refused, would he ask her again?

'Well . . .' She took a deep breath to calm herself. 'It's a bit difficult . . .' Without realising it she had clenched her hands. Fenn watched the knuckles whiten. 'It's a sort of long-standing arrangement . . .'

He knew if he kept silent for a few moments longer she would suggest breaking the imaginary date. He also knew she would probably resent the silence.

'Couldn't you get out of it? Ring him up? Make some excuse.' He took a step towards her. 'Please?'

'You're very persuasive. He won't like it but . . .' She made an open gesture with her hands, indicating the extent to which she had been overwhelmed, '. . . all right.'

'Great! Write your address down. I'll pick you up around seven-thirty.'

But not in these clothes he thought as, half an hour later, he entered a large men's shop near Piccadilly. The audition story had worked once but there'd be no reason for him to turn up in the same gear this evening. He wandered happily around the high-ceilinged rooms, all glass and chrome.

He chose some trousers, narrow and sludge-coloured corduroys, a green sweater with an Italian name tab and a stylish *blouson* in greyish-brown antelope. He explained to the assistant in separates that he was taking the jacket and trousers to the ground floor to choose a shirt and told the assistant in shirts that he was taking the one he had chosen back to separates to check against his jacket. Both men smiled agreeably.

He slipped into a fitting room, cut off the plastic, antitheft device tags with his knife and put on the clothes. They were perfect. They made him look taller. His skin too seemed to change colour, become warmer, almost tanned. He transferred money (nearly thirty pounds), keys and knife to his new trouser pockets and moved the curtain aside.

Saturday was a good day to shop. There were a lot of people milling about. He opened the curtain a little wider. He could see only one assistant and he was trying to attend to two customers. Fenn took a deep breath and stepped out. He crossed the floor. There was a mirror near the top of the stairs. If anyone spotted him he could pretend he was just looking for a glass to admire himself in. Just as he reached the mirror a lift came. The doors opened. He slipped in with a couple of other shoppers and two minutes later was out in the street.

He felt wonderful. He was sweating slightly (he could feel it cooling on his upper lip) but as high as a kite. And he was wearing – he dug the price tickets out of his pocket – three hundred and ninety-six pounds' worth of extremely posh gear.

He got so carried away by his new persona that he only just stopped himself hailing a taxi. His thirty quid wouldn't last long at that rate. He hated the thought of returning to the crappy area where he lived; killing time before he met Sonia. His footsteps slowed down. He was outside the Royal Academy. Warm, free, but boring. Opposite, Fortnum's clock struck two, the famous figures trundling out and in again. He crossed over. Fortnum's too was warm and free and far from boring. He stepped inside.

He moved over the deep-pile carpets inhaling, evenly and deeply, the rich, ambrosial air. A compilation, on the ground floor, of ripe fruits and coffee, of chocolate and spices and honeyed sweetmeats and, overlaying all these, an indefinable scent, a distillation of all that was exclusive and exquisite and expensive. The scent of money.

Just inside the door on the right was a great basket of fruit. Everything was tumbled in, apparently artlessly. Peaches with blooming, downy skins; blushing pomegranates, waxen and pitted; perfect nectarines. They lay on fresh ferns and grasses. Next to them were baskets of tiny strawberries, no bigger than a thumbnail. He wondered where, in November, they all came from.

He moved over to the wine department. Here there were desks and elegant chairs, in one of which a heavyweight in a pin-striped suit was sitting discussing a wine list with a young man who was offering the most impeccable and courteous attention – in spite of being wreathed in his customer's cigar smoke.

Fenn sauntered past pyramids of honey and preserved-ginger jars, beautifully painted in the Chinese manner with flowers and dragons. He passed the cold food section, all sorts of glazed pies, (some with little feet sticking out) and charcuterie. The tea and coffee were in large, dun-coloured tins that looked as if they had been there since the store first opened. Although business was being contracted there was no hustle. A man in a morning suit asked Fenn if he would like any assistance and, on being told no, melted away after making a welcoming gesture as if Fortnum's was his home and Fenn the sort of guest he had been long awaiting.

Fenn mounted a few steps and found himself in the patisserie. Here were rows and rows of wonderfully feather-light cakes; spun sugar and caramel and fresh cream. A woman in a pale mink coat was pointing along the shelves and an assistant lifted the cakes with silver tongs, very skilfully, never disturbing the decorations or squeezing them out of shape. She lowered the cakes into a large box as reverently as if they were the crown jewels. The woman's pug, rolls of brindled fat bulging out of a jewelled collar, lifted a leathery lip and snarled at Fenn.

He made his way to the second floor. Here the scent was different. Frankly feminine, almost voluptuous. Make-up, clothes, accessories. Pure silk and real lace; alligator handbags and French perfume. He touched a nightdress and *peignoir* set: shimmering waterfalls of ivory satin. He imagined the sort of person who would wear it: slender, high-breasted, her skin always faintly gilded. She would have long, wavy hair, expensively tinted and streaked, tumbling over velvety, youthful shoulders. He crossed over to one of the perfume bars.

Afterwards, when he had time to think, he was amazed at what he did. He certainly had no such idea at the time. Around the other side of the counter the assistant was bending, with grave seriousness, over an elderly lady, and was sniffing, alternately, her freckled wrists. Fenn's hand closed over a cellophane-wrapped box, he glanced around, dropped his hand to his side and walked away.

This time he felt no apprehension. He knew he was safe. So certain did he feel that he made no attempt to leave the store, but simply made his way back to the ground floor, the box in his pocket. Behind him he could hear the clatter of cutlery and chatter of voices. He turned and walked to the entrance of the Soda Fountain. The tables were full but there were one or two spaces at the bar.

Suddenly he wanted terribly to be sitting there; to be legitimately part of the crowd that was shopping or whiling away the afternoon at Fortnum's. He had no idea what dinner would cost and to spend any of his money, even on something as austere as a black coffee, was mad. He moved across the crowded floor, picking his way around the parcels and bags lying at the feet of the affluent, and climbed on to one of the stools. He got a shock when he looked into the mirror. He already felt so at home in his new clothes that he'd forgotten he was wearing them.

Behind the bar a pretty girl with a mop of curls and a carnation pinned on her overall smiled at him.

'Could I see the menu please?' At once he felt silly. As they served very little in the way of food it would hardly be a menu, would it? Perhaps he should have asked for a price list.

But she just smiled again, said: 'Certainly sir,' and handed him a large card.

He didn't look at it straight away but watched the crowd behind him in the mirror. There seemed to be an awful lot of children around, all tucking into cakes and ices with gusto. Some were in school uniforms, some in jeans and bright sweatshirts. One child had a baseball cap and catcher's mitt, another wore a Mickey Mouse T-shirt and a horror hand, large and rubbery and hairy, with dripping bloody nails. There were Japanese and Arabs among the

grown-ups and a very compelling American, of indeter-
minate sex, in a checked bowler hat.

'Have you decided what you'd like?'

'Sorry . . . no . . .' He studied the card. He felt now that
he did not wish to order anything as banal as a coffee,
delicious though it would probably be. There were all sorts
of elaborate sundaes and pastries and toasted sandwiches.
He felt quite lost and determined to conceal the fact.

'I'll have . . . a granita . . .'

'Al caffè?'

'Yes. Yes, fine.'

He was about to look at the price then didn't. What was
the saying? If you had to ask the price you can't afford it?
He closed the card with a brisk movement and handed it
back. Moments later she put before him a tall glass almost
full of mushy-looking, brownish-black crystals topped with
a swirling pile of cream. There was a long silver spoon, a
napkin and a bill. He slipped the latter, unperused, into his
jacket pocket.

He dipped the spoon into and through the cream, feeling
the granules grate against its edge. Then he withdrew it,
half full of granita, half full of cream. He looked at it for a
moment – the cream was already taking colour from the ice
and turning a rich, toffee shade – then put it in his mouth.

He had never tasted anything remotely like it. It was
both bitter and sweet, with the fragrance of newly roasted
coffee. The cream had the faintest hint of vanilla which
seemed to emphasise the granita's coffeeness. In the warm
cave of his mouth the flavours remained separate for an
instant then melted and mingled, were divinely present
then, just as suddenly, gone. He took a second, wonderful

spoonful. Then another. Now there was just a small, fawn puddle in the base of his glass which he couldn't get out without tipping the glass up and pouring, which he wouldn't demean himself to do. He laid his spoon down.

Lapped by the sounds of eating and conversation he no longer had any sense of his own separateness. He felt warm and secure. Then, for no reason, he remembered the pile of clothes he had left behind in the fitting room. Irritated he thrust the picture from his mind. It had no part in the perfect present. But it would not stay removed. It niggled, like the first sound from the real world in a sleeper's dream, and gradually the bright feeling of belonging slipped away. Feeling cold he took the bill from his pocket.

Jesus F. Christ! He put some of his loose change in the saucer, paid at the grilled cash desk and stepped out into the driving rain of Jermyn Street.

Chapter Three

'What an absolutely marvellous smell.'

Outside everything was bleak. A cast-iron November sky; black and spiky plane trees. Inside Roz's office the air was like a spring day. Warm and green and fresh with the opening of flowers and blossom.

'Oh . . .' Sonia spoke casually but her face and neck turned red with pleasure. 'Do you like it?'

'It's heavenly. What's it called?'

Sonia's brows fretted as if fifty bottles had to be considered each morning before a choice could be made.

'Ummm.' She turned her hand over and sniffed the scaly skin, 'Joy . . . I think . . .'

'Joy! My God. How do you do it? I think we'd have to take out a second mortgage before I could afford Joy.'

Sonia gave Roz a hard, cool stare. The remark about the reporters' room still rankled and Roz needn't think sucking up to her would cancel it out.

'Gracious Mrs Gilmour, I never buy my own perfume.' This was nothing more than the truth. After rent, clothes, fares and a bottle or two there never seemed to be anything left for frivolities. 'My boyfriend gave it to me. On Saturday evening actually.' She fumbled in her bag. 'Perhaps you'd like to try some?'

She passed the box casually over. Roz's face. It was worth losing a spot of scent for. Roz took the box hesitantly.

'Is it a birthday present?'

'Oh no. No special occasion. He's just like that.' Her tone suggested an endless caravan of exotic gifts. Apes and ivory and peacocks. Jewelled robes and sandalwood. Silks from Cathay.

Roz undid the stopper. 'Are you sure?'

'Help yourself.' Sonia started typing.

Roz tipped the bottle quickly once on to her wrist and restoppered it. She rubbed her wrists together then put the bottle back on Sonia's desk.

'That's very sweet of you. He must be terribly rich.'

'Who?'

'Your boyfriend of course.'

'I don't think so. He lives over a chip shop in Islington. Why – is it expensive?'

'Are you kidding? A bottle that size must have set him back a couple of hundred.'

Sonia stopped typing. She stared across at Roz, swallowing hard. 'Pounds?' It was no more than a squeak.

'Didn't you know?'

Sonia, now quite pale, shook her head. No wonder Fenn hadn't been able to take her out to dinner.

He had arrived almost half an hour late. She had been ready for an hour by then, after trying on nearly everything in her wardrobe at least twice. She had bathed, put her hair up, let it down, put it up again and painted her nails. Then panicking in case he arrived early she had put her tights on before the varnish was dry and had to peel them off and start all over again. By eight-thirty, convinced he was not going to turn up, she had opened a bottle of wine and was well into the second large glass when the doorbell rang.

She hardly recognised him. She had been carrying his likeness, as she thought, in her mind since they parted, but now he looked completely different. He seemed taller and more handsome and he was wearing the most beautiful clothes.

He stood smiling down at her for a moment then said: 'Aren't you going to ask me in?'

'Ohhh of course.' Trying to draw in what she knew was a huge grin of relief she opened the door wide and Fenn stepped forward. 'I'll just get my coat.'

'Sonia – wait.' She stopped halfway to the bedroom. 'Look – I'm awfully sorry but—'

'You can't stay.' She turned quickly before he could see the look on her face. The look which said: 'I might have known.'

'Silly.' He crossed to her. 'Of course I can stay. It's just that . . . oh, before I forget.' He handed her a white, cellophane-covered box. 'A little present.'

'Fenn.' Her fingers shook as they pulled at the paper. 'How lovely.' She tipped the bottle against the hollow at the base of her throat. A little trickle of perfume ran down the neck of her dress. She reached after it demurely with her little finger then tried to put some behind his ears but he stepped quickly away. 'What a nice smell. You are good to me.' She spoke as if their relationship was already long-standing. 'Now – what is it you're sorry about?'

'After I left you I popped into Fortnum's for some lunch

and to buy you something nice and spent all the cash I had on me. And of course the banks are closed and I've exceeded my cashpoint limit so . . . I can't take you out.'

'Is that all? Heavens – I've got some money.'

'Oh no – I couldn't. Not in a restaurant. What would people think?'

She liked that. It showed he was sensitive. But she hadn't been able to eat a thing since those awful canapés and now her anxiety had died down she was absolutely ravenous.

'I know.' She clutched his hand. 'We'll eat here. There's a couple of takeaways across the road. And a Falafel House.'

'Only if you let me pay you back.'

Now it was her turn to say: 'Silly.' She wrapped herself in a tartan blanket-like coat, picked up a carrier and took her purse and keys from her handbag.

'Hey . . .' He beckoned her with a little finger and, when she crossed to him, kissed her lightly on the corner of the mouth. 'Don't be long.'

Sonia queued up for the takeaway in a dream, occasionally gently touching her lips with a knuckle. She came back with hummous, sheftalia, pitta, salad, olives, Turkish delight drenched in powdered sugar and smelling of roses, and a large bottle of Frascati.

They sat in front of the little gas fire, he on the settee, she at his feet and fed each other olives and, later, pieces of Turkish delight. The meatballs were hot and spicy and they scooped up the hummous and olive oil with their bread. Fenn drank a little wine, Sonia a great deal.

It must have been this, she decided in retrospect, which persuaded her to allow him such privileges, and on their first night together too. At the remembrance of the form the privileges had taken Sonia felt her skin prickle. To be absolutely fair to him he had not meant things to go so far. He had been terribly worried and terribly apologetic, wondering what on earth she would think of him. She also felt that, in these matters, it was largely up to the woman to apply the brake and, if she had not had so much to drink, she would have been more able to do so.

Afterwards he had not stayed as long as she'd hoped (she was looking forward to telling him about her unhappy childhood), hurrying away, she was sure, out of simple embarrassment. But she would be seeing him again soon. He had promised.

She became aware that Roz was looking at her expectantly. 'I'm sorry?'

'I said what does he do?'

'He's an actor. I mean – in reality. At the moment he's between jobs so he's doing PR for a rock group.'

'Well,' Roz stood up and started to dump letters and folders into her capacious bag, 'If I were you I'd hang on to him. Anyone who lets Joy be that unconfined must be a real prize.'

Imagine that, she thought, travelling home on the Tube. And fancy Sonia not mentioning him before. Roz would never have thought her the sort of person to keep quiet about having a handsome swain in the background. It was quite chastening really, how wrong you could be about someone. He was obviously a good influence. There had been barely a touch of 'lo hear the gentle lark' this morning. And the frost had definitely started to thaw. She'd forgotten to ask Sonia if she'd enjoyed the *Saturday Show*. She was glad Toby had let her go. And she had taken a vow against saying unkind things in the future. Roz felt the last shreds of guilt disappear.

At Camden Town she hurried through the bitter driving wind, picking her way through wet cabbage leaves and splintered bits of boxes and rotten bits of fruit in the Inverness Street gutters. At last, the skin of her face feeling almost solid with cold, she stepped into her own front hall. Immediately she was enveloped in warmth. She moved over the deep-pile carpet. From the sitting room the grandfather clock ticked softly. Today Mrs Jollit had included the hall and stairs in her whiparound. The paint gleamed white, there was a very faint smell of pine. Roz shrugged off her greatcoat and went down to the kitchen to make coffee. It was lovely to be home.

Fenn had decided to ask Mr Christoforou downstairs if he could use his private phone to ring Roz. He had already checked with the studio and she had left for home over an hour ago. Getting hold of her number had been easier than he had expected. Easier even than getting hold of Sonia, and that was saying something. Going out for the food she had taken her purse and keys but left her handbag behind. The address book was in there. A Snoopy one – which was pathetic enough, he thought, at her age – but when he opened it . . . A couple who he assumed were her parents, Euston Station Passenger Enquiries (the couple lived in the Midlands), a local dry cleaner's, a female who lived in Tulse Hill, the National Theatre, Selfridges and Roz. The bare bones of a dreary life. He copied down Roz's name and address and replaced the book.

He could have left then before she returned, but for his plan. He hadn't forgotten Sonia's letter even though it had been straightaway destroyed. He would be attentive, act the lover, get what he could and then, when she was madly in love (and that wouldn't be long if Saturday was anything to go by) he would dump her. He pressed the thought of how he would do it – and her reaction – to his heart, like a small nugget of gold. When he woke in the morning now there was first a generalised feeling of pleasantness, then he would locate its source and smile.

Meanwhile, for the next couple of weeks, there was plenty of delicious food – Chinese next time or perhaps Indian – and easy sex. She had been, as he suspected, almost totally inexperienced. He could still see quite vividly the amazement in her eyes, the round O of her mouth, as he had entered her. And talk about eager to please. He could work through his whole bookshelf with Sonia and she'd still be coming back for more. The only thing that worried him was that he'd as good as told her where he lived. It wasn't like him to be careless but he'd been distracted at the time (sending his tongue after some powdered sugar that had fallen down her neck opening). Of course he hadn't given her his actual address and he didn't think she'd really taken it in. She'd just given him a goofy, doting smile. Still, it was a warning to keep his mind on things.

Before he left the room he crossed to his table to look at Roz. He placed the tip of his finger gently between her shining lips where the knife point had made its mark. How vulnerable she looked. He loved women like that; beautiful and successful but not hardened into the career-woman mould or cut off from reality. He knew they would get on, become friends. He checked his watch. She would be home by now. He ran down to the hall, picked up the pay phone for Mr Christoforou's benefit, made exasperated noises and went into the shop.

'The phone's out of order, Mr C. I've got to make a rather urgent call. Could I use yours? I'll leave some money on the table.'

'Sure.' It was not as if he made a habit of it. The boy had never asked before. 'Have you reported it?'

'Yes. Told the operator.'

Fenn hated Mr Christoforou's sitting room and never went in if he could help it. It was like being sealed up in a stuffy, garish box. The walls were smothered with crudely coloured hangings and pictures of Christ in various stages of torment. The Christoforous were Greek Orthodox. Carpets, madly patterned and already deeply piled, were covered with rugs and runners; silver filigree incense burners converted to electric lights hung from the ceiling. There were no books. A vast television set dominated a room already filled to bursting with brocaded furniture and knick-knackery. The phone was on a chrome and gilt cocktail bar next to a shiny little train with open trucks full of peanuts and olives, crunchy bits and After Eights. Fenn closed the door.

Roz had reached the point in her work where Michael Kelly was about to open a wine shop in London. His friend, Richard Brinsley Sheridan, had suggested that 'Composer of Wines and Importer of Music' should appear after his name on the shop front. Roz liked that. She thought, if you could tell a man by the number and quality of his friends what a very likeable person the tenor must have been. She was finding it easier as the work progressed to slip into the period.

The biographer must have a novelist's imaginative gifts and an historian's discipline, and the need to walk a tightrope between the two was always present in Roz's mind. Too much of the first and her work would not be taken seriously: too much of the second and hardly anyone would want to read it.

So real was the scene she was describing, the chattering crowd of men, the pipe smoke, the smell of fresh cakes and hot chocolate and the rustle of journals, that the telephone bell took a second or two to penetrate. When it did she ignored it, struggling to hold on to her coffee-house, knowing the twentieth-century clamour would soon stop. But it didn't stop. Long after most people would have given up her caller persisted. And then – oh God! – it must be the school . . .

The nearest extension was in the sitting room. She ran down the next flight of stairs and flew across to the telephone table.

'. . . Hello . . .'

'Roz?'

'Yes . . . yes . . . what is it? What's wrong?'

'Roz. We haven't met but I wrote to you a couple of weeks ago.' She sat down limply. It wasn't the school. The voice carried smoothly on. She tried to pay attention. Not at all resentful now at being interrupted. Just consumed with relief. The children were all right.

'. . . and when I saw the signature of course I realised that it wasn't from you at all.' A little laugh. 'So I thought a personal approach was called for. Man to man. Or rather,' the voice became softly sly, 'man to woman.'

'I'm terribly sorry. What is it you actually want?'

'Haven't you been listening?'

'I was working when you rang. It takes me a while to collect my thoughts.' Roz sounded crisper now. She was getting accustomed to the idea that the children were safe. She knew that, given another minute or two, she would be growing annoyed. The man started again from the beginning. After a moment she interrupted him.

'I can assure you that anything you received from my desk, even if it was signed by my secretary, came from me.'

'Doesn't she answer your post then?'

'Certainly not.'

He was silent for a moment then said: 'This alters things entirely. This puts a whole new complexion on the matter.'

Roz glanced at her watch. Half an hour before she had to leave. There would be no point in going back to her study now. It would take at least ten minutes to work her way into the scene she had, she now saw quite pointlessly, abandoned.

'If, as you say, you want to work at City Radio I should write in—'

'I've already written in!'

'—to Toby Winthrop. He's the studio head and he'll be able to advise you far better than I ever could how to set about things.'

'I can't do that, Roz. It's too late for that now. You've been chosen. There's no way I can go back and start again. *You're* the person who's going to help me. When can I come to see you?'

Dear God. Roz tried to be patient. The poor guy sounded as if he wasn't all there.

'Look, I'm sorry – I really am but there isn't anything I can do. I'm just an employee at the station. I don't have a position of authority. I don't make any decisions. I can't hire or fire anyone. I just run a radio show twice a week.'

'Come off it, Roz. I'm not just a member of the public. I'm going to be where you are one day. And that day, futuristically speaking, is looming pretty large, I can tell you. You don't have to give me all that balls about only being a presenter. I'm *au fait* with the media scene. I know the score.' When she made no reply he went on: 'How would it be if I came to the studio after Friday's show? We could have a pre-luncheon drink.'

'There's no point in continuing this conversation . . . I've given you what advice I can. Now you'll have to excuse me.'

Roz hung up. It was only as she was parking outside the school half an hour later that it occurred to her to wonder how on earth he had got hold of her number.

Fenn never knew how he replaced the receiver, called 'thanks' to Mr Christoforou, and got back to his room. His legs, his whole frame, were shaking. He moved like a palsied old man. He was gripped by a raging fury. It was like being snatched up by a hurricane and thrown forcefully about. There was nothing he could do about it. His earlier resentment against Sonia seemed to have the force of a zephyr compared to this.

He sank to his knees in the centre of the floor and waited for it to pass. There was no question of disentangling various emotions, or of analysing what he felt. When he closed his eyes he seemed to see a tidal wave of red towering over him, ready to crash down and destroy. He felt very sick. Time was arrested. His brains were clotted with emotion. He was unable to think or reason.

When the storm eventually passed, ebbing away, he sat up – amazed to find that he was not worn out and depleted but narrow and cold and strong, like a blade forged in fire.

He had recognised, down in the sitting room before the tempering process had begun, a moment of real rapport between himself and Roz. A true meeting of minds. He knew she'd felt this too; he had sensed it very strongly. But she had chosen not to build on the moment. She had rejected him and now it was too late. She would only have herself to blame. No use to remind him of it in the future. To cry: 'Please Fenn – don't you remember when we first spoke together how it was . . . I want another chance . . . *please* . . .'

He got up from his knees feeling like a young warrior blessed by a priest before a crusade. He burned with the justice of his cause yet felt almost humble. A mantle of divine authority had been laid across his shoulders. His life, his mind, suddenly became wonderfully unscrambled. He crossed to the table and carefully, even tenderly, picked up Roz's picture. He was aware of feeling sexually as well as emotionally excited, but everything was under control. Buried somewhere deep in his mind was a centre, stripped of all human feeling, directing operations. He handed himself over to this authority without hesitation, almost with relief. Things were out of his hands now. What will be will be.

He staked her out on the table, pushing drawing pins

firmly into each corner, then he took his knife and made the first cut. A sweeping one, without hesitation and full of command, clean across the throat.

'You always say you've never got time.'

'Because I never have.'

'You're constructed like all the rest of us, Roz. You have to throw fuel in sometimes, otherwise the wheels don't go round.'

Duffy was perched on the edge of Roz's desk wielding the guillotine. She was emptying the envelopes, sorting the letters into piles.

'If I have lunch in the canteen with you, we eat then we have a pudding then we have a cup of tea then we have a talk then it's three o'clock. If I have something on a tray at home, I've done an hour and a half's work by then.'

'Oh drat Michael Kelly. He doesn't care how much love and time you lavish on him. He's been dead for years. Whereas here, pulsating at your side, is a real live human being; ripe in experience, aflame with adoration, full of needs and desires, longing only to lay his heart at your feet.'

'It all sounds very messy to me.'

She looked at Duffy and smiled. She never knew how seriously his protestations were meant but knew that taking them seriously would be a mistake from any angle. It would be easier if she didn't like him. He had a dry vein of humour that she found refreshing and he was basically very kind. If she hadn't been in love with Leo she might have found him attractive; certainly other women in the studio did. He had honey-coloured hair, receding slightly at the temples, which contrasted strangely with a skin which had weathered, after a thousand outdoor broadcasts, to a tough, even caramel. His eyes, strong blue, were amazingly clear considering the amount of Irish lowered on the same outdoor broadcasts, 'for insulation'. He had a slight Irish accent but was mercifully free of professional brogueishness. She knew little about his private life (Louise had said she thought he had been married) and felt she'd like to keep it that way. She had got her own life precisely as she wanted it – happy, constructive and well organised – and was anxious that it should not be disturbed.

'I hear,' Duffy whispered seductively, his lips to her ear, 'that it's salmonella fishcakes garnie.'

'Garnie with what?' Roz moved her head away with an irritated gesture. Duffy immediately withdrew.

'Baked beans of course. What else?' He paused. 'You're not going to come, are you Roz?'

'No.' She had reached the last letter on her pile. A large, square envelope. It gave a rich crackle as she opened it. Inside was a stiff ivory card. It was embossed with the words 'In Memoriam' and edged in black.

'Duffy—'

'Mm?' Duffy turned, already at the door. 'You've changed your mind?' He was smiling.

'Look at this.' Roz held out the card and he crossed over and took it.

'Someone on holiday? Makes a change from bazooming ladies and little men with knotted hankies on their heads. Who's it from?'

'I've no idea.'

'Isn't there a message? Weather is here, wish you were wonderful?' He turned it over. 'Oh.'

'Let's see.' He handed the card back. On the other side she read: 'Anticipating, Yours, F.'

'Who do you know who's died, Roz?'

'What? . . . No one . . . What a peculiar thing to send.'

'Well, if you want to borrow a black tie you've only got to ask.'

'But it's not a funeral invitation. It's one of those cards people attach to wreaths. And what does he mean "anticipating"? It's as if the person isn't dead yet.'

'I shouldn't worry. It won't be anyone you know, will it? Otherwise whoever sent the card would have been in touch before. In the proper way.'

'I suppose you're right.'

'Some idiot playing about.' Then, as Roz continued to stare with a serious frown at the card, he reached out, took it from her and tore it in half. He dropped the two halves in the waste basket. 'There. Best place for that.'

Roz threw the envelope away as well, then turned her hands over and regarded the tips of her fingers. They were tingling as if she had touched something warm and vibrant. 'By the pricking of my thumbs . . .' What was the rest of it?

'I won't stay for lunch Duffy, but I think I would like some coffee.' She knew it was foolish but she wanted to postpone leaving the building, being alone, until the taste of the card had faded.

'Wonderful.' He put an arm around her waist and almost scooped her out of her chair. 'Get your bag then and come on.'

Duffy's good humour, his delight in her company, his ordinariness would, she thought, blow any shreds of disquiet away and so it seemed until, a couple of hours later, she entered her study and settled at her desk ready to work.

She sat for a while but Michael Kelly's world, usually just a brief, imaginative step away, today seemed slippery and insubstantial. She read a little then pushed the book aside. Her brown study today seemed more oppressive than soothing. Darkness everywhere. Dark walls, heavy furniture, the dead sky outside adding nothing but a pall of gloom. Even her treasured rug seemed unillumined. She switched on the light.

She must change this room. She couldn't go on working happily in it until she did. This decision made, straight away Roz felt better. There were pieces she must keep, of course. Most of the furniture, her rug. But she wanted light, bright walls, springlike curtains (perhaps something with poppies), fresh prints or even posters. She would go to Air France tomorrow. Perhaps they would have something on Provence. She saw baked earth, wavy terracotta tiled roofs; white doves and olive trees under a blazing sky. She felt warmer. Afterwards she could drive over to the Designers' Guild or Harvey Nichols' to look at fabrics.

She started to take down the engravings. They could go in the junk room for now. She had them piled on her desk and was just rummaging in one of the drawers for a ball of string when the phrase she had been seeking unsuccessfully earlier dropped into her mind.

'By the pricking of my thumbs . . .' her hands stilled and she repeated the second part of the quotation aloud:

'. . . something wicked this way comes . . .'

'Can the Birdman fly?'

'Of course not stupid.' Roz wondered if Guy was as

patronising at school and hoped, if he was, someone sat on his head. 'People can't fly.'

'Why is he called the Birdman then?' Kathy persisted.

Guy took so long over his condescending, elderly sigh that Roz was able to start first. 'Because he's passionately interested in birds and their habits. And in comparing them to people.'

Kathy said: 'You can't compare birds to people. They're absolutely different.'

'Oh I don't know.' Guy had decided to cut his sigh short for the more direct pleasure of a quick come-back. 'They've both got two legs and some people, not a million miles from here, have very bird-like brains.'

'You wait till I'm twelve as well. Then you won't be able to talk to me like that.'

'Weak thinking, bird-brain. When you're twelve I'll be seventeen.'

'You won't! You won't! Will he Mummy?'

Guy laughed. Leo rustled his paper. Kathy turned tearfilled eyes to her mother. Roz took her hand.

'He will darling, but it won't be like you think. You'll be so grown-up then you'll feel differently. You won't mind. Honestly.'

'Do you promise?'

'I promise.'

'Guy said the other day he'd stay twelve till I catched up.'

'Then that was very unkind.' She looked across at her son. 'You're old enough to know better.'

'Unkind *and* stupid.' Kathy's tears vanished, she beamed at everyone.

'I haven't got all day to listen to you lot nattering.' Guy pushed his chair back. 'Can Madgewick have the residue of my kipper?'

Roz said: 'There's only bones left and you know he won't touch those.'

'They'll stick in his throat and he'll die! Daddy – Guy's trying to kill Madgewick!'

'Get all your stuff together, children.' Leo folded up his paper and smiled across at Roz. 'Good morning, darling.'

'Good morning, Leo.'

They had stumbled across each other briefly and blearily in their bathroom half an hour before and now, a pint of strong Colombian and a couple of newspaper leaders later, felt alive and ready for the real world. Leo picked up their bedtime discussion.

'Are you sure you want to rip out the entrails of our home and festoon the place with ladders and paint and paper, and men in white overalls drinking us dry? I thought we'd done all that.'

'Don't be ridiculous, Leo. It's just my study.'

'But your study's beautiful. You've always loved it.'

'Well now I don't. It's depressing.'

Actually it hadn't seemed so bad when she had nipped in this morning to pick up her bag but she was reluctant to let go of the sparkling transformation scene that had so changed her mood the previous day, although the feelings of anxiety that had conjured up the mood now seemed very shadowy.

'There's no harm in just picking up some samples and paint cards. I don't have to do anything about it.'

'Let's hope you don't.' Leo liked everything working smoothly. 'It's not like you to be whimmish, Roz.'

Roz kept quiet. They were to part for the day in a few minutes and there was no point in bickering but really . . . 'whimmish' . . . The word implied the sort of female personality she most disliked: cooing and petulant, demanding little frivolities and surprises. Women who thought a day on the sunbed or with the hairdresser was a day well spent.

Leo was putting on his heavy greatcoat and his real Russian hat. It was black Persian lamb and Roz, catching a sudden glimpse of his profile, as clean and dark as a hawk's, felt her heart turn over in her breast.

The children were bundled up like Eskimos. Leo opened the door on to driving grey hailstones, then they were gone. Roz fed Madgewick, forgetting that she had done so when making the early tea. He did not remind her but scoffed it quickly, with many a winning glance over the edge of his bowl.

She checked her bag and poured another cup of coffee. Today the theme of the programme was 'Communications'. In a few days' time *Roz's Roundabout* would be nearly two years' old. Working in radio was the last thing she expected to be doing in her thirty-third year. She had been asked to research the background to an hour-long evening programme on the great London strikes of the nineteenth century. She had had several meetings with the programme presenter and Toby Winthrop, who admired her approach to her work and her method of presenting her material. Her voice was pleasant and her manner friendly without being unctuous and he had asked her to take part in a phone-in after the programme. She had been so successful that a six-month contract had been offered which had now been renewed three times.

Roz was not without a natural amount of human vanity and had been pleased, even excited, at the thought of having her own radio show. She had also genuinely wished to help people. But the repetitious nature of so many of the calls and her inability to follow up any contacts made (there was no way of knowing if she had actually helped a single soul since the show started) had gradually changed her belief in the validity of her work. She was also aware that a certain amount of blandness – almost glibness – was lurking in her responses, and although she strove rigorously to weed this out the fact that it was there at all was not a good sign. If Toby offered a renewal of her contract next month, and she felt sure he would, she had almost decided to refuse. She wanted to finish Michael Kelly, then take a new look at her professional life. She glanced at the clock and got up hurriedly. Ten more minutes would bring Mrs Jollit and her malady of the month.

'I'd feel ever so much better asking Doctor Gilmour's advice, dear,' she had said to Roz. 'Pass it on. I'm afraid it's cancer of the spine.'

But Leo had said: 'Tell her not to let it go to her head,' and laughed.

Roz had laughed too, then felt dreadful. 'What if it really is?'

'Nonsense. Her poor GP must be a bag of nerves by now. She'll see us all buried.'

Roz had almost half an hour in her office, wondrously Sonia-free, to go over the possible shape of the programme. She scribbled down some headings. 'The media's role in communication. Have wider and more accessible methods of public communication meant less contact between

98

individuals? Why is group communication often easier than one to one? Or talking to a stranger?' Perhaps it might be possible to touch on themes in current films and theatre . . . 'Lack of C,' she wrote. Question-mark. She read through her notes again then went down to the studio. The programme held no surprises. The Birdman came on eight minutes before the end.

'Our hopeless failure to communicate with each other, Miss Gilmour, is really a question of lack of clarity. We have so many ways of concealing what we really feel even when we are, ostensibly, trying to make contact. What we need is to refine our methods, paring away all the little obfuscations until we have something as clear and shorn of misunderstandings as the method used by the birds.'

'That would be their songs?'

'Their feet! Their feet!'

'I beg your pardon?'

'The footprints of a bird are like hieroglyphics, you know. We are of course denied the key to all this secret knowledge. When you or I see birds walking about what do we think they are doing?'

'Walking about?'

'Exactly. But to another bird it's a different pair of shoes.'

I really don't think I can stand much more of this, thought Roz and saw, with relief, the hand of the studio clock jump to eleven-fifty-five. She exchanged a look with Louise, who had removed her Peruvian slipper socks, put them on her hands and was making wild ear shapes on the top of her head. Somehow Roz ironed the laughter out of her voice:

'But humans have their signals too. Their body language.'

'Humans are full of deceit and chicanery, Miss Gilmour. Their body language, as you so coarsely put it, is used as much to mislead as to illustrate true feeling.'

'Do all birds read each other's signals?'

A long ponder. Then he said, as sadly as if the discovery had shortened his life: 'I fear not. It wouldn't be necessary, you see. But it's a lovely thought isn't it? No. Each species can read its own foot-writing. Any extra knowledge would be superfluous and our Creator abhors waste, as we know.'

That's a matter of opinion, thought Roz as her interconnecting light came on. She flicked the switch.

Louise said: 'One more.'

'We're nearly through.'

'He says he'll be brief.'

'He'll have to be. OK – put him on hold.'

Roz thanked the Birdman and eased him out. She put the final caller on. A soft voice, courteous. Almost too much so. Boneless but full of shy persistence. There were so many who sounded like this. The fact that they had nothing original or even slightly interesting to say never deterred them. They would ring and ring until they got through, then trot out run-of-the-mill prejudices and threadbare clichés with an air of triumphant discovery that Roz had found quite touching the first couple of times.

'The line's free now.'

'It's . . . about a death.'

Roz only just stopped an audible 'tsk!' of irritation. They had broadcast a programme on bereavement only a couple of weeks ago; why couldn't he have rung in then? His statement started to evoke Pavlovian responses: send information on supportive organisations, perhaps suggest Samaritans, ask the usual questions. She watched this brisk pigeon-holing, suddenly shocked. Whatever happened to compassion?

'I'm so sorry. Was it someone close to you?'

'No. Nothing personal.'

A strange voice. Not quite at ease with itself. A touch too carefully paced, with a London intonation which she sensed was once much stronger. A manufactured voice then, but whether it was put on for the call or by now second nature there was no way of knowing. It also sounded faintly familiar.

'I don't quite understand. Is it something you've seen in the papers that's distressed you? An account of a killing? Something in Northern Ireland?'

'Oh – I'm not distressed.' She could hear the laughter now, running underneath the words, threatening to surface and break them up.

She snapped, with some asperity: 'Well, what are you ringing up for then?'

Out of the corner of her eye she saw Duffy, waiting in the control room, move to stand behind Louise. She sensed them both staring at her.

'I just thought . . . as the death hasn't happened yet . . . I should tell someone.'

Roz sighed. This was definitely not going to be her day. Two of them before she'd even digested her elevenses.

'Do you mean you're some sort of clairvoyant?'

'Did I say that?'

'You haven't actually said anything yet.' Roz could hear

her voice fraying. Yes – I've definitely had enough of this. If her patience was on so short a rein it was time to get off the roundabout. 'And you've now got less than fifty seconds to get whatever it is off your chest.'

'I have to kill someone you see. I wanted you to know.'

Roz sat up, impatience fled. 'What?'

Louise had half risen and was leaning forward, her hands on the control panel. Duffy, just behind her, stood very still, his glance pointing with retriever-like intensity towards Roz. A thread of alarmed excitement suddenly yoked the three of them together. Roz mouthed 'Hold' at Louise.

'. . . as you're involved . . .'

Louise cut him off the air and signalled, thumb raised, to show she'd still got him on the line. The second hand closed to the minute and Roz started to wind up, aware she was gabbling. Duffy left the control room, news sheets in hand.

'. . . all from *Roz's Roundabout* for now . . . see you Friday . . . if I'm still here . . . Goodbye now . . .'

Louise started the closing music tape. Roz removed her headphones and handed them to Duffy, who slid into her seat saying: 'What are you going to do?'

'I don't know.'

What was she going to do? She moved without hurrying to the control room. The excitement was ebbing fast. It had been aroused, she now saw, purely by the novelty of the incident. The team who monitored the calls had, until now, sifted out the nutters and odd-bods and (the Birdman excepted) kept them off the air.

Louise held out the phone, tapping the side of her head significantly. Roz hesitated. Her reasons for not taking it were purely instinctual. The basic human impulse to turn away from deformity; the wish not to acknowledge the existence of thought and behaviour patterns wildly, unknowably different from one's own. Her reasons for taking the phone would be rational. She had been paid, very well, for the past two years to present herself as a caring interviewer with a concern for her fellow man. And she had never questioned this basic assumption. She had never felt she was taking money under false pretences in spite of inevitable irritations with some of her callers.

But when had she been asked to make any sort of commitment? The calls were as brief as she wished to make them, she simply cut people off when she had had enough. How caring was that? Here was an opportunity to really help someone. Not just slap a stereotyped letter into the post or give out a few follow-up addresses, but to listen at some length and try to understand.

Yet instinct would not be quenched. As she reached out her hand for the phone a ripple, a crawling sensation, ran over her skin.

'Hello. Are you still there?'

'Oh yes.' It was like silk, his voice. As if someone had poured warm oil down the line into her ear. She was sure she had made a mistake. Taking the call, treating it seriously, would encourage him to fantasise further. If it had been an obscene call she would not have spoken to him. And what was more obscene than the idea of deliberately taking a human life?

'I'd like to help you . . . if I can.'

'Oh you can.'

He laughed. It was a terrible laugh. As innocent and

merry as a child's. Louise, watching her face, rose and made as if to take the phone but Roz shook her head. She sensed the door opening behind her and Duffy coming into the room. She said:

'How? Would it help to talk about it?'

'I don't see why we shouldn't chat a bit. First.'

Roz felt her throat tighten. 'What do you mean ... first?'

Duffy moved before she could stop him and snatched the phone. 'Listen. There are specialists to help people like you. Give us your name and address and we'll put you in touch with someone.' They all heard the prompt click. 'Thank you for calling.'

'You shouldn't have done that, Duffy.'

'Look at you. Pale as a barn owl. I'm not going to stand here and watch you taking all that crap.'

'I might have been able to help him.'

'Rubbish – he's a nutter. If he wanted help he'd go to a doctor. Not come here to torment you. How the hell did he get through anyway?'

Louise said: 'He was very crafty. He told the girl who took the call that he ran an encounter group specialising in communication without words. She buzzed me back before Roz came off the air in a high old state. She's afraid she's going to get the sack.'

'I'll go down and talk to her. It'll be all right.' Roz sounded more confident than she felt.

'I'll bet Toby won't think it's all right.'

'For heaven's sake, Louise. It's the first time anything like this has slipped through. Even Toby's got to allow for human error.'

'I should go and see him before you tell Fiona her job's safe.'

Duffy took Roz's arm. 'I've got a feeling you're both worrying about nothing. But let's go and check.'

As soon as they emerged into the corridor it was obvious the buzz was round. Everyone they passed looked at Roz curiously; a clutch of typists by the lift stopped talking as they passed. One of the reporters put his head around the door next to Toby's then clapped a hand around his throat and withdrew, crossing his eyes and gargling: 'I wanna kill somebody baby . . .'

'That's much better, Colin,' said Duffy as they walked by. 'You looked almost human there for a moment.'

Roz smiled at Duffy – or tried to. They knocked on Toby's door.

'Come.'

She had hardly stepped inside before Toby had sprung from his chair and rushed across the room. He was beaming.

'Darling – here you are. Come and sit down. I see you've brought one of your cohorts. Clear off, Duffield.'

Duffy sat down. Toby led Roz to his large leather sofa. 'Come and relax on my auditioning equipment. Would you like a drink?'

Roz felt both puzzled and wary. 'Why?'

'Fine.' Toby spoke over his shoulder without looking at Duffy. 'Make yourself useful. There's some goblets in the fridge. Open the Pouilly Fumé. Two large ones.' As Duffy was opening the wine he continued: 'Now look, darling. I think we might be really on to something here. The switchboard's jammed with ghoulish calls already. Did you talk to this man after the prog?'

'. . . Yes . . .'

'What else did he say?'

'He just repeated what he'd said over the air.' Roz could not bring herself to use the words. 'Then he said I could help him.'

'Great! That's what I wanted to hear.' Duffy handed Roz a drink. 'How are you going to make contact?'

'I don't know. Duffy took the phone and he straightaway hung up.'

'You interfering shit.' Toby turned a face like a magenta balloon towards the drinks cabinet. 'Hey! What the bloody hell do you think you're doing?'

'Drinking my wine.' Duffy lowered his goblet, looking mildly pained.

'The two glasses were for myself and Rossi.'

Roz hated it when he called her Rossi. Something unpleasant was usually about to ensue.

'Now sod off.'

Duffy poured a third glass. 'Why this radiance of spirit, Toby? The gargoyle grimace that serves as a smile?'

'Don't presume too much, Duffield. Sports reporters are ten pence a dozen, you know. Jumped-up PE instructors. Uncultured beer-swilling louts with the intellectual equipment of a wombat.'

Apart from his radio work Duffy wrote for an upmarket Sunday newspaper and was in the running for Sports Reporter of the Year. They both knew that his job was as safe, if not safer, than Toby's. He took the second chair now, setting the bottle on the corner of the desk. Toby ignored him.

'Don't you see darling, what something like this could do for the ratings?'

Duffy made a disgusted sound. Roz looked puzzled, then incredulous.

'But Toby – you can't mean what I think you mean.'

'Can't he though.'

'Don't you go all grand and mealy-mouthed on me. This is a tough, competitive business and there's no point in pretending it isn't. We're fighting LBC and Capital, not to mention Auntie Beeb up the road, so stop behaving like a Victorian maiden lady and get your finger out.'

'A Victorian maiden lady would hardly—'

Toby carried on over Duffy's interpolation. 'We can really develop this, Rossi. OK – maybe when it comes down to it this guy won't really kill anyone,' Toby sounded genuinely sorry, almost wistful, 'but if we can string it out, get him to phone again, we can really build it up. I've already got onto PR.'

'Great. Maybe when the time comes we can coax him into the studio. Get him to strangle his victim over the air.'

'If you're going to insist on sitting in uninvited Duffield, at least try to make some practical suggestions.'

'Oh – I didn't mean we'd let him go through with it. Just a gurgle or two then the Keystone Cops could rush in and restrain him. Of course it'd go even better on television.'

Toby, with the look of a saint tried beyond endurance, continued talking to Roz. 'I didn't hear it myself, darling . . . up to here with work as usual –' he waved at the central light fitting. Duffy gave a mordant chuckle – 'but my secretary had the Tannoy on and she said it all sounded rather . . . well . . . personal. What did he actually say?'

'That he had to kill someone and he wanted me to know.'

107

'Why you, I wonder?'

'He's a case,' said Duffy. 'He's just picked her out with a pin. It could have been anyone.'

'He said I was personally involved.'

'He's trying to frighten you, Roz. He's just a bloody wanker.'

'Just a minute . . . I'll decide who, if anyone, round here is on the wank.' Toby looked firmly from one to the other, sensing his authority slipping. 'What did he say afterwards? Before this interfering clown cut him off.'

'I asked if it would help to talk about it—'

'Good! Good girl!'

'—and he said he didn't mind chatting a bit first.'

'First? That sounds promising.'

Duffy got up quickly, hesitated for a moment, then poured some more wine: 'You make me want to throw up.'

'So it all hinges now on him following this through. And I'm sure he will. Especially once the press office gets going. They like to feel important, at the centre of things, these loonies. There'll be no stopping him then, you'll see.'

Roz shuddered, then remembered something. 'I wonder if that card I received the other day has anything to do with this?'

'What? What card?'

Roz described the In Memoriam card and message. Toby reacted like a greyhound in the slips. 'Bound to have. God – the man's an artist. Go and fetch it Roz – let's have a look.'

'Well . . . um . . .'

Duffy said: 'I tore it up.'

'*You what!* I've just about had enough of you.' Toby got

up and lumbered to the window, pointing with injured but vibrant intensity at his empty chair. 'Perhaps you'd like to sit there and run the place?'

'Somebody should.' Duffy crossed to Roz. 'Come on Rosetta.' He took her arm.

'I haven't finished yet.'

'What else is there to say? Until he rings again there's nothing we can do. And there's no point in chewing it over indefinitely. Can't you see it's upsetting her?'

'People with fragile sensibilities shouldn't be journalists.' Then, as he caught Duffy's change of expression: 'OK. OK. Fair enough.'

Duffy glanced back as they left the office. Toby, reseated, had the look of an unknown, not very successful actor who had just been offered the lead in a Spielberg movie. He wasn't going to let go of this in a hurry. Duffy found himself hoping, disproportionately, that the man would not ring again.

'Mummy?'

'Mmm.'

'If you had to give me or Guy away which one would you keep?'

Roz wished Leo would contribute more, or even something, to the breakfast ritual. She had to cope with preparing and dishing out food, checking the right schoolbooks were packed, that socks were holeless and clothes reasonably tidy, and now she had to answer daft questions as well. There was something about this morning. It looked the same. The children were alternately giggling and grumbling. *The Times* was open and doing its usual effective screening job. The clutter on the table was no different from the usual clutter. Madgewick lolled lordlily by the Aga. There was even the bonus of a hard November sun adding a chill gloss to the plates on the Welsh dresser. But somehow the effect on Roz was not the same. Instead of providing the usual launching pad for her day the dirty dishes, Leo's complacency and the children's bickering had started to irritate her.

'What's brought this on?'

Kathy said: 'We're all asking our parents. I was supposed to ask you yesterday but I forgot.'

'I couldn't bear to choose. I love you both the same.'

'That's what all the parents said. Except Francesca's.'

'And what did hers say?'

'They said they would have to pick her because they loved her better than her big brother or the new baby or all the children in the world rolled together.'

Roz smiled. 'Did they really?'

'But no one believed her. She tells such dreadful lies.' Kathy stared at Guy defiantly but he was filling in a coupon on the cornflake packet and not listening. Roz wondered what new bit of junk would be coming through the letter box to add to the mountain already only just contained by the four walls of his room. For the first time she felt she couldn't be bothered to ask.

'Don't forget to take an apple.'

The children slithered off their chairs, Kathy scraping hers over the buff stone tiles. *The Times* was lowered to half-mast then, reluctantly, to table level. Leo never took the paper to work. He had no spare moments during the day and Roz suspected that he frequently worked straight through without lunch. When he came home in the evening he was too tired to do anything but unwind, eat and talk, in a rather desultory way, to the children. So she was being very selfish, grudging him a semi-quiet read at breakfast. But she felt that he should know that this morning was different. That things weren't quite right.

Now he was bending over her chair, kissing her somewhere between the eyebrow and ear. 'Are you going in today? Or is it Michael Kelly?'

'Oh *really* Leo.' Two years of *Roz's Roundabout* and he still had no idea of how her week was organised. 'I never go to the studio on Wednesday.'

'Sorry, sorry.' He crouched down so that their faces were level. 'What's wrong?'

He'd obviously completely forgotten their conversation the night before. She had waited until the children had gone to bed and he was almost asleep on the chesterfield before mentioning the phone call. She had been thinking of it all evening and this seemed to have fed her anxiety so that by the time she broached the subject her whole body was rigid with tension. She had been shocked by Leo's response, although common sense told her she should have been comforted. He had been almost casual.

'Shouldn't be a celebrity, darling.' Quick, warm kiss. 'Don't worry. He probably rings up a famous name every day. You know – if it's Monday it must be Gilmour.'

'It wasn't Monday!'

Leo swung his legs to the floor and stood up, drawing her to her feet. He smoothed her hair back and traced the lines of tension on her brows and temples. 'You are in a tizz. Let me make you a drink. We can't have tears before bedtime.'

They had sat, close together in their large, downy bed drinking hot chocolate and then made slow, sweet love and the world went away as it always did in Leo's arms. Afterwards she had drifted into secure, contented sleep only to wake suddenly and fully in the middle of the night to cry: 'Leo – we're all right aren't we? Whatever happens we're all right?'

He didn't open his eyes but slipped an arm around her shoulders and she spent the rest of the night dozing uneasily with her head on his chest.

Now, in answer to his questions, she said: 'Nothing, darling. Just a bit tired.'

When he had left, the children clattering down the steps behind him, Roz took her coffee up to the study. She liked to get in safely and close the door before Mrs Jollit arrived. It was understood between them that she was then working and not to be disturbed. She sat at her desk and started by re-reading her previous day's notes. She read three pages before realising that she had taken in nothing. She pushed the work aside.

Stacked up on various chairs around the room were swatches of fabrics, paint chips and cards together with carpet samples. She walked over to the nearest and picked up a Warner's curtain selection. This was not what she wanted to do. She wanted to write: to enter the calm, ordered, enlightened world of the eighteenth century, but she couldn't concentrate. The disciplined energy which she called on so carelessly and without question was today simply not available.

She stood by the window, flicking through the cottons and chintzes. Holding them up against the white frame, seeing how the colours looked in direct light. She especially liked one splashed with large flowers. Bold, strong aggressive colours. Making a definite statement. She was sick of subtle, wishy-washy shades and twee little prints. She took a handful of paint chips. There was a high-gloss mimosa that seemed especially appealing. Plain union canvas on the sofa and masses of brilliant cushions. Embroidered, tapestry, maybe some of those pretty appliqués with padded satin clouds and stout funny sheep. Yes. 'Get on with it then Gilmour,' she murmured, and hunted around for her tape measure.

Downstairs the front door slammed. Mrs Jollit. Roz stood on a chair to measure the curtain drop. She made notes on a scrap of paper. From the kitchen she heard crashing and banging and then a shrieking soprano telling the world the owner had done it her way.

Roz returned to the paint colours. White was too cold, on the other hand with mimosa gloss on the door and woodwork and those curtains it had to be something fairly understated. Greys were out for the same reason. A sort of putty ... or vanilla. Muffin looked too dark, primrose banal, the walls were a bit big to take a huge expanse of beige. She finally settled for strudel: vanilla but with a warm, lemony undertone. Almost without realising it her depression was slipping away. Now for the carpet.

The deep brown of the present one was far too heavy. She rather fancied green then decided, what with the flowers and the walls, it might be a bit like working in a public park. There was a nice milk-chocolate with a cream fleck. Almost tweedy. She knelt down and measured the floor. Although everything would have to be ordered and would, no doubt, take weeks to arrive, she'd made a start.

She could have phoned the curtain order through but decided to drive over to the Guild and return the swatches at the same time. She could pick up the paint on the way back. In her large address book was the telephone number of a freelance decorator and his daughter who had painted, most beautifully, the top floor of a neighbour's house the previous summer. They were probably booked up for months but it was still worth a try.

She sat at her desk, got the book out of the drawer and turned to P, then D, then F for Freelance. No luck. She had probably foolishly entered him under his own name, then promptly forgotten what that name was. She sighed. It was a vast book, full of every address and number she might ever need. Personal (going back years), family, business. She started on the A's and had got to Arundell (Fran) when the phone rang. Damn. That meant exposure to Mrs Jollit. She hurried downstairs.

'Hullo Roz.' She didn't, couldn't reply. 'It wasn't very nice of you to hang up on me yesterday.'

'I didn't – it wasn't me.'

She was pleased that her voice sounded so even. There was no hint of the turmoil churning in her stomach. Or of how much worse it seemed, speaking to him when she was alone.

What had she decided yesterday? That she would try to help him? Wasn't that her business? But what could she do? Disturbed people needed professional help. And Duffy had said if that's what this man was after he'd have gone to a doctor. But perhaps his doctor was unsympathetic and a stranger more approachable. And all this time the words were pouring out. She couldn't distinguish one from the other. There was just a warm oily rustle; a river of silk.

The white receiver was slipping in her hands. Occasionally a phrase pierced the fog. 'Community service . . . utter nonentity . . . putting affairs in order . . .'

And then, the first signal of returning life, the tips of her fingers began to prickle. She slammed the phone down and returned to her study ignoring a yell that might have been 'good morning' from the basement.

She moved quickly round the room grabbing the fabric swatches and her handbag. She had to get out; into the fresh air. Visit shops, talk to calm, rational people about calm, rational things. How many Coxes to the pound and was English lamb available. Guy needed some grey socks. There should be fresh coriander in the Greek shop. Then, walking through the hall, she stopped.

He had rung her home. But she was ex-directory. How easy was it to get hold of an ex-directory number? She went into the sitting room and picked up the phone feeling a ripple of distaste as if he would still be on the line, waiting. Then she thought, how supine can you get? Frightened to use your own phone. She dialled directory enquiries, gave her name and address and asked for the number. After a brief pause the girl said: 'I'm sorry but this number is ex-directory.'

'But it's terribly urgent.'

'I'm afraid we can't help you.'

'I simply must get in touch with Mrs Gilmour. It's terribly important. Absolutely vital.'

'We can't give this number out under any circumstances. I'm very sorry.'

'Not even to the police?'

'Are you the police?'

Roz hesitated. '. . . Yes . . .'

'Then if you will give me your number and the address of your station my supervisor will call you back.'

Roz hung up. So it wasn't all that easy. She wondered if the man was a member of British Telecom's staff. This comforted her a little. It meant, if they could get his name next time he rang, he could be traced.

But then, quickly on the heels of this thought came another. If he knew her number he probably knew her address. She felt, coldly, how much worse this was. She crossed the room and looked out of the window then, feeling nakedly exposed, stepped back shrouded by the curtains.

Yet the street seemed empty. Gradually she stepped up to the glass again. There was the usual jam of cars parked nose to tail on either side, her own Golf directly beneath the window. The trees, so fresh and bright and sheltering a few months ago, now seemed to be clawing at the sky with stripped, whiplike branches. She saw Jonathan Miller leave his house, his tall rangy form muffled in an overcoat and scarves. A man pushing a Camden Council dustcart went by. She was half expecting him to look up and felt a small hurdle had been cleared when he walked on, prodding at rubbish in the gutter, then disappeared around the bend.

The phone rang again. Between the first sound and the moment, half a minute later, when she picked it up, something happened to Roz. She became angry. Resentment flowed in her veins against this unknown man who was disrupting the calm, even tenor of her life; making concentration impossible, spoiling even, it seemed, her pleasure in her family. She didn't give him a chance to speak.

'Listen. If you ring here again I shall tell the police. You should be in a mental hospital. I don't want to know about your sick plans or what's going on in your sick mind. People like you ought to be locked away. Just leave me alone, do you hear? *Leave me alone*.'

'. . . Roz?'

'Oh God.' She sat down weakly, anger evaporated. 'Duffy.'

'What on earth's wrong?'

'He rang up. Here.'

'When?'

'Just a few minutes ago.'

'What did he say?'

'I don't know.'

'What d'you mean you don't know?'

'I suppose I switched off. Just odd bits . . . filtered through . . .'

There was a pause then Duffy said: 'What are you going to do now?'

'. . . um . . . I was going over to Sloane Street to see about curtains.'

'I'm just going up to Accounts to collect my expenses. I can't think of a better way to spend them than taking you to lunch.'

As she began automatically to demur, Duffy said: 'I'm not asking you, sunshine, I'm telling you. You know The Gay Hussar?'

'Yes.'

'Come just before one.'

'Listen Duffy—'

'Don't argue with me.'

'I wasn't going to argue. I just wanted to say thank you.'

'Quite right too. See you later. Oh and Roz—'

'Yes?'

'Before you come out get on to British Telecom. Get your number changed.'

It must have been ten years since she had been to The Gay Hussar but nothing seemed to have changed. Duffy was there when she arrived. She slid into a banquette and sat for a moment with her eyes closed, listening to the clatter of conversation and cutlery and the rain on the window. Duffy said nothing until she opened her eyes and she was grateful.

'Hello.' He was pouring some Magyar wine. It had a delicate amber, almost greenish tinge. The glasses showed a bloom where the cold wine struck them. 'I've ordered the cherry soup.'

'Do they still do cherry soup?'

'Specialité of the maison.'

It was very cosy, almost homely. The net curtains shut out the grey light and the waiters bustled about covering snowy tablecloths with steaming dishes. Lamps glowed. Roz breathed in the scent of her wine. Their first course arrived. She had wondered slightly about cold soup on a day like this but it was delicious, the cherries and the sour cream blending beautifully, any tartness offset by the flowery, slightly honeyed taste of the wine.

Duffy seemed completely at home. She was so used to seeing him in heavy outdoor clothes or sweater and cords

118

that the three-piece suit in a narrow pale grey pin-stripe was something of a revelation. His shirt was also pale and of soft cotton. She couldn't decide whether it was grey or white and asked him.

'The man in Turnbull's thought it was blue. As long as you like it, darling.' He smiled across at her, the lean tanned planes of his face softened by the diffused light.

Roz smiled back. 'I hate nylon shirts don't you?'

'God yes. They seem to go with string vests and tie and hanky sets.'

'And men who wear socks with open sandals.' Yet if she had thought of Duffy's shirts at all she would have assumed they would be nylon. Something easy for a man living on his own to rinse through and hang up in the bathroom. Perhaps he didn't live on his own. Perhaps there was a pair, or more than one pair of willing hands washing and ironing his Turnbull and Asser shirts. She was aware that she had stopped feeling sorry for him. A dangerous sign.

'I'm having the goulash. What about you?'

'An omelette please. I never eat much during the day. We eat . . . well, later.' She felt suddenly shy as if she had, by dragging the pattern of her domestic life into the conversation, committed some social gaffe.

But Duffy just said: 'What sort of omelette?'

'An egg omelette.' They both laughed, far more heartily than the weak joke deserved.

The omelette came, fat and light and smothered with poppy seeds. She had salad with it. Duffy's goulash smelled richly of paprika and tender meat and came garnished with rice and okra. They ate companionably together.

It was not only Duffy's clothes that were different. In the

studio, she had always felt that he was casually posing. Playing the bluff outdoor reporter who had a yen for Roz Gilmour. It was as if making a pass or issuing a lunch invitation was part of the act. Now the performance was laid aside and, although pleased, she was also slightly disturbed. She found herself wanting to question him. To fill in the background of which she knew so little and to discover what paths had led him to City Radio. And what his future plans were.

She tried to picture his home. It would probably be a flat. She wondered what books and paintings he would have – if any. Then she thought how patronising that amendment was. Why shouldn't a sports writer own paintings? Duffy was a very good writer. He probably had a library that would put her own to shame. Perhaps after lunch he would ask her back to his place. She would refuse of course. She hoped he wouldn't. It was so good to have him as an ally and a friend. She just didn't want to have to handle anything else.

'Don't worry.'

'What?' She felt the warm colour touch her cheeks.

'You know what.'

'I certainly don't.'

'Come on, sweetheart. I can read you like a book. Look –' he lifted his hands to shoulder level, palms facing her – 'no hands.'

She smiled. 'I'm sorry.'

'I love your smile, Rosetta. Much better than your stony look.' He paused. 'Ho ho?'

'More ouch.'

He turned the conversation quickly and skilfully: 'You

must be wondering what I rang up about. I wanted to pinch a new tape for my Uher. I'm vox popping in Oxford Street tomorrow morning.'

'As long as you put it back.'

Duffy's face was suffused with outraged innocence. 'I always put them back.'

'Duffy – you *never* put them back. What's it on, anyway?'

'Shoplifting. Asking people if they're ever tempted. Whether they resent paying extra to cover the stores' losses. The usual. You ought to try it some time.'

'No fear. I like to be tucked away in the studio. Safe from the madding crowd.'

And there it was. The perfect opening to discuss the reason they had really met for lunch. Roz, in her interested reassessment of Duffy's personality had, for minutes at a time, forgotten it.

He said: 'You've changed your number?'

'It's in hand. They're blocking calls till then. It should only be for a day or two.'

'Fine. He won't get on to the air again – that's for sure. Of course there's the post. We should have kept the envelope from that ghastly card. Then you'd recognise the writing and just chuck anything else away unopened.'

'But if he got my home number before, I assume he can always get it again.'

'I've been thinking about that. Who actually has it?'

'Oh – a few close friends. The children's respective schools, St Thomas's, Leo's parents, my mum. The studio, Sonia—'

'I hate to sound depressing but that's an awful lot of people.'

121

'But they can all be ruled out, surely. Can you imagine my mother or the Gilmours or even St Thomas's handing out our number to a complete stranger?'

Maybe he's not a stranger thought Duffy, but would not have said so for the world. 'Are you sure you can't recall anything he said? I know you don't want to deliberately dwell on it but there might be something that would help.'

She didn't want to dwell on it. Within seconds it seemed the insinuating whisper was threading itself around the restaurant, dirtying the white cloths, muddying the smiles of the departing diners.

'He said something about killing a tramp. And a lot of people mourning.'

'Are you sure? I mean, they don't sound as if they go together.'

'No I'm not sure!' Her voice rose in pitch and volume, exasperated. People at the next table stopped talking and stared. 'I was trying to blot him out – not give him my undivided attention.'

'Come on, darling.' He stretched out a hand and, without thinking, Roz slipped hers into it.

'I'm afraid, Duffy.'

He didn't say any of the trite things she was longing to hear: 'Don't worry' or 'He's probably perfectly harmless' or 'It'll be all right. I'll look after you.' Just covered their two hands with his other one.

'I don't know why you're doing all this.' She gestured at the table meaning much more than the meal. There was a pressure on her hand so slight she wondered, afterwards, if she had imagined it.

Then he said: 'I'm sure you do, Roz.'

After she had refused coffee he signalled for the bill.

Outside, within seconds the feelings of warmth and security vanished. The wind bit into their skin, snatched the breath out of their mouths. She wanted to smile but felt her lips were frozen together. Even her eyes hurt. She was wearing a hooded coat of mock ocelot.

Duffy buried his head in the fur close to her ear. Her heart jumped as she saw his face come nearer, go out of focus. He shouted above the wind: 'You look like Miss Arctic Circle '94.'

Around their feet Soho debris swirled. 'I'll get you a taxi.' He stepped into the road, arm raised.

As she got into the taxi she said: 'Won't you come? I can drop you somewhere.' She did not want to part from him and realised, with a shock, that this was not only because she did not wish to be alone.

She had felt happy in the restaurant, almost secure. Standing close to him but exposed to the elements, less secure; now, as the cab drove away not only did she feel insecure but peculiarly bereft. He had made no attempt at a goodbye kiss, not even a brief friendly peck on the cheek.

Turning, she looked through the rear window and saw, through the pelting rain, that he was already walking away.

Chapter Four

It was about halfway through their conversation that he became aware that she wasn't listening. He couldn't give a reason for this. He wouldn't have thought you could tell; it wasn't like talking face to face. He knew she hadn't put the phone down, just that she'd switched off. He'd got through to her at first, though. Heard her indrawn breath. She'd been upset all right, but then she'd somehow got away.

But she *would* listen. He'd make sure of that. It was only right that she should know what was going to happen. No one would be able to say afterwards that he hadn't played fair, scrupulously fair with her, even though she'd never played fair with him. Leading him on then letting him down.

And he probably wasn't the only one. How many other people had written to her or rung her up and been pushed aside like so much worthless garbage? The blow he struck would be a blow for them all. All the ones born to the wrong people in the wrong place, the ones who hadn't had the luck. He felt again the cleansing rush of moral certainty. To see justice done was satisfying but to be the instrument of that justice . . .

He pulled his notepad towards him. The first thing was to repeat his side of the telephone conversation and to make sure that this time she listened. Which meant writing it all down or, better still (she might read the first few words then throw the letter away), taping it. He realised this would make things much more risky, other people might listen to the tape for instance, but this couldn't be helped. Making his plans much more clear to her was the next step in his campaign and there was no honourable way he could miss it out. And he wouldn't send a tape through the post to be dumped into the waste basket with the rest of the unwanted mail. No. He'd deliver his message on to her own machine. That would be more difficult but difficulties were made to be overcome.

He wrote DELIVERING THE MESSAGE and underlined it. Then: 1. HOW TO ENTER THE STUDIO. He knew the layout, exactly where her office was. And the set-up at reception. There'd be no wandering up there blind this time. What he needed was a legitimate-sounding reason for getting in. Not an appointment, they'd just ring through and check. He thought hard but without anxiety. He felt confident, knowing his cause was just, that inspiration would come.

It occurred to him that a studio as small as City Radio would probably not have much of a maintenance staff. If things went wrong they would use an outside firm to put them right. Also it would take time for the girl at the desk to check up on who had actually called in a workman. He could just breeze in with his bag of tools and say: 'Plumber . . . it's all right – I know where to go,' and that – if he kept a cool head and kept walking – would be that. He might wear a bit of a disguise. Perhaps a moustache, in case anyone from the *Saturday Show* was on. Nothing elaborate, he didn't want to draw attention to himself.

Mr Christoforou kept an old canvas bag full of tools in a cupboard near the hall phone. It shouldn't be difficult to smuggle them out and replace them before they were missed. No need to wear a uniform. In weather like this he'd be wearing outdoor clothes anyway. Jeans and his old reefer jacket would do.

He must make sure Sonia was out of the building. She was the only one who would recognise him. That wouldn't be difficult. He'd arrange to meet her outside Holborn Tube, ask her to get off a bit early. There was no chance she'd come back. The silly cow would stand there waiting for ever, even if he asked her to meet him in the fast lane of the M1. He was sick of Sonia. In the short time he'd known her she'd already got as bad as his mother. Always asking if he loved her and would she see him tomorrow. She was incredibly obliging, though. He was not only getting as much as he wanted but, for the first time, something like the variety he wanted. When he had taken one of his books along the previous evening Sonia, although she had turned deep crimson all the way down to her ankles, had bravely attempted three or four of the less convoluted postures. She'd had to agree that when two people were in love and (more important) going to be married, it didn't really matter what they did.

Leo was late. Roz had been watching television with the children and was now watching the kitchen clock. They had seen a cartoon in which a dog with a nose like a liquorice golf ball worked part time as a janitor when he was not solving crimes which had baffled the police of five continents. Roz had thought, wryly, we could do with him here.

She was feeling better. This was partly the lunch with Duffy, partly the sheer normality of collecting the children, listening to their chatter, getting tea. Now she chopped celery and walnuts and peppers for salad. Chicken joints in wine, stock and herbs had been in the slow cooker all day. She was looking forward to a glass of wine and could quite easily have poured one but this was something Leo usually did as soon as he came in. The first step in the slow, unwinding ritual of their evening together. He should have been home nearly half an hour ago. Guy appeared at the kitchen door.

'Where's Daddy?'

Roz marvelled at the confidence of children. Where's my science book? Football boots? The longest bridge in the world? Mars?

'He won't be long.'

'It's nearly Kathy's bedtime. Perhaps she'll have to go to bed without seeing him.'

'Don't be mean. Anyway even if she did he'd go up as soon as he came home.'

Guy did not seem displeased at this. 'I know.'

They both heard the door at the same time. 'There he is!'

He ran up the basement stairs and she heard Kathy scrambling down from the floor above. The two of them talked solidly at Leo as he took off his coat. Roz heard their voices fade as he went with them into the sitting room, then, ten minutes later he entered the kitchen. He came up behind her and slipped his arms around her waist.

127

'Something smells good.' He kissed the back of her neck. 'Mmm – it's you.' He pressed her close for a moment then let her go. 'What would you like?'

'Some hock darling, please.' Then, as Leo took a slender glass from the dresser, 'And some Perrier. I had quite a lot of wine at lunch.'

'Really?' Leo replaced the glass and took down a large balloon, 'That's not like you.'

'I went to The Gay Hussar.'

'Curiouser and curiouser.'

'There's some M and S open in the fridge.'

Leo half filled the balloon, opened a small bottle of Perrier, topped it up and took the glass and the rest of the mineral water over to where Roz was dressing the salad. He poured a large Irish for himself, adding a little Malvern water.

'And who took you off to The Gay Hussar?'

Roz rather resented the assumption that she could not have taken herself off to The Gay Hussar or lunched there on equal terms with a friend. Then resented even more the fact that Leo did not wait for her to answer.

'I'm sorry to be late. I tried to ring but there's something wrong with the phone. I'd better report it.'

'Oh.' Everything seemed to be whirling in on her. She had planned to tell him about the phone call later in the evening when the children were settled. 'That's my fault, I'm afraid.'

'What?'

'I had an unpleasant call. That man I told you about, he rang here. I don't know how he got the number. So I'm having it changed.'

Leo stared at her. 'I've got a private patient in a very critical condition. I might have to get to the hospital at any time. Perhaps in the middle of the night. And you're telling me that I can't be contacted because you've had the phone cut off?'

'I thought you'd be pleased.'

'Pleased! Of course I'm not pleased.'

'I mean that I'm not going to get any more calls like that.'

'So why not get an answerphone?'

'We've been through all this before. I *hate* answerphones. And you can still hear what people are saying. I want to stop the sound of his voice. Not have it recorded on tape for all time.'

'All you have to do if he rings again is to put the phone down. He'll soon get fed up. Instead you disrupt everything – we'll have a new number to circulate to everyone—'

'Not everyone. I thought we'd be very careful, until he's apprehended. Anger tinged her voice. 'You seem more worried about your private patients than you are about me. What about your poor National Health patients? Don't they get the same devoted attention?'

'There's no need to sneer at my private patients. They've been the cream in our coffee for a very long time as well you know.' Leo paused, then, obviously making some effort to diffuse the tension: 'What did he actually say – this chap?'

'. . . Hello Roz . . .'

'Well, that doesn't sound too horrendous.' Leo smiled.

God he's patronising, thought Roz. Why have I never noticed it before? 'Then a long stream of stuff about community service . . . cleaning up mess . . . or something . . .'

'He didn't threaten you?'

'I don't think so. I tried not to listen.'

'I'd have thought the most effective way of not listening was to hang up.'

'Yes.' How could she explain the paralysis that had seeped into her bones? She now appeared, to herself as well as to Leo, as both witless and spineless.

'Can you still ring out?'

'Yes.'

'That's something. I'll call the hospital and explain what's happened. And the exchange to make sure any emergency calls get through. Did they say how long it would be – the new number?'

'No.'

'Oh marvellous. I suppose you realise that as he's discovered the old one he's perfectly capable of discovering the new?'

'Yes it had occurred to me Leo, but thank you very much for pointing it out. That makes me feel a lot better.'

As Roz turned back to the salad, her hands trembling, Leo slammed the kitchen door. When they eventually sat down to eat he hardly spoke. Usually there was at least one story about his day, a comment on the meal, questions about her day, or they would both talk about the children. This evening, when she asked about Guy's homework, he had replied briefly: 'Biology. Never any problems there,' and carried on eating.

They finished the chicken and brown rice. For pudding Roz had bought some baklava from the Greek shop. She usually loved these but tonight the mixture of honey and nuts seemed sickly and she left most of it. Their argument didn't seem to upset Leo, she thought as she watched him polish his off and pour a second cup of coffee. She had not realised he could be so insensitive. Her thoughts returned again to the scene at The Gay Hussar and Duffy's reaction to the phone call. Again she seemed to see him across the table, hands raised, smiling, understanding her without a word being said. And this time she did not push the picture away.

Fenn stood at the corner of Southampton Row and Great Ormond Street. A stream of traffic charged by, churning filthy water from the gutters over the pavement's edge. It was chucking it down and the sky was bulging with more rain, like a grey waterlogged blanket. He studied himself in the window of a gents' outfitters. He wore a flat, black plastic peaked cap and a little blond moustache gummed neatly into place. He carried Mr Christoforou's tool bag. Occasionally he glanced over at the entrance to City Radio. Time was getting on.

He was just starting to get worried when he saw Sonia come out. He stepped quickly back into the shop doorway. He watched her walk away, heading for Holborn Tube. She had a heavy shopping bag and a plastic carrier from Victoria Wine. Good. That meant a large meal and a glass or two when he eventually caught up with her. He'd look forward to that.

There was no point in hanging about. He joined the bunch of soaking, miserable-looking people at the traffic lights and crossed the road. As he approached the swing doors he struggled to recreate his feelings of rightness, the certainty of success that had so consumed him when he made his plans. He felt the omens were right, yet longed for a sign that luck was with him. Through the doors he could see the tall, fronded palms and gleaming glass and metal desk, the rich, dark carpets. He made himself walk on. To stop would be fatal. Up the steps. Across the carpet.

The girl behind the desk was very young and pretty. He couldn't help contrasting her with Sonia. If circumstances had been different . . . Her face was creatively painted with lovely colours and her yellow hair stood up in dozens of soft quilly spikes. She looked like a sweet sexy little hedgehog.

He walked straight past her, saying: 'Plumber . . . gents' downstairs toilet . . .'

She was rising. About to speak. 'Just a minute—'

'It's all right. I know where to go. Done it all before.'

But she was moving out towards him from behind the desk. And then he got his sign. A large man in a camel coat who looked as if he knew how to put it away came through the swing doors and called:

'Louise? What are you doing here?'

'Waiting for Felicity, Mr Winthrop. I'm standing in while she gets her coat.'

'Val Berry here yet?'

'I'll check for you.' The girl studied the book on the desk.

By this time Fenn was through the second door and halfway along the corridor. He knew now that the girl would not ring anyone to see if a plumber had been booked. Just as he knew that he would record his message undisturbed. The omens were right for him. The lavatory was empty. He had thought about tinkering with a spanner or fiddling with a cistern while he waited but there was always the chance that one of the people using the place would be the man in charge of maintenance. Although his luck was holding there was no point in pushing it.

He entered one of the cubicles and put his bag of tools out of sight on the cistern. Someone had left a copy of the *Sun* behind, which would pass the time. He turned to page three. He thought it was absolutely disgusting that some girls would show all they'd got to any yob with the price of a paper. Some people would do anything for money. If any girl of his did anything like that he'd give them something to remember. He thought of Sonia lying in the bottom half of a bikini licking an ice-cream cone and giggled, stopping quickly when someone came into the room.

He knew the office staff finished at five-thirty, in about five minutes, and he planned to stay hidden for a further quarter of an hour after that, giving them time to get away. He'd picked up all sorts of information from Sonia. He knew where the studios were and that there'd be staff around there till midnight. The fact that she disliked Roz Gilmour had been a real bonus. Endless information and unkind personal remarks poured forth. All he had to say was: 'And how was Madam today?' and she was off.

Cisterns were flushed. Hands were washed. Two men spent ages arranging a dinner, the first man giving a never-ending list of things his wife couldn't eat because she was pregnant, the second man sighing and saying, intermittently: 'Don't tell *me*.' Smoke from an expensive cigar drifted over into Fenn's cubicle. Then it was quiet.

He came out carrying his tool bag. The corridors seemed deserted. A few feet away was the lift. He pressed the button then retreated again to the lavatory just in case the lift was occupied. The doors opened automatically; it was empty. He dodged in and pressed the fourth-floor button. When the lift stopped, in spite of his overwhelming sense that the Fates were with him, he had to admit to a moment of anxiety. If he stepped out now and met someone it would be difficult to explain his presence. There was not much to plumb on the fourth floor. But there was not a soul. He walked straight to Roz's office.

Sonia had told him where the tape recorder was kept during one of his naive question sessions where he'd pretended to want to know absolutely everything about her office routine: 'So that I can picture you at work, darling.' He sat at Roz's desk, slipped on his gloves and placed the recorder in front of him. He had got everything he wanted to say written down and he opened the paper and spread it out, knowing it wouldn't really be necessary. The words were branded on his mind. He started to speak.

Sonia had been waiting forty-five minutes. At first she stood inside by the ticket machines to keep dry but then she thought Fenn might approach the station, not see her outside and walk away. This thought filled her with such panic that she ran into the street to check every three of four minutes and was now as wet as if she'd spent the whole time standing in the rain.

She had now reached the 'if' stage. If I close my eyes and count to twenty and don't open them no matter how much I want to, when I do he will be the first person I see. She counted to twenty and opened her eyes. A fair-haired young man was pushing his way through the rush-hour crowds. 'Fenn! Over here—'

But close to he didn't look like Fenn at all. As he put some coins in the ticket machine his eyes swept over her almost derisively. He bought two tickets then turned back into the crowd. He joined a rather striking girl in a leather mini skirt and thigh boots. He whispered and she turned and stared at Sonia and they both laughed. Oh! how she wished Fenn had come then, so that she could take his arm and stick her nose in the air. She pretended she hadn't noticed.

He'd been attending an audition this afternoon but had said nothing about being late. Perhaps he'd had to stay on and read again. It would be wonderful if he got a job, although Sonia couldn't help being worried about the actresses he might be working with. Ten more minutes dragged by. What if he'd had an accident; been run over? Or even mugged? She didn't really believe this. There was something about him. He seemed not exactly indestructible but grandly and secretly confident as if he knew something the rest of the world didn't.

Looking back over their few meetings Sonia still couldn't quite see how they had got to such an advanced stage in their relationship so quickly. He no longer seemed at all shy and although he never ever said so, she had somehow reached the conclusion that if she refused any of his 'physical demands' he would leave her. She often wished that he were a little more tender but perhaps that would come later. She was sure fatherhood would change him. And if things went as she planned there would definitely be children. She wanted a girl first, with Fenn's colouring but her own kind nature. And pretty. You could even manage without a kind nature if you were pretty.

'Hello.'

He had come up behind her. She flung herself at him, relief shining out of her face. Her bottle of wine cracked him across the knee.

'Ow. Give me a kiss then, Sony.'

He sometimes called her Sony because, he said, she could change channels at the flick of a button. Sonia never quite got the point of this remark but liked the idea of a nickname; it was friendly and indicated togetherness. On the Tube she snuggled up close.

'Darling,' she touched his face gently, 'your top lip's all red.'

He jerked away. He hadn't minded her kissing him in the ticket place which had been very crowded; here they were painfully visible. It occurred to him that everyone in the carriage must think she was the best he could do.

'It's spirit gum. This part I told you about – well it was one of these public-school snots. You know, toffy voices. So I wore this little moustache. Fair. Edward Fox type.'

'Was it old-fashioned then?'

'What?'

'The play. I mean they don't wear them much nowadays.'

'Yeah. Set in the thirties.'

'What was your part like?'

'Not a big one. One or two good scenes though.'

'What's the play about?'

'I dunno, do I? You only get to read a few pages. Not the

whole play.' God he was hungry. Ravenous. Now it was over and successful he could eat a ten-course dinner. 'What's in your bag then, Sony?'

She prepared pasta and there was a meat sauce that she had made the previous evening when she hadn't seen him, chopping everything carefully, watching over the slow, patient simmering. Her happiness had struck her then with a new, wondrous force.

Sometimes, just to enhance her feelings of joy, she would recall the evenings before they met and how bleak they were. An egg or a meat pasty, not eaten till eight-thirty to break up the hours. Watching the television just to pass the time, washing underwear that wasn't really dirty. And the endless, dusty summer evenings when she would take a long walk before bedtime, averting her eyes from couples lying in the park or groups of young people sitting outside pubs, laughing and drinking in the late sunshine.

The wine was Rioja – wine of the month the salesman had said – and it was really very nice. 'Fruity' was the adjective he used.

'Not as fruity as you, darling,' said Fenn just before he started what she called his little tricks. He drank very little as always, one glass to her four. When she had turned obediently towards the single narrow bed he had guided her away and towards one of the hardbacked dining chairs.

'Come *on* . . . no, don't sit down silly . . . here . . . like this . . .'

He gazed into her eyes and moved quickly. She made a tiny noise, rising up the scale, on an indrawn breath. 'Sorry. I'll have to cut my nails.'

But he didn't stop. Her eyes darkened. Moonishness

overcome by something else, a wistful yearning mixed with apprehension, the beginnings of fear. It added so much to his pleasure and almost made up for her lack of response. Then, in a rare moment of insight, he realised that it was her very lack of response that stimulated him.

God – that was better – it was amazing the chairback didn't break. What the people underneath must think. Delighted, he laughed into her bewildered face, altering her position for his final move.

Louise was in Roz's office drinking lemon tea. She had come in to discuss her future. She had been offered a course, the successful completion of which would make her eligible for promotion to Production Assistant, and felt that talking it over would help to clarify her thoughts. She was very happy working in the control room and wasn't sure she wanted to change. However their discussion had been abruptly terminated when Sonia had come in, fizzing with excitement and bearing a copy of the *Sun*, which she placed, like a dog with a ball, in front of Roz.

Toby's news conference had been a bit of a let-down, the quality papers either not turning up or giving his startling revelation a para on the back page, but the tabloids had been a bit more cooperative and here, above a publicity still of Roz, were the stark black headlines: DEATH THREAT REVEALED TO PHONE-IN STAR. The story underneath said nothing they didn't know already, but said it in terms pregnant with sinister implication.

Louise said: 'I think Toby's making a mistake. It just encourages exhibitionists – going to the papers.'

'That's what he wants. Good for the ratings.'

Louise screwed up her face: 'Not very nice for you. And anyway he's deliberately misled them. He's made it sound as if you've been threatened personally.'

'Oh, that's one of the perks of the job, didn't you know? You can have your own pet loony.' Roz was angry with Sonia for bringing in the *Sun*. She had been feeling better today: bright and fairly positive. The paper had set her back.

Between Roz's office door and the corridor was a tiny cubby hole. It had three narrow shelves holding rarely used files, a swivel chair and a rather wider white melamine shelf which could double as a desk-top in an emergency. Sonia always retired, very ostentatiously, to this space whenever Louise or Duffy came to talk to Roz. She retired there now, firmly closing the door. Roz, just as firmly, opened it and left it ajar. She resented the unspoken assumption that she and Louise were having the sort of conversation that should not be overheard; perhaps a conversation that included unkind remarks about her secretary.

'It's tomorrow's chip paper Roz. A couple of days and it'll be back where it belongs. In the gutter.'

'Not if Toby has his way.' Roz's voice was filled with distaste. 'He's trying to build this up. You know – will he won't he? Is his future victim even now walking the London streets blissfully unaware that her life is soon to be cut murderously short? It makes me sick.'

'Got to be a woman of course.'

'Of course. Where's the thrill in a man murdering a man?' Roz crumpled the paper up and stuffed it angrily into the waste basket. 'Sod that girl. I'm sorry Lou – we were supposed to be talking about your job.'

Louise opened her bag. 'That's all right. I suppose I've decided really. People always say they want advice and then do what they planned to do all along don't they?' She produced two familiar-looking oblongs. 'Want a Mars?'

'No thanks.' Somehow Roz did not have the heart to enter their usual routine. 'It's only ten minutes to lunch.' Then, on impulse:

'Duffy took me to The Gay Hussar yesterday.'

'So that's what it was.'

'Did he talk about it then?' Roz was disappointed, unreasonably she felt.

'No. But I saw him at half-five and he looked like a very fashionable cat that had just eaten at least half a dozen canaries followed by whipped cream.'

'He . . . seems very fond of me.'

'I've been telling you that for yonks.'

'I know but I've always felt it was a pose. A bit of a joke. I suppose it suited me to believe that. After all there's no point in it, is there? And I'd hate him to be unhappy.'

Louise said: 'I shouldn't worry about Duffy. Men are very good at looking after number one.'

Sonia entered, taking her coat from behind the door. 'I'm going for lunch now, Mrs Gilmour. Back at two p.m. sharp.'

She always said that. Roz was never sure if it was an assurance or an admonition. When the door closed she said to Louise: 'Sonia has a boyfriend who buys her Joy.'

'Wow! Even in my palmiest days I've never rated anything higher than Rive Gauche.'

'There you are, you see. There are obviously hidden assets.'

'Totally submerged I'd say.'

'Stop it. I'm not saying anything unkind about Sonia. I've made a vow.'

'Well I haven't. She must be worth it –' Louise spoke through a mouthful of Mars – 'perhaps she's on the game.'

The idea of Sonia being on the game was so ludicrous that they both burst out laughing. Louise continued: 'Are you going home to work now?'

'No, I don't think so.' A short while ago Roz could not have imagined a time when she would rather stay in her office than go home. 'I've got quite a lot of letters.'

Louise got up. 'How's Michael Kelly coming on?'

'Slowly.' She pulled the tape recorder to her. 'That's funny.'

'What's funny?' Louise stopped at the door.

'I put a new tape in here before I went home the other day and someone's used it.'

'Perhaps it's a message from Toby.'

'He leaves a scrawl. Or sends a minion. How odd.'

Louise came back then and sat down. 'Well go on then, play it.'

As Roz still didn't move Louise reached across, pressed the rewind button then the one marked 'play'.

'Hello Roz . . .' Her hand flashed out to the stop button. They looked at each other.

'Is Duffy here?'

Louise nodded. 'He's in the reporters' room.'

'Please ask him to come up, Lou. I don't think I want to listen to this by myself.'

Louise was not offended at the suggestion that her presence rated less than nil but when she returned not only Duffy but Toby Winthrop was with her. Roz's heart sank.

'What is it, Rossi? What's the buzz?'

Louise looked sympathetically at Roz and lifted her shoulders. 'Toby was in the reporters' room. Sorry.'

'Is it your eccentric, darling? Or should I say nutter?'

'What's the difference?' Duffy sounded ready for anything, aggressively so.

'Oh, class of course. Ruling and upper-middle eccentric – lower-middle and working, nutters.'

'There's a message on my tape recorder.' Feeling sick she pressed the start button.

'. . . Roz. How unkind of you to hang up on me at home. But you see how persistent I am. And how clever. I've penetrated your little stronghold. Aren't you surprised? I wish I could see your face. Now, about this death. I want to be absolutely fair about it, Roz. I mean, I think you should know why. The point is that, like a lot of very famous and successful people, you're really just a pile of filth, aren't you – as a human being? In fact I think we can dispense with the term human being altogether. Once we've tidied that out of the way things become much simpler. I mean anyone who gets rid of a pile of filth is doing the community a service. They even get paid. So I'm doing an awful lot of people a favour, Roz. All the others you've let down. People like me who turned to you for help believing all this shit you vomit over the airwaves. I expect you thought I was just another nonentity. Like everyone else you've kicked aside. That was your big mistake. I might even say your last mistake. There's a photograph of you facing me, Roz. So beautiful. You won't look like that when I've finished with you. You'll be glad when it's over. I won't keep you any longer now. I have plans to make and of course you'll have your affairs to put in order. To be honest and quite fair with you I can't promise to be in touch again. I mean before the day. I feel by giving you the warning in a general sense like this I've played as straight as I should. We don't want to tip the scales too far the other way, do we? Goodbye Roz.'

There was a silence which lengthened. Roz sat crumpled in her chair, waiting for it to be broken. Eventually she said, through a parched mouth: 'Switch it off.'

Duffy reached over and did so. Toby said: 'Well, apart from the fact that he seems to have the bodily functions a bit confused that seems to be pretty straightforward.'

'For Christ's sake, Toby.' Duffy sat on the desk corner and took Roz's hand. Her face was deathly pale. 'Get some water, Lou.'

'It's all right . . . I'm all right.'

'Of course she is.' Toby was blustering, almost exploding with pleasure. 'Takes something like this in her stride, don't you – our Rossi? They never do anything anyway, these barmies. They're like the hijackers, always going to blow up the plane, always going to shoot the passengers. They never do.' He pressed the rewind button.

'You're not going to play it again!'

'Remember who you're talking to, Louise, and watch your tone.' Toby waited till the tape clicked off and flipped it out of the machine. 'I shall take this away –' he slipped it into his pocket – 'and submit it, suitably edited of course, to the press who, I must say, took my previous hot tip a touch casually. Perhaps this'll perk them up.'

'You might make enquiries while you're at it down at Security,' said Duffy. Louise looked at him with surprise. She had never seen him so angry. He was almost as white as Roz.

'Security?'

'As he seems to have walked in here, made his way to Roz's office, used the machine and walked out all without anyone noticing anything was amiss, I'd have said that Security was the place to start!'

'You're right.' For the first time Toby showed traces of alarm. 'We've got some bloody expensive equipment around here.' He glanced at the clock behind Roz's desk. 'Eight minutes to. I should be able to get this on the news.'

'Pity you're carrying the tape, isn't it?' Toby at the door looked blankly questioning. Duffy continued: 'It stops you rubbing your hands together.' Then, to Louise: 'There's a hip flask in my overcoat pocket – in the newsroom. Could you get it, sweetheart?'

After they left he said: 'I hate to say this lovely, but for once Toby's right. I know it's a foul thing to have to listen to but they hardly ever do anything.'

She sat very still, looking more disbelieving than frightened as people do who have been given appalling news but have not quite taken it in. She said, in a still, reasonable voice: 'Sometimes they do, Duffy.'

Yes. Sometimes they did. The voice had sounded terribly relentless. He obviously saw himself as a divinely appointed avenger. And there was no way you could reach them, the mad ones with a mission. Duffy tried to keep these apprehensions out of his voice as he said: 'We must contact the police.'

'I suppose so, although I don't see what they can do.'

A call to Southampton Row station resulted in a visit from a sergeant accompanied by a young policewoman.

'For all the world,' as Roz later said to Leo, 'as if they were bringing news of a bereavement.'

They had been to Toby's office and listened to the tape and were now sitting with Roz and Duffy drinking coffee out of plastic cups from the machine in the corridor. The policewoman had a notebook and pencil. Roz, after a couple of hefty slugs of Duffy's Glenlivet, had a little colour in her cheeks.

'You see Miss Gilmour,' said the sergeant, who had glossy moustaches the colour of conkers, 'although I'm sure this can't have been a very pleasant experience for you it's all a bit run of the mill to us. I don't know if you've discussed this with any of your colleagues in the media—'

'She's hardly had time to discuss it with anyone,' Duffy cut in.

The sergeant drank a little of his coffee and mopped his moustaches delicately with a snowy handkerchief '— but if you do I think you'll find most of them have received something similar to this at some time or other. Obscene phone calls, threats, demands for money, it seems to go with the job. Something public figures have to learn to live with. These people very rarely follow the threats up, you know.'

Personally he didn't like this at all. There had been genuine enjoyment in that voice. He wouldn't be surprised if the chap was psychopathic. But there was no point in saying so at this stage.

'But surely there's something you can do. The man must be committing an offence.'

'Indeed he is Sir.' The sergeant had taken against Duffy. He could do without Galahads and heated, nudging remarks. He liked things to proceed at a certain pace. He could see too, out of the corner of his eye, that WPC Palmer seemed to be taking down every single syllable that everyone was saying. He would have to speak to her afterwards. The day was proving to be full of revelations, not least of which was that coffee existed which was worse than that at the station canteen. He placed his half-full cup carefully on the corner of Roz's desk and repeated: 'Indeed he is. A threat is a form of assault. But we have very little to go on. I shall question the reception staff, of course.'

'I doubt if he gave his name and intentions at the desk.' Duffy knew he was being unreasonable but couldn't stop. Talk about Mr bloody Plod. 'Can't you check for fingerprints?'

'Yes,' nodded the sergeant, patience on a monument, 'but I'm not hopeful. At least three people have handled the machine since the tape was made and if our chap's half as clever as he thinks he is he'd have been wearing gloves. Can you tell me,' he turned to Roz, 'when you think the tape might have been made? Make a note of this, Constable Palmer.'

The policewoman looked startled, blushed and stopped writing.

'I left about three. My secretary left a little earlier than usual for a dental appointment, about five past five. Her usual time is five-thirty.'

'Does that apply to all the office staff?'

'Yes. This floor would probably be empty by around a quarter to six. Of course the ground floor and the studios are still busy. We transmit till midnight.'

'And the morning?'

'Sonia – my secretary – gets here at nine. But the station's open from seven.'

'I'll have a word with her before I go. You have absolutely no idea who this man might be?' Roz shook her head. 'Was the recorder put away in a cupboard?'

'No. Anyone opening the door would see it.'

'But they'd have to know which door to open. There's no card outside. Which seems to indicate some knowledge of the layout here.'

'Yes.' Roz paused. Constable Palmer's pencil, which had been flying over her pad again at the speed of light, was momentarily still. 'He contacted me before. I got a postcard. And he rang me at home.'

'That may be helpful. May I see the card?'

'I'm afraid it got thrown away. I didn't attach any importance to it at the time. An In Memoriam card. Black-edged with a cross.'

'Very artistic. What did he say when he called you at home?'

'I don't know. I know that sounds unlikely but when I heard his voice I just sort of cut out. I've got an ex-directory number. I can't think how he got hold of it. It's been changed now.'

'Did you tell the police?'

'Yes. At my local station. They said there wasn't anything they could do.'

'I'll get anything from there sent over to us.'

'That sounds ominous. As if you're expecting to build up a file.'

'Not at all.' The sergeant smiled as he rose. A slightly superior smile; calming Galahad as well as his lady. 'We've probably heard the last of him. It's sensible though to keep all information in one place.'

'Of course.' Roz smiled back. She felt encouraged. He seemed so solid and unruffled. And there were thousands like him. A whole armoury of men, cars, equipment. Forensic laboratories. Computers. Telecommunications. Guns.

'I believe I heard your secretary returning from lunch?'

'Yes indeed.' Roz had heard the outer door slam. 'Would you like to talk to her in here?'

She left Sonia, agog with excitement and pleasure, answering questions and went to the canteen. The news bulletin blared from a tannoy on the wall.

'Roz Gilmour, host of top phone-in programme *Roz's Roundabout*, has received a death threat. We can now reveal that the message, cleverly smuggled into the building on tape, is the latest in a whole series of particularly unpleasant attacks on this popular, well-loved personality.'

In spite of herself Roz almost smiled. How typical of Toby. Oddly enough, instead of fuelling her alarm she found the melodramatic announcements comforting. The hype seemed to work in reverse, making the tape less, instead of more, important. Of course she was a million miles from taking it as a joke. She never would. But the policeman was probably right. It was some poor little pervert, desperate for attention, who had chosen her to work it off on. What was it Leo had said? If it's Monday it must be Gilmour? She stood up, then sat down quickly. Duffy's whisky on an empty stomach had made her feel very light headed. Just time to fill up with Salmonella Fish Cakes garnie before driving home. She wondered if Duffy was still in the building and decided to check the reporters' room before placing her order.

*

When Fenn woke the next morning he knew immediately there was something very wrong. Settling down to sleep the previous night he had been aware that his state of mind, which should have been perfectly tranquil, had something, some tiny unnamed anxiety, snagging the edges. He had gone over the day a step at a time. It seemed supremely satisfactory. He had accomplished his mission at the studio with cool bravura; he had dined very well, drunk very little and fucked a lot, leaving Sonia more or less shattered. Everything should have been perfect. But by the time he fell asleep the worry had not been resolved and it had waxed fat in the night so that he felt not refreshed, but cumbrously burdened.

He got up, dressed and made some very strong instant coffee. He sat at his table and got out his plan. He went through everything for the umpteenth time. He was sure, with his cap and moustache, that the girl at reception would not recognise him again. Sonia, the only person who could, had not been in the building. Although he had no record or prints on file he had still worn gloves: safety first. So what had he forgotten? Nothing. Then why this overwhelming feeling of anxiety?

When it hit him it seemed so obvious. It came like a mighty punch from behind or a bucket of icy water in the face. He couldn't move. Just sat there while he absorbed the blow. He was finished. Cheated. Worse, on the point of capture. Because as soon as Sonia heard the tape she would recognise his voice. The enormity of his stupidity was almost more than he could bear. How could he not have thought of this? He clenched his fist and pounded his forehead again and again, wanting only to damage the feeble brain that had betrayed him.

And she had his telephone number. He had rung her up once from the phone in the hall and she, wanting to coo and ramble on, had rung him back. He hadn't worried about it at the time. A pay phone wasn't listed in the directory and so wouldn't give her his address. But the police would soon trace it. They must have been called in by now. He looked at the clock and his blood ran cold. It was nearly two-thirty.

He must have slept until lunch time and then sat, a lot longer than he realised, at his table. He got up and started to pace about frantically. Even if Sonia didn't give him away when she heard the tape she would give herself away. He snatched at a straw. Perhaps she would be alone when she first heard it. She had told him how she typed some letters from replies Roz had put on tape at home. Perhaps Roz had simply carried on using the machine without playing back the beginning. In that case she would not have heard the message and the police would not yet have been called. It was a slim chance. Of course Sonia herself might have called the police but he didn't think that likely. She would know it would mean the end of their relationship. His head ached from the pounding of his fist and such maze-like speculations.

The thought of Sonia having any sort of hold over him made him shake with nausea. She would cling and whine and dribble hints of honeymoons and three-piece suites and, vilest of all, babies. And always, behind the words, would lie the unspoken, that other hint that was so nearly a threat. No. He could never stomach that. He would just have to vanish. Other people did. He would get on a train and go to another city. Birmingham, perhaps Bristol. He'd survive. Pick up some sort of casual work. And find some other doting female to feed him. That shouldn't be difficult. But oh! – the black bile of disappointment welled up and over in his heart – to have to abandon his grand design. To let Roz Gilmour get away with it. Still it needn't be for ever. He was young. People would soon forget about the tape. And then he would return. And strike.

He moved quickly, taking a canvas holdall from under the bed. He put in first half a dozen of his books, the rarest of his collection, then his new clothes, the watches and wallets and some underwear. He put on his coat and collected such money as he had. He decided to take a train from Paddington to the West Country as far as fifteen pounds would take him, and hitch the rest of the way to Bristol. He left the room and found the landing door to the fire escape locked. He would just have to trust to luck and use the stairs.

He was three steps down when the phone rang. Mr Christoforou was passing through the hall. He picked up the phone. Luck, fawning all over Fenn yesterday, was spitting in his eye today. He put his bag behind him out of sight on the landing and made to step back but it was too late.

Mr Christoforou, backed by the radiant smile and glowing, vulgar pendulous fruits of the Caribbean poster, was holding out the phone.

'Hey,' he called. 'It's for you.'

Chapter Five

'What sits in the middle of Paris and wobbles?'

Kathy said: 'I know *that*.'

'No you don't. In any case I was asking Mum.'

'I know more than anyone thinks I know just because I'm seven.'

Roz was forming and re-forming various sentences to open a conversation with Leo. He had come home, concerned this time, after hearing the news on the car radio, but had been reassured by the stoical, almost optimistic attitude that had held through her lunch with Duffy and the rest of the day, fortified by fairly frequent trips to the wine rack. But in the cold light of morning she felt far less confident and was searching around for ways and means to bolster her morale.

'I wouldn't give you two out of ten for that last sentence. As far as structure is concerned, grammatically speaking that sentence was an absolute shambles. Mum – what sits in the middle of Paris and wobbles?'

Her worries about the children had proved quite unnecessary. Kathy mercifully hadn't seemed to grasp what was going on at all, Guy thought it was all very thrilling and she should contact MI5.

'I don't know. What does?'

'The trifle tower.'

'Good heavens – I knew *that*,' said Kathy.

'No you didn't. You don't even know where Paris is.'

The wine had made Roz sluggish. Her head felt heavy and her mouth sour. She couldn't seem to wake up properly. 'Leo . . .' An all-purpose sound from behind *The Times*. 'Oh do put that down. I'm trying to talk to you.'

'Sorry.' Leo put down the paper and smiled. 'Good coffee.'

'It's what we always have. Leo – I think we should change all the locks.'

'What on earth for?'

'I should think it's obvious what for.'

'Ohhh him. He hasn't got a key has he?' Leo's eyes were already straying back to *The Times*. Roz leaned over and removed it. He frowned. 'We've had enough of a hoo-ha with the phone without whizzing around ripping all the locks off.'

'Then we should get someone to watch the house.'

Leo said: 'Have you any idea what that would cost? They charge something like twenty pounds an hour, these people.'

'I thought perhaps as it's my life at stake you might think it would be worth it.'

'Don't be so melodramatic, Roz. Do you think if your life really was at stake I'd be talking like this? The police would have a man watching the house for a start.'

'They say they can't spare anyone. Not on such slight grounds.'

'There you are then. They're very experienced in

assessing situations like this. If they think the grounds are slight they're probably correct.'

'Probably's enough for you, is it?'

'Where do spiders play football?' Guy paused. 'Mummy, where do—'

'You seemed concerned enough last night.'

'I was concerned. And I am. But we've got to keep this in proportion. The chances are it'll come to nothing.'

'I see. And what am I supposed to do while we wait and see if it'll come to anything? How am I supposed to live? Permanently looking over my shoulder? How long for, Leo? A week? A month? The rest of my life?'

'Mummy . . . *Mummy* . . .'

'How am I supposed to work?'

'You could stop work. We could more than manage on my salary.'

'Guy knows where spiders play football, Mummy.'

'Ahhh . . . now we're coming to the real point. You've never wanted me to work, have you? You've always been jealous.'

'Roz!' Leo looked astounded. 'You know that's not true.'

'Thanks anyway for your wonderful suggestion. My problem's solved then. All I have to do is secure all the windows, bolt all the doors and never go out. I could stay in the kitchen all day baking wholesome things and making patchwork quilts and brewing mead like the pioneer women.' Her voice tore up the scale. 'With a shotgun by my side in case of Indians.'

'Mummy . . .' Kathy reached out to clutch at her mother's arm and knocked over a tall glass of orange juice. Roz slapped the child hard across the face. The bright liquid spread over the checked cloth and started to drip on to the floor. She stared at her children in disbelief and amazement. They stared mutely back. She had never hit them in their lives. Guy pushed his chair back and went to his sister. Kathy, too shocked to cry, buried her face in his blazer.

'. . . I'm sorry . . .' Roz looked across at Leo, who got up and walked out of the room. 'Leo . . .' – it was almost a whisper – 'don't go . . .'

Some of the juice was dripping on to her cream skirt. She watched it spread: a jaundiced comment on the whole awful turn her life was taking. Leo came back carrying his case. He rested it on the Welsh dresser, opened it. He took out a dark brown bottle and shook out a couple of tablets. Then he went to the table, poured out some juice and bent over Roz.

'Here. Take these.'

'Oh Leo – I don't want to spend the day stupefied.'

'You won't. They'll just take the edge off things. Help you cope. Are you going in today?' Roz shook her head. 'Will you do some work here?'

'I can't, Leo. I can't seem to concentrate. Everything seems to be . . . breaking up around me.'

She watched him making a visible effort to be patient as he sometimes did with the children.

'I'm sorry I can't stay. I'll be home as soon as I can. When I get a break I'll ring and see how things are.'

'. . . Thank you . . .' Roz felt ashamed when she heard the gratitude in her voice. She swallowed the tablets, put the glass down and looked again at the children. Guy looked hard and accusing. Kathy had started to cry, the tears

CAROLINE GRAHAM

running over the angry, scarlet mark on her cheek. 'Oh darling. I'm so sorry.'

'Listen Roz.' Leo took her hand. 'You're under a lot of strain. You lost your temper and slapped your youngest. Don't over-react and lash yourself into a state of self-abasement. It happens in families all the time.'

'Not in ours, Leo.'

'No.' Leo paused. 'I suppose we're exceptional. Or perhaps it's just that we've never had to face any really tough problems before.'

Roz gripped his hand. Maybe that was true. Certainly their lives, until a few days ago, had now obtained in her mind a patina of golden, innocent happiness that had an almost Eden-like quality. Before the serpent. Before the fall. She struggled to keep a sense of perspective. She simply couldn't let one single human being, some demented soul that she'd never even met, affect her like this. And the lives of the people most dear to her. And how pleased he would be if he could see the unhappiness and upheaval he had already caused. It was this thought more than any other which made her take a deep breath and say to Leo: 'I feel better now. I'll be all right.'

'Mrs Jollit will be here soon. She'll cheer you up.' They both laughed and she saw the tight, apprehensive looks on the faces of her children dissolve like snow under sunshine. 'If you'll drop Guy off I'll keep Kathy home today.'

'That's not fair!'

'Come on, Guy. I'm ten minutes late as it is.'

Grumbling, Guy followed his father up the stairs. 'I should have a treat then to make up for it. I should have something.'

'Where do spiders play football anyway?'

'Poor Guy.' Kathy sighed, a rather smug sigh. 'Why aren't I going to school, Mummy?'

This guileless enquiry struck Roz straight to the heart. She wondered how long the mark would take to fade. 'We can look at the frozen teddies this morning. I have to go to Marks and Spencer's. And perhaps this afternoon you'd like to go to the toy museum.'

Kathy's smile lifted her cheeks into soaking wet cushions: 'Ohh yes.' She loved the toy museum with its poky stairs and tiny, dark Victorian rooms crammed with dolls and cardboard theatres and puppets. 'Perhaps we could buy a present for Guy, because he couldn't come as well.'

'We'll find something. Let's mop you up.'

'I'll do it in the bathroom.' Kathy climbed down and started for the door.

'No – don't do that.' She meant don't look in the mirror. 'Look – over here. Let's do it with a paper towel.'

As she dabbed at Kathy's face with exaggerated tenderness she glanced at the clock. No avoiding the voice of the sibyl this morning. And Mrs Jollit took the *Sun*, which would no doubt add fresh fuel to her tragic utterances. None of this would be good for Kathy. At least they shouldn't overlap by more than a few minutes. She took Kathy to the hall and helped her into her coat and balaclava. The day was cold though brilliantly sunny.

'Wait in the sitting room darling. I'll just get my bag and keys.' Back in the kitchen, hunting for her purse, Roz began to feel a bit more cheerful. It looked as if they might miss Mrs J. after all. She was late – due at nine-thirty and it was now nearly twenty to ten. She was just starting to climb the stairs when the phone rang.

Her first reaction was one of alarm. All her apprehensions came rushing back until she remembered that their number had been changed. Only half a dozen people had the new one. She hurried to the sitting room.

'Hello?'

'Mrs Gilmour? It's me.'

'Oh Mrs Jollit. Aren't you well? I was wondering where you were.'

'I'm at home where I'll be safe. And at home I'm going to stay.'

'Why? What's the matter?' As if she didn't know. The jaundiced stain spread a little further, bringing disruption now as well as unhappiness.

'Well – you know about this cancer problem I've got.'

'Yes.'

'I saw this programme on the telly. It said one of the main causes was stress. Well, with my prepondancy to the disease I've obviously got to keep well away from any situation that's going to get me into a state. You get my drift, Mrs Gilmour?'

'Oh yes.'

'I mean I could come over to your place and get murdered in me bed.'

'He's not at my place. We have locks and bolts and the house is quite secure.' And, she added silently, it's not you he's after. 'I do wish you'd reconsider. It's really going to leave me in the lurch.'

'And I've got my Albert to think about. I can't go and catch some terrible wasting disease just because you might be left in the lurch. I'll be back when they've caught him.'

'Don't bother.'

'Pardon?'

'I can't manage with no one at all so I shall have to get someone from an agency. I shall deduct the no-doubt astronomical fee from your money.'

'I'm entitled to a week's wages.'

'Not if you don't work a week's notice. Goodbye.' Roz banged the phone down. She turned to Kathy. 'I'm sorry darling but Mrs Jollit can't come in today, so we'll have to tidy up a bit before we go out. Will you help like a good girl?'

'What shall I do?'

'You could make your bed and Guy's. And I'll start washing up.'

After Kathy had disappeared upstairs Roz turned on the taps, piled all the dishes into the sink and seized the canister of washing-up liquid. She pointed it into the breakfast debris and fired it, with all her force, like a gun.

He knew the minute she spoke that it was all right. At least for now. He could tell by her voice. She wasn't smart enough to fake.

'I know you said I shouldn't ring you at home dear, but I'm going to be a bit late tonight and I didn't want to think of you standing about in this weather. I thought we could meet in our little coffee bar.'

He wondered which one that was. She was so nauseatingly sentimental. Any place they had visited more than once became 'their' coffee bar, pub or restaurant.

159

'Why are you going to be late?'

'Wouldn't you like to know?'

Jesus wept. Of course I'd like to know, you stupid bitch. Why do you think I'm asking you? She sang in a little-girl voice: 'Tellyouwheniseeyou.' Then: 'At the Donatello. I must go, I'm all behind.'

Chance'd be a fine thing, he thought sourly. 'You sound very excited, Sony. What's up?'

'Tell you tonight. I promise.'

'And I promise that if you don't tell me now I won't be there tonight.'

Pause. 'Well – Madam's had a death threat. The real thing. On a tape. I've been with the police for absolutely hours. Talk about the third degree.'

The flicker of fear was instinctive; his rational mind doused it straight away. Until she heard the tape there was nothing she could tell them. 'Are they going to talk to you again?'

'No.' He could tell how much she wanted to say yes. 'Love you.'

'See you later.' He hung up.

What was he to do? Anything could happen between now and six o'clock. The old Bill could change their minds and talk to Sony yet again. Perhaps winkle out vital info. Even play her the bloody tape! Fenn knew he should cut his losses and run. No question.

On the other hand, how could he throw away a golden opportunity to discover what the police knew or didn't know? What they'd done with the tape (*if only he could get it back*) and, most important of all, how Roz had reacted when she heard it. God – he'd have given the world to see that. See her shake and tremble and cry. Hearing about it would be the next best thing.

He decided to keep his date but conceal himself till Sonia arrived. One glance would be enough. First sight, he would know.

The Donatello was appropriately situated in an Italianate passage ending in a courtyard near Dombey Street. In the summer there were tubs of bay and oleanders and hanging baskets of flowers with tables and benches. The paved yard looked almost like a piazza. Now the courtyard was empty. There were six lamp standards, the milky globes of light cupped in filigreed metal. They shone on dripping shop signs and were reflected in still puddles.

Fenn stood in the shadows where he could see the approach. For the first time since they met he could hardly wait to see Sonia. Before leaving he had written down every single thing he would want to know. He planned to space the questions out of course, lest she became suspicious.

She was late. Another first. As he waited Fenn became gripped by cold anxiety. What if, after all, she had been faking the phone call? He might have underestimated her. The police could have been there, at her elbow, telling her what to say. Setting a trap. Perhaps were, even now, all about him. Hiding in the apparently closed stationery store and Ski and Sand boutique opposite. Or sitting, plainly clothed, in the restaurant, sipping an aperitif.

But then he saw her and knew straightaway his fears were groundless. She flew past shimmering with excitement, her whole demeanour shouting: 'hold the Front Page!'

He watched it all seep away as she entered Donatello's, realised he was not there, presumed he had been and gone and sat down, uncertain what to do next.

He gave it five, long enough to bring her to the verge of tears, then sauntered in.

'Fenn!' she cried, her face lit up like a car headlamp. She was talking nineteen-to-the-dozen before he'd even sat down.

'My God, sweetheart. What a day it's been! Well – I never want to have another like it.' The opening lines of her dramatic recitation thus untruthfully declaimed Sonia got up and took off her coat and woolly hat. Doing the rounds at the radio station, she had discovered quite a talent in herself for telling a tale and sensed that a pause near the opening was a great way of creating suspense. She folded her coat and put it on the chair next to her, placing her hat on top. She removed her wet gloves slowly and carefully, tugging at each finger and eyeing him the while with dreadful roguishness. Fenn watched this grisly parody of a strip routine, keeping his mouth closed by a tremendous effort of will. He could have choked her.

'I thought I'd never get away.' She started watching the waiter and signalling in the aggressive way unconfident people often have. 'I've simply got to have a coffee . . . I just can't tell you . . .'

After three or four minutes of this Fenn got up very suddenly, walked across to the counter where there was a Gaggia and came back with a cup. He placed it with extreme care directly in front of her and said: 'There you are, lovely. Let's hear all about it then.'

'Ohh Fenn,' she inhaled the steam as if it were the rarest nectar, 'you *are* good to me.' Then, as if sensing she had gone far enough: 'Well – I was with the police for absolutely—'

'Hold on, hold on. Start at the beginning. You said something about a tape?'

'Someone's got it in for Roz all right. He actually entered the building, found her office and taped the death threat on her own machine. You've got to admire his cheek.'

'You mean ...' Fenn sounded amazed, '. . . he just walked in?'

'Just walked in.'

'But haven't you any security?'

'Of course. There's always someone at the desk. She says no one got by her.'

'He must have got in the back way,' said Fenn, who had checked this out.

'There isn't a back way. You see what this means? If he didn't come through the front *and* he knew exactly where her office was . . . ?'

The coyly arched brows and leading pause with held breath prompted him to spoil it for her. 'An inside job?'

Sonia's adoring gaze became tinged with peevishness. 'Obviously. The police are working on that line. Although my understanding is that they remain baffled.'

He asked: 'And didn't you get to hear this horror job?'

She sighed, genuinely regretful. 'No.'

'Never mind. Perhaps Roz'll play it for you tomorrow.'

'She hasn't got it. The police have taken it away.'

'Are you going to have to go to the station for a listen?'

'No.' She sighed again. The party was definitely over. 'They seem to think he won't do anything. He's just one of these nutters. You know how it is,' a collective twinkle, one celebrity *manqué* to another, 'if you're famous you're very open to this sort of thing.'

Whilst one part of his mind flamed with resentment at this evaluation another was overwhelmed with relief. For the moment he was safe. And he had more than made his point. He had frightened her to the extent that she had called in the police. It had been on the news. It had been treated seriously.

'And how did *she* take it?' It suited him to subtly bolster Sonia's dislike of her boss. It made her feel he was on her side and kept the information, albeit biased, forthcoming.

'Madam?' Sonia snorted. 'Scared out of her wits. You should have seen her. Trembling like a leaf. White as a ghost. Of course they were all dancing around her. All the men. Old Duffield was rushing around getting her whisky and glasses of water. I could hear them through the door. And she was encouraging him. As if she didn't have a perfectly good husband and children at home.' She stopped, remembering that now she had no cause to be jealous of Roz. She too would soon have a husband and children of her own. Fenn watched her face change, correctly sizing up the reason and thinking: in a pig's eye.

He wondered if she had Roz's new phone number in her address book. Roz hadn't lost much time in changing it. He had decided to ring before coming out, just to reinforce the threat on the tape. To let her know it wasn't someone playing games. But he got the number-unobtainable tone. He couldn't help laughing. As if something like that would stop him. Nothing would stop him.

The relief had made him relax for the first time in several hours with the result that his sphincter relaxed as well. He stood up hastily. 'Shan't be a minute, Sony.'

In the loo, emptying his bladder, washing his hands,

smoothing his hair back in front of the full-length mirror, Fenn began to feel the sense of destiny seeping back into his veins.

The police obviously weren't going to make a big thing of this. Sonia hadn't even been in the building when the tape was made so they wouldn't be talking to her again. All the same he felt time pressing on his heels. He had been looking forward to having a bit of a game with Roz. Now you see me, now you don't. One or two more tasty little telephone threats. But all that would have to be cut a bit short. A pity. Sometimes when he pictured the end of the hunt the images would almost stop his heart, such was their terrible and exciting power. Yet there was an awful lot to be said for the chase. Each detail, each twist and turn, the lure, the smell of fear, the appearance and disappearance of his quarry. The need to be supple and think fast; to anticipate and backtrack.

Even earlier today when he had thought himself beaten he had never felt so alive! The days no longer dawned grey and monotonous but new-minted, as if polished up specially for him. In a way he would be sorry when it was all over but he also knew that he would be transformed. He didn't know quite how or what the result would be, only that in his own eyes, and those of the world, he would be completely different.

Back in the restaurant Sonia was quietly studying his list.

The agency had promised to send someone within twenty-four hours. It was the sort of agency prepared to tackle anything. The voice on the phone had such an indecisive, flute-like timbre that Roz's response must have sounded uncertain because it went on to assure her that satisfaction 'however *outré* your request' was guaranteed. 'Only last week we supplied a steeplejack, a pixie for Selfridges and escorted a camel from Stanstead airport.'

'Fine.' Roz's voice was heavy. Not so long ago she would have relished such a delightful juxtaposition of jobs, saved them up to tell Leo. 'He'll be here in the morning then?'

'Nine-thirty.' The voice, about to hang up, added: 'Oh – I hope you don't mind actors?'

'Good heavens no.'

'A lot of our staff are. They're always resting, you know.'

'Well as long as he doesn't rest on my time.'

This acerbic note did not go down at all well. There was a cracked note in the flute as it said: 'Goodbye Mrs Gilmour.'

Now Roz was waiting for this unnamed actor to make his entrance. She was looking forward to the company. She who had previously looked forward, more than anything else, to having the house to herself. She doubted if he would be as efficient as Mrs Jollit. On the other hand she wouldn't have to cope with terminal neuroses. The doorbell.

As she entered the hall and saw a tall, dark shadow outlined behind the stained glass she felt a fleeting tinge of disquiet. She should have had a chain put on the door. She would organise that today before going to the studio. There was a locksmith in the high street. She opened the door a fraction of an inch and peered out.

'Mrs Gilmour? Greg. From the agency.'

'Come in.' She smiled, swinging the door back. 'Sorry to seem suspicious. It's just . . .'

'I heard, dear.' He followed her into the hall and down to the kitchen. 'Too hairy for words.'

'Would you like some coffee?'

'Well . . . you're paying for the time, Mrs Gilmour.'

'Roz.'

'Coffee would be lovely.' He put his leather jacket on the back of a chair and looked admiringly round the kitchen. 'Super house.'

'Yes.' She put the kettle on. 'We got it just before the prices exploded. You'd have to be almost a millionaire now. Where do you live?'

'Palmers Green. I share a flat with a friend.' He perched on one of the bentwood stools. 'Do you have a set routine you'd like me to follow? Or is it different every day?'

'Mrs Jollit had a fixed routine but she'd been here quite a long time and knew what I wanted. I think we'll just sort it out from day to day.'

'Why did she leave?'

'Because of this awful business . . . you know.' Greg nodded sympathetically. 'She thought she'd be murdered in her bed.'

'Did she live in then?'

'No.' Greg snorted with laughter and Roz smiled too. 'I've got to advertise for permanent help and as Leo and I both work I have to have someone to fill the gap.'

Greg glanced at the pile of washing-up in the sink and on the draining board. 'See what you mean, dear.' Then: 'I say. What a divine mog.'

Madgewick, hearing a new voice, had lumbered out of his basket to investigate. Roz gave a brief rundown of his origins.

'Poor beast. I just love the motley.'

'Yes. It is a bit like Joseph's coat.'

CAROLINE GRAHAM

Greg watched Roz pour coffee into two heavy dark green breakfast cups. He thought how pale she was beneath the skilfully applied make-up and wondered what it must be like to have someone you've never seen announce that they're going to kill you. Moved suddenly by her predicament he said: 'I know it's easy for me to talk but I shouldn't worry too much. They—'

'—never do anything.' Roz spoke with him.

'Sorry. I expect everyone says that.'

Roz sat at the table with her cup. 'Everyone who's never been threatened.'

He was really very nice, she decided. He was curious but not pruriently so and seemed genuinely sympathetic. He was tall and rangy with a long narrow bony face like a kind rocking horse's. He had pale green eyes and a lot of reddish curly hair. He wore the inevitable jeans and a hand-knitted Fair Isle sweater. He sat at the table with her.

'Do you want to talk about it?'

'I don't know. Sometimes I think if I don't I'll forget about him. Or he'll go away. But it doesn't work like that.'

'Best not to be on your own if you can help it. I don't mean that you're really in danger, but so's you don't brood. Just till they catch him.'

'They're not really bothered. The police I mean. They seem to think this sort of hassle goes with the job.'

'They're not far wrong. I used to char for a newsreader. A famous telly face. I won't give you his name – he's fallen on ever such hard times, poor darling, what with the gin and other little peccadillos – but he got hundreds of letters from dementos. You know the sort of thing. He used to

168

read the daftest out to me. We'd spend hours in fits on his Liberty's sofa.'

'What sort of thing?' Roz had already decided that Greg was worth six pounds an hour even if he never lifted a finger.

'Well, one woman wrote, after he'd cleared his throat once or twice, to say she was putting a little glass of Pulmo Bailley on top of the set every night for a week or until his cough got better. And he was always getting letters from frustrated old ducks in the Home Counties. You can guess the sort of thing . . . if you feel the same as me don't shuffle your papers at the close of the programme next Friday, stand them on end. And there's a Freudian slip if you like. One night he forgot and did and the drawings she sent through the post . . . my dear . . . explicit wasn't the word. And a Gerrards Cross postmark too.' Roz shook her head in disbelieving mock disgust. 'If only she'd known. His current madam was just seventeen and too androgynous for words. Flexibility personified. Nice to meet someone straightforward. If we ever are.'

He drained his cup. 'I really feel I ought to hurl a pot or two about. I mean – I don't come cheap, you know.'

She got up. 'Yes. And I should go. I've put a key on the dresser for you. The days I'm at the studio you'll have to let yourself in.'

Greg said: 'Only a Yale? Should have something tougher than that in present circs.'

'We've got a Chubb but not a spare key. I'll get one cut when I see the ironmonger this morning. There's a vacuum cleaner in the pantry.'

'A pantry!' Greg sounded delighted. 'How Edwardian.'

'With a mile of flex, because of all the stairs. If you could do the kitchen, make the beds then vacuum as much as you can before twelve. The cleaning stuff's in the cupboard under the sink.' She hesitated at the door. 'I'm glad they sent you.' She emphasised the you.

'Have a nice day at the office.'

It wasn't quite a parody. Roz felt more cheerful when she left the house and even better after she had visited the ironmonger and made an appointment for a man to call and fix a chain at four that afternoon.

After she had left Greg spent five minutes looking at everything in the cupboards and on the dresser, then started washing up. He had no sooner plunged his hands into the suds than the doorbell rang. He dried his hands and hurried up the stairs muttering: 'Never get a po emptied at this rate.'

Then he was sorry he had grumbled for there, on the steps, was the most delicious boy. Not too tall, no hips to speak of and a profile to match Antinous. Eyes a touch too close together perhaps but the lashes . . . And wonderful petalled hair, like a pinkish-bronze chrysanthemum. He let his glance fall, quite deliberately. Well hung too from the looks of things, although you never knew these days, what with codpieces and all. He looked into the boy's rather unusual eyes and produced his most appealing smile.

'Can I help?'

'I was looking for Chalk Farm. Do you know where it is?'

'Terribly sorry dear but it's not my manor. I'm a maverick. From Palmers Green.' The boy looked blank. 'There's an A to Z in the kitchen though.' He had noticed it on the dresser. 'Hang on a sec – I'll go and look. What part of Chalk Farm?'

The boy hesitated. 'Chalk Farm Road.'

Greg ran down to the kitchen and picked up the A to Z and turned to the index: 2D 45. He stopped at a mirror to check his hair, pulled out a comb and rearranged a curl or two. No harm in asking him in for a sec. The details on the map were quite small. Whilst pointing it out their heads would, of necessity, be very close together. He sprang expectantly back up the stairs but as soon as he entered the hall all expectation fled. The boy had gone. Greg ran to the front gate and stood a moment, shivering, looking up and down the street. But there was no sign of him. Greg sighed. He had been looking forward to the back view; to watching the boy walk away.

Sonia, murmuring 'excuse me', 'would you mind . . . just . . . thank you' pushed and edged her way through the jam-packed mass of people on the Piccadilly-line train. Months of travelling on the same route at the same time each day and you got to recognise people. She had spotted a woman – fur-booted and ear-muffed, with a plastic Pink Panther shopping bag – who always got off at Gloucester Road. As she did, Sonia, perfectly positioned, dropped into her seat. Once settled she could devote her attention to her thoughts. They were, as always, of Fenn.

She was glad he hadn't wanted to come home with her the previous evening. Apart from feeling absolutely exhausted – and very sore – from the evening before that, she had wished to be alone with her dreams . . .

At first the list had puzzled her. After taking it all in she had replaced it carefully under the bill. She did not wish to embarrass or anger him. But later, sitting by the gas fire in her camel dressing gown, with her Horlicks and hottie, she had begun to understand. Knowing, from her phone call, how excited she was by what had happened to Roz, he had prepared a list of questions on every single aspect of the crime. He wanted to make sure she missed nothing out; to give her the most receptive setting possible to tell her story.

The thoughtfulness of this gladdened Sonia's heart. She had to admit he was not always thoughtful but then men weren't, that was something women had to learn to live with. As she had sat there, snugly half-dozing before the popping fire, the thought occurred to her that really she was much happier on the evenings when Fenn wasn't there. When she could sit dreaming about him. In dreams you could obliterate all the little things about a person you didn't like and they always did and said everything you wanted.

But finding the list had been very encouraging. All right, in making it he had revealed a tiny bit of the voyeur in him, but so what? He was no worse than all those people who read the *News of the World* or the *Sun* looking for the salacious bits. It was human nature. Perhaps (Sonia revelled in her honesty) she was not without a trace of it herself . . .

The heat generated from so many bodies was causing the snow on boots and brollies to melt and clothes to smell damp and even faintly mildewed. She raised her eyes, gazing through a bunch of cross or indifferent faces at the advertisements. As long as she could remember there had been ads on the Tube for Bravington's rings. Next to this one was a picture of houses on a new estate at Milton

Keynes. They were semi-detached with sliding glass doors on to a patio, with tubs of flowers as well as gardens. The garden had a swing in it with a pretty little girl being pushed by a young mother. On the patio a handsome man in jeans was crouched with his son. They were tinkering with a bicycle. The wave of longing that consumed Sonia as she regarded this scene was so intense and poignant that she felt tears prickling behind her eyelids. Quickly she switched her attention to the Bravington bride and her band of gold. After all, first things first.

It was obviously going to be up to her to plan the wedding. It was all right Fenn saying he would think about things. Thoughts weren't plans. Plans were so much more solid. The train stopped at Green Park. Two more before Holborn. There was time to look at her list. She rooted in her bag and produced the little notebook she had bought, with silver bells on the cover and pencil attached.

She would definitely wear white. After all no one would know. And how many traditional brides were virgins these days anyway? Some were even pregnant. She flicked the pages till she got to her guest list. She was for ever revising this. Her father and stepmother were constants, if only so she could crow over the old so and so, and the friend from secretarial school that she had kept in touch with and had lunch with once a month. It was the people at work who caused a certain amount of indecision. Some days they were all over you, others you might as well not exist. Mrs Gilmour especially. Sonia was torn between wanting to ask Roz so that she could show Fenn off, flaunting her happiness, and markedly leaving her out. One could do this in a delicate way. Dignified but pointed was the effect to aim for. Yes. Sonia licked her pencil and scored, yet again, through Roz's frequently rewritten name.

Fenn cautiously turned the handle of the wardrobe, slowly pushed open the door and listened. The house was silent. He stepped out into the bedroom. He opened his mouth and gulped down air. Another few minutes in that dark interior and he was sure he would have choked. Jammed in with scented velvet and brocade. After the first hour they seemed to take on a life of their own, twining around his arms and legs, nestling against his mouth. But he had not dared to move until he heard the front door slam. Until that bloody awful queer had gone. Fenn shuddered at the memory. He still felt queasy. People like that should be put away.

He had been watching the house without any definite aim in view when she emerged. And had simply felt that he must do something to close the gap, to tighten the connection between himself and his victim. He recognised her immediately from the blow-up on the office wall. She was rather taller than he had expected but very slim, with elegant, breakable bones. He had moved quickly, throat clotting with excitement, as she came down the steps, so that he was able to pass her on the pavement. He was strongly tempted to say 'good morning'; indeed it rose in his throat but got so tangled up with a gleeful chuckle that, when he was level with her, he couldn't get it out.

She was almost as beautiful as her picture, with ashen grey smudges under her eyes, her lipstick gleaming against a too-white skin. He turned and watched her round the corner then hurried to the house and rang the bell.

Thinking about it afterwards he couldn't explain why, and had been amazed when someone opened the door. He said the first thing that came into his head, remembering a name from a group of Northern-line stations on a list at Camden Tube. And when the poof had disappeared back into the house he had, again on impulse, run in, soundless on the thick carpet, and up the stairs. On the top floor he had found himself in a bedroom and stood there, tense and listening to noises from the kitchen. Then, after about a quarter of an hour, he heard the whine of a vacuum cleaner. Gradually it came nearer. The stairs were being cleaned.

Fenn touched his inside pocket where the knife was always kept. He felt excited. He attempted to rationalise the compulsion which seized him. After all if he was discovered all his plans would have to be abandoned. That could not be allowed to happen. And some people, let's face it, were better dead. Gays for example. Going from one to another, pestering decent men, spreading disease. Looked at that way, he'd almost be doing the human race a favour. The vacuum cleaner was humped on to the third-floor landing.

Fenn got into the wardrobe. Now things were out of his hands, left to that red-headed nance outside. If he opened the wardrobe he was asking for it. He heard the cleaner running over the bedroom floor. Chairs were dragged out and put back. The cleaner actually banged against the base of the wardrobe – Fenn felt the vibration judder up his spine from the soles of his feet. Then it was switched off. He stood, immobile, holding his breath. There was no sound through the door. The guy might have been walking about of course. The rugs were so thick you couldn't tell. Then there was a sound, like glasses or bottles being disturbed and a sort of wheezy sigh, repeated several times. Fenn made a fastidious grimace. The poncey sod was spraying himself with perfume. Then he went, bumping the cleaner down the stairs. Five minutes later the front door slammed.

Fenn now stood in the centre of the bedroom a little uncertainly. He felt, though safe, at a bit of a loss. He was in sole possession of his enemy's house and that must be advantageous. But how to take advantage of the situation? He tried to think strategically, like a soldier. The more you knew about your opponent and, conversely, the less he knew about you, the better. He decided to explore.

At first he had to admit to a feeling of disappointment. The wardrobe was a huge, old-fashioned thing. Satiny dark wood with a gold and mother-of-pearl inlay which could have belonged to his grannie. The bed was made to match with a scroll design in gold at each gracefully winged corner. There wasn't even a dressing table. Then he saw why. A door leading off opened on to a bathroom. An ivory bathroom suite and lots of ferny plants. One of the walls was mirrored with patterned glass like you see in ancient pubs. This reflected all the plants making it look, Fenn thought, like Father Christmas's bloody grotto. Bottles and jars were everywhere and scent from a large atomiser labelled Fleurs de Rocaille still hung in the air.

There were three rooms on the floor below. One full of dolls and dozens of soft toys almost covering a plain little bed which had a matching wardrobe. The curtains were covered with buttercups. There were mobiles hanging from the ceiling; iridescent fish and jokey frogs and one of white seabirds which, as they turned against each other, made gentle whispering sounds.

Next door was a room with the same sort of bed and wardrobe crammed to the ceiling with stuff. There were piles of games in boxes, Lego, a fort, soldiers mounted and on foot flanked by weaponry. A couple of hundred books, shelves with dishes of pebbles; dried leaves and flowers, sea urchins, a long fish skeleton, some animal's jawbone, a musical instrument in a case, a handsome microscope. There was a cork notice board next to a poster of Nirvana. It had a programme for Wimbledon and one for a rock concert. A list of fixtures and two or three scribbled notes: Remember ring Speed re. Science Museum. Remember entry form Crystal Palace Dinosaur race – close Dec. 20th. The curtains here were khaki and pale grey stripes. From the ceiling hung a splendid kite in the form of a Chinese dragon. There was a trestle table of the sort used by interior decorators acting as a desk. It held pens, pads, paints and pencils. And a computer.

Fenn wondered how old the boy was, the lucky little bastard who possessed all these things. He wondered how he had come by the shells and the skeleton and pictured him walking along a deserted sea shore, perhaps with his father, beachcoming. Some distance away on the sand his mother and sister would be unpacking a wicker basket for a picnic: laying out a cloth and real china cups and plates. He wondered how many Christmases and birthdays had had to go by before such a cave of treasure could be accumulated. How many hugs and kisses and loving greetings; how many sheets of colourful paper and yards of glittery string? How big a network of grandparents and aunts and uncles who all thought he was the bee's bloody knees? Black, overwhelming hatred for this unknown child gripped his heart. He wanted to crush the little shells, to grind the jawbone to powder beneath his foot, to smash the microscope against the computer until both were destroyed.

But that was not part of his plan. He did not intend even, at this stage, that she should know he had been in her house. It would have been so easy to destroy things, to tear and rip his way through the place, even to leave his own filthy signature in their bed as he had heard certain burglars did. But that was not his way. So far he had displayed a certain amount of style. He had been stylish, clever and resourceful and he didn't want to blot his copybook now by behaving in a coarse and ugly manner. Also owning all the possessions and all the love in the world wouldn't, when the time came, bring the boy's mother back. When he felt envy rising like a toad in his throat he would dwell on that.

The third room was full of books and papers and painted brown, and a few steps below that was a long room, the width of the house, with tall white-painted dividing doors which had been pushed right back. There was no carpet here but lots of rugs in warm, sunny colours and long, silky curtains.

Fenn walked slowly around the room, running his hand along the gleaming oval table. In the centre were a silver candelabrum and a dish piled high with perfect, polished apples. He picked one up. Rough, reddish stripes on green. There was a huge jar with branches covered in tiny pink, powerfully scented blossoms. In one corner a narrow grandfather clock ticked quietly. The enamelled face had a painted, pastoral scene: a plump shepherdess sitting beneath a spreading tree while her lambs gambolled in the distance. On the walls were three paintings done on gilded wood and some watercolours of seaside towns. There were eight lyre-backed chairs with seats of apricot velvet around the table. Fenn pulled one out and sat down, biting into his apple. It was funny the things people liked. Probably none of this was cheap yet he couldn't see his parents buying it, not if they were rolling.

On a narrow sideboard, matching the design of the table, were several bottles and decanters on a silver tray. He opened the sideboard, found a cut-glass tumbler and half filled it with whisky. He drank perversely. He didn't like alcohol and despised undisciplined people who couldn't manage without it. But he wanted to siphon off some of this affluence without actually stealing something that would be missed.

There were a chesterfield and two armchairs at the far end of the room, facing the garden, covered in lemon and green fabric, a pattern of water lilies. He lowered himself into an armchair, resting his feet on an embroidered foot stool. He drank a little (it tasted foul) and leaned back, closing his eyes. The clock ticked gently on.

He felt his body uncoil. What was it about this room? One minute dissolved into the next. Time passed not in blocks as it did when you had tasks to do, appointments, people to meet, but like a river, almost soundless, indifferently flowing away. It was the quiet that was getting to him.

For the first time he made the connection not between money and possessions or money and sex but between money and silence. He could not remember ever living anywhere without a constant background of noise. Other people's blaring television sets and ghetto blasters through the walls, yelling kids, yapping dogs. He had not realised until now that there was an alternative. That there were fortunate people in existence who lived with only the self-imposed sounds of their own lives. Advertisements never told you about that. They told you about cars and videos and drinks and clothes; not about silence. The whisky and the peaceful, quiet air were combining to dilute the strength of his venom. More than that, it seemed to hold an almost healing quality that he sensed could unman him. He felt the will to destroy, his very *raison d'être*, being leeched out of him by subtle and invidious means.

He stood up quickly, grabbing the back of the chair to steady himself. What a fool he was! Just because the house was empty did not mean that he was safe. It was still his enemy's house. He almost ran from the room.

A final flight of steps from the hall led him to another bathroom, a loo and the kitchen. He would splash his face with cold water, perhaps make some coffee to sober himself up. Expecting gleaming fitted units and bright lights he was surprised by the homely scene that faced him. It was lovely and warm, the heat coming from a large scarlet stove. The room smelt of fruit and herbs. He saw a dresser of dark wood covered with pretty plates and wooden bowls and a stone pot full of berries and everlasting flowers. Kids' drawings were on the back of both doors and a calendar, of huge white squares, scribbled all over with notes. Everything looked neat and orderly but not in the strained, attention-seeking manner of kitchens in shop windows or magazines.

He looked out of the window with possible re-entry at a later date in mind. A long walled garden backing on to another long walled garden. Nothing doing there. The back door was bolted on the inside and the window double locked. He put his face under the cold tap and turned it full on. That was better. The stinging icy water shocked the bile back into his bloodstream. By the time he had dried his face he was again his true avenging self. He decided not to push his luck by stopping to make coffee.

There was a sound down by the Aga. Alarmed he swung round. A cat came into view, stepping daintily, then arching and stretching. Christ – he'd seen some funny-looking objects but this one took some beating. It looked as if it had been put together from two or three different kits. He liked that joke and chuckled. He bent down and held out his hand.

'Here kitty.' Then, chuckling again at the measure of his inaccuracy: 'Pretty kitty . . . come on . . . here kitty . . .'

Chapter Six

Duffy was waiting to take Roz to the canteen. They had got into the habit of lunching together. Roz had still not acknowledged to herself just how much she looked forward to it. Louise sat in the low chair facing the desk. All three of them had just been discussing whether she should go on the Production Assistant course and she had now definitely decided to do so. Today Louise was looking almost subdued. She had on black barathea culottes, a peacock-blue velvet waistcoat and a mulberry and gamboge patchwork jacket. Her hair was spattered with silver dust.

Roz said: 'Are you coming with us to lunch?'

'No. I'm slimming. Just one Mars today.'

'They'll be going out of business.' Duffy smiled across at her. 'We shall all have to look to our jobs now you're going up in the world.'

Louise asked if Roz had heard anything more from the police, then was sorry. The atmosphere darkened perceptibly. Roz shook her head.

'No. They've given up bothering, I think. Although to be fair they did what they could. Questioned everyone, people in reception . . .'

'I was in reception. They didn't question me.'

'Were you?' Duffy's voice was full of surprise.

'Only for five minutes. I was going back to Felicity's flat. We were going to the new club in Frith Street. Wild Horses? I didn't want to go all the way home to Redbridge and back. I sat in for her – just while she got her coat.'

'Did anyone come to the desk while you were there?'

'Only Toby. Oh – and the plumber.'

Duffy frowned 'What plumber?'

'Just a plumber.'

'Did you check with Maintenance before you let him through?'

'No. I was going to ring down but that's when Toby came in. He asked me if his five o'clock visitor had turned up and I had to check in the book. By the time I'd done this the other guy had disappeared. I'm sure he was genuine, though.'

Roz asked: 'Why are you sure?'

'Oh, he'd obviously been here before. He said . . . "Don't worry, I know where to go," and he had a bag of tools . . . you know . . . he just looked right.'

They looked at each other. Roz said: 'He's the only person not accounted for.'

Duffy reached for the internal phone and dialled Maintenance. 'Easy enough to check.'

'He said it was the gents' downstairs loo.'

'Hullo Robby? Duffield. Fine – how are you? Look – did you book a plumber on Tuesday for the downstairs loo, gents'?' Pause. 'Perhaps someone else did. Would you mind checking the book?' Pause. 'Fine. Thanks a lot. Yes, I think

183

it may be.' He hung up and turned to the others, his face flushed. 'No plumber.'

Louise said softly: 'Zowie.'

'Do you remember what he looked like?'

'Dark clothes, a cap. And I think he had a moustache but I'm not sure. He went by so quickly.'

There was a discreet tap at the door which was wide open. Sonia entered. 'Yesterday's letters for you to sign, Mrs Gilmour.' Her eyes made a note of the coffee cups, Duffy's familiar placing on the edge of Roz's desk and Louise's ultra-relaxed position in the low chair. 'If you have a moment to spare, that is.'

'Oh I think I can squeeze in a few signatures before lunch,' Roz said drily. 'If you'll just leave them in the tray.'

'Guess what, Sonia,' Louise levered herself upright, 'I'm the one who let the phantom threatener in.'

'I beg your pardon?'

'Oh come on. Don't tell me you don't know—'

'Hey,' Duffy cut in, 'would you recognise his voice? I mean we'll tell the police anyway but that would really clinch it. Otherwise it's all pretty circumstantial.'

'I might.'

'We'll play the tape.'

Roz said 'Can't. The police took it away.'

'Perhaps they'll ask me to go to the station. To help with their enquiries.'

They had all forgotten Sonia who hovered by the door torn between the need to show her complete indifference to their cosy little chats (talk about living in each other's pockets) and her wish to partake, however spuriously, in any drama that was going.

'What about the *Roundabout*? When he first rang up.'

'Oh I've got that.' Roz swung her chair around. Behind the desk were narrow shelves stacked with tapes all neatly labelled. 'It was "Communications". I remember because the Birdman's contribution was especially bizarre.' She put on the tape and pressed the wind-on button. Louise went across to the desk and stood over the machine with an intent, serious, listening air. Roz pressed the play button.

'. . . full of deceit and chicanery . . . their body language as you so . . .'

Louise said: 'A bit further on.'

'I know, I know.' Roz whizzed a fraction more.

'The line's free now.'

'This is it, Roz.'

'*I know*.' Her voice was loud with irritation. She didn't want to listen. But at least they were trying to help, which was more than you could say for Sonia. All bright-eyed stares. Gloating would hardly be too strong a word. 'I'll let you have these after lunch.' Roz indicated the letters, the dismissal plain in her voice. Sonia moved reluctantly nearer the door.

'. . . about a death . . . nothing personal . . . I'm not distressed . . .'

Hearing him again with hindsight was much worse. It was as if he was in the room with them. Breathing noisome air into her face. Roz turned her head from the machine.

'. . . hasn't happened yet . . . I should tell someone . . . did I say that? . . . have to kill someone you see . . .'

She looked at Louise whose pretty face was screwed up with the effort of concentration. '. . . wanted you to know . . . as you're involved . . .'

Roz pressed the stop button and Duffy said: 'Well?'

But Louise's reply was never uttered. There was a sound from the doorway. They all turned. Sonia was gripping the door frame for support. Her face was stamped with incredulity. The mouth wrenched open and downwards in a rictus of disbelief, the eyes dark holes, the skin the colour of whey. Before any of them could reach her she had slipped to the floor.

Things were not going according to plan. Snatching the cat had seemed a brilliant idea. He hadn't thought any further at the time. Just zipped it into his jacket and taken it home on the Tube. But during the journey it had come to him just what a prize he had there. The beloved family pet, no less. What delicious sorrows and anxieties could be brought into being once the Gilmours knew in whose tender care the animal was. He could start by popping a few whiskers in the post, just to prove he wasn't having them on.

But back at the Oasis, although he had got safely through the shop, trouble had been waiting for him in the hall. He had run up against Mrs Christoforou. The bloody animal had started to wriggle, she gripped his arm, shouted: 'What you bringing in my house?' and started pulling at his jacket zip. The cat struggled out, fell awkwardly to the ground, shot through their legs and disappeared into the night.

Sitting fuming afterwards in his room it was some time before he realised that, although he knew he had lost the cat *they* would not know he had lost the cat. He could still distress and worry them all. And they'd have to believe him. After all, how would he know the animal had disappeared unless he'd had something to do with it? That was how they'd reason. He didn't like it, though. He felt it was ominous, the cat getting away.

Then there was Sony. Or rather there wasn't. He'd been ringing on and off for ages and getting no reply. It wasn't like her. Usually she snatched the phone off the hook and was gobbling away at him before he'd had time to open his mouth. He was afraid to ring her at work. He thought there was just a chance that whoever he spoke to might recognise his voice and ask him to hold, then try to trace the call. For all he knew there might now be a direct line from the studio to the police.

'What's the new daily like?'

Roz and Leo were sitting together on the large chesterfield. The curtains shut out the winter night and the lamps were lit. As well as the central heating there was a gas fire with flames and glowing logs. Kathy was in bed, Guy in the kitchen doing his homework. Roz had kicked off her shoes and was leaning, legs tucked beneath her, against Leo's shoulder. She was aware, even as she assumed this relaxed position, that it was an artificial posture. She did not feel relaxed and she wondered if Leo, stretched out comfortably with his feet on the foot stool, was also faking contentment.

'Wonderful. Good entertainment as well as a whizz with the Windowlene.' She had been pleasantly surprised to find the house so neat and clean. She had been afraid Greg's frivolous conversation augured an equally frivolous attitude to household chores. 'Only one snag.'

'What's that?'

She nodded to indicate the sideboard. 'He's like the archetypal butler. A secret tippler.'

'Really?'

'Mm. A fair bit of whisky seems to have gone. I wouldn't have noticed but for the smell in the room. And he left the glass.'

'Are you going to act the *châtelaine* and start marking all the bottles?'

'Of course not. I don't really mind. What's a nip between friends? Anyway it's not as if he's permanent.'

'Have you advertised for someone?'

'Not yet.'

'Better get a move on while there's still a drop left in the house.'

Roz tried to stem a feeling of resentment. She thought, why me? Then, you're being unreasonable, Leo's working all day. But *I'm* working too. But you're at home. Unspoken but assumed was the fact that it was up to her to attend to these matters because it was she who would be doing the cleaning if no one else was engaged. Irritation was creeping in. She sought to get off the subject before she said something acrimonious.

'As if there isn't enough drama in my life already, Sonia threw a fainting fit today.'

'Good God. Is she pregnant?'

That possibility had not occurred to Roz. So sudden and dramatic had been Sonia's collapse that for a moment all three of them had stood there simply staring at her in amazement. Louise had reached her first and tried to lift her up, then Duffy had taken over whilst Roz had brought some water.

Sonia was out for less than a minute. When she came round she didn't speak, just looked at them all in turn then burst into ugly, raucous sobs. At a nod from Roz the others left them alone. The sounds coming from Sonia were appalling, rent with something far beyond despair. She cried as if the end of the world had come. Roz was glad they hadn't been able to play the second tape if she reacted like this to the first. She attempted to hold the girl in her arms. It was like embracing a plank of wood.

'Try to drink some of this.' Roz proffered the glass but Sonia pushed it away violently, spilling the water on the floor. 'I'm sorry if the tape upset—'

'It's not that. It's nothing to do with that . . .' Sonia seized Roz's arm. Her eyes had a supplicating, feverish shine. 'I . . . it's my nerves. I've been feeling ill for some time . . . I meant to tell you . . . to ask for a break . . .'

'All right Sonia, all right.' She took Sonia's hand. The awful tearing sounds had stopped. Sonia was now crying quietly, tears pouring unchecked down her cheeks. 'Of course you must have some time off. Look, take the rest of the week.' With the weekend that would be four days. 'Then ring me on Monday morning and say how you feel. I'll take you home now.'

'Oh no – I can—'

'Don't argue, Sonia.' She smiled and let go Sonia's hand. 'Do you want to go to First Aid before we go? See if they have something to calm you down?' Sonia shook her head. 'Come on then. Baron's Court isn't it?'

'Edith Road.'

'I'm all right till the Cromwell Road, then you'll have to direct me.'

Sonia hardly spoke on the journey except to give directions. Roz parked outside a seedy, three-storeyed terraced house. She imagined Sonia sitting in there after she had driven away, lonely, perhaps ill, weeping quietly into her pillow.

'Would you like me to come in, Sonia? Make you some soup perhaps? Do you have something in to eat? Perhaps I could pick up some shopping for you?' She was about to add: 'Would you just like to talk?' but Sonia had got out of the car and slammed the door. Roz was not offended. The abject misery on the girl's face had precluded good manners.

'I'm sorry, Leo?'

'I just wondered if she was pregnant. After all I assume he wants some return on this highly expensive scent you told me about.'

'What an insensitive, chauvinistic remark. The girl was in absolute despair.'

'Oh come, Roz. It's the sort of thing you might have said yourself any other time but now.'

The truth of this remark stung Roz to the quick. 'Don't be so bloody avuncular. I'm not one of your patients, you know.' She shrugged out of his encircling arm. 'Is that how you cosy them along? Now, now Mrs Smythe-Willoughby. You're in very good hands you know. Pompous ass.'

Leo was quiet for a moment, then said: 'You haven't told me how the show went today.'

'*I haven't had a show today*. Surely after two years you know which days I broadcast.' She stood up, a little uncertainly. She had had two large gins before he had arrived and although he must have smelt it on her breath he had said nothing. She was starting to drink earlier and earlier. 'And stop laughing at me.'

'Darling, I'm not laughing.' Leo stood also. 'Come on.

You toss the salad tonight and I'll do the fish. I wouldn't trust you within a mile of a naked flame.'

He watched her lower lip jut out. Just for a moment she looked very like Kathy. He was aware of a great tenderness towards her, tinged faintly with disappointment. He had hoped that his love, the children and the stability of their family life would have weighed larger in the balance, against this outside threat, than they had. He kissed her gently on the ear. She jerked her head away. Guy appeared in the doorway.

'Where's Madgewick?'

'Isn't he in the kitchen?'

'Uh-uh.'

'Then I expect he's on our bed. I'll have to tell Greg to make sure he's shut in the basement.'

'I've looked in your bedroom.'

'What about the airing cupboard?'

Madgewick had a passion for the warmth and snug of the airing cupboard and was in there like a shot if the door was open, generously distributing hairs of assorted colours over all the ironing.

'I looked in there as well. I've looked everywhere. And under all the beds.'

Leo said: 'He must be somewhere. We'll look together after supper. Even if this new chap had left a door open he wouldn't go out.'

That was true. Since the first day they had brought him home he had never gone out apart from his first session for extensive repairs at the vet's. His previous experiences, only to be guessed at but quite dreadful if the condition in which they found him was anything to go by, had given him a disinclination for travel verging on the paranoid. In the summer he could occasionally be coaxed out into the yard if they were all in the garden, when he would curl up in the sun about two feet from the back door with an alert air, ready to race back to safety at a moment's notice.

After supper they looked all over the house. He was definitely not there. Leo went out into the bitter night, calling on people up and down the street. Roz rang the police to report the cat missing. The voice at the other end of the line didn't sound too concerned. 'We do keep a register of lost and found dogs but not of any other animals. Of course we'll make a note of it.'

'That's nice. I don't suppose you think a cat matters. Well – he matters to us.' She was shouting and aware of Guy's worried frown. She banged the phone down. That night, puzzled and anxious, she slept badly.

At breakfast everyone was subdued, the children on the verge of tears. Roz missed Madgewick's odd, funny face and parade of naked flattery more than she would have thought possible. She stood in the garden until the very last minute before leaving for the studio, facing the leafless trees with their black wind-whipped branches, calling and calling but to no avail. The cat had simply vanished.

Sonia was lying in bed. She had lain there since the afternoon when Roz had brought her home. The rest of that day, the dark early evening, the endless night, the next wretched, grey day had dragged by. But then she had lost track of time. What did time matter? Only, she was so cold. The flat was cold. The sheets were cold and damp, her pillow cold and soggy with tears.

Now, having cried herself out, she lay stiff and rigid with loss. She had had nothing to eat or drink and felt that to swallow would choke her. The telephone rang three times. She ignored it. Having reached rock bottom, pursued by black despair and utter misery, she now sensed her numb feelings painfully quickening into life. And with the return to awareness came a new emotion.

At first it was just resentment. How he had used her! She thought of the hours they had spent together in her flat. All the meals and wine she had provided. And the things he had made her do. The fantasy of courtship discarded, she now saw them for what they were: filthy, degrading things. And she had allowed them all because she had wanted so much to be wanted. To have a white wedding with a Bravington's ring and a little house with a child playing in the garden. Now, as strongly as she had deceived herself before so, with equal, brutal strength, did she rip away all the half-truths and downright lies with which she had so stupidly supported her illusory happiness. Stiffly she sat up (she was still wearing her office clothes) and swung her legs out of bed.

She still felt shaky and sick with so much crying. But resentment was warming her, and burgeoning by the minute was a second, subsidiary emotion. Something which flickered in the bleak area of her heart and warmed her chilled breast. Blood, only seconds ago coagulating in her veins, started to shift and run. And this warmth was no illusion to be dispelled by another violent, accidental discovery. This was generated by hard reality.

Sonia felt the floor steady beneath her feet. Railing thoughts, wasteful tears, smashed hopes and ruined dreams

193

all coalesced and were transformed into an elixir more powerful, more self-renewing than love had ever been. As hatred made itself known and the flicker blazed into a consuming fire Sonia felt fear lurking behind her excitement. The force of the hatred was so overwhelming it seemed to have a life of its own. She half expected it to open doors, snatch at curtains, bowl her off her feet. She clung to the edge of her bed until it subsided a little.

She felt only pleasure, totally free from any trace of regret or guilt as she dialled 999. When the operator answered she said: 'Give me the police.'

Roz was aware that Leo was watching her. The pans seemed to be clattering about on the top of the stove almost of their own volition. She told herself this was because the handles were slippery with steam. Today she had done the unthinkable. She had asked the children to collude with her against their father.

It had been one of her home days and she had drunk almost a whole bottle of wine before and with her lunch. At three-fifteen she had almost decided to ring the local taxi rank and ask that a cab collect Kathy and Guy and bring them home, then decided against it. Kathy would probably be very apprehensive driving with a stranger. Roz rang the mother of Guy's friend Speed to see if she could help but no one answered. So at three-twenty she had got into the Golf and driven, very slowly and carefully, to Kathy's school.

With both children in the back she had got to Bayham Street when a sense of being home and dry took over and she picked up speed, driving straight over the 'Give Way' lines and into Greenland Road. An approaching van screamed to a halt and Roz swerved into the gutter. Miraculously the two vehicles did not collide. A young man got out of the van, his face white with shock and anger, and came over to the Golf. Roz wound down the window.

'I'm . . . I'm terribly sorry . . . I didn't . . . I'm sorry . . .'

'You want locking up. People like you. You're not fit to be in charge of a bloody pushchair never mind a car.' His handsome young face, made ugly with rage, pushed in at the window. 'You're bloody pissed aren't you?'

Roz shook her head, tears falling. '. . . No . . . no . . .'

'And kids in the back.' He said again: 'You want locking up before you kill somebody. I've a good mind to have you for dangerous driving.'

Roz rested her head on the steering wheel, her shoulders shaking. He seemed about to say something else but perhaps the wretched picture she made stopped him. He got back into his van, eased it into the traffic stream and drove away.

A few people had gathered on the pavement. Before she closed the window Roz heard a woman say: 'Poor little mites' and another: 'And it's not even tea time.' She stayed a few moments on the yellow lines, then saw a traffic warden approaching and drove, shocked into sobriety, carefully home. It was then she had asked the children not to mention the incident to Leo.

'If Daddy knew I'd been . . . ill he'd be terribly worried. And unhappy.' She added, despising herself: 'I know neither of you would want that.'

Kathy had agreed immediately, climbing on to her knee; Guy after a lengthy pause and reluctantly, not looking at her. But grown-ups always know when children have a secret. Kathy and Leo had so ostentatiously not spoken of the incident that the very intensity of their unspokenness gave them away. However Leo had said nothing and, now they were alone, still said nothing. It was the waiting for him to speak that was getting on Roz's nerves. He cleared his throat. She lifted the Le Creuset from the oven.

'Darling, that smells gorgeous.'

'Carbonnade. And I've made some noodles. There's no veg. I can't be bothered preparing vegetables when I'm busy all day.'

'Why don't you ask Greg to do some cooking? I thought they were supposed to have a flair?'

' "They" indeed. Don't be so coy, Leo. Anyway he's not coming again. I've rung the agency and asked them to send someone else.'

'Why? What happened?'

'We had a row.'

'But I thought you liked him. And he seems efficient enough.'

Both of these things were true. Roz found it hard to explain how the row had suddenly developed. They had started off as before that morning, companionably sharing a pot of coffee. Greg had told her he had an audition for the RSC at the Barbican the following week.

'What are you going to do?'

'I thought I'd treat them to my Tamburlaine. And then a little something in a comical vein.'

'How about Lady Bracknell?'

He gave an exaggerated shriek. 'Not in cold blood dear. No – I thought some Malvolio. Although I rather think everybody does him. I might try Garry Essendine.'

'And what will you wear?'

'Well,' he pushed his chair cosily close, ready for an all-girls-together, 'I've got a dear little *cache-sex* embroidered with Nelson's flag on a pole. Some clover tights and a lime-green doublet with deliciously full sleeves.'

Roz laughed. 'What are you really going to wear?'

'Jeans and a National Theatre T-shirt. I don't want them to think I'm toadying.'

It was only minutes after this when he was clearing up the breakfast dishes that Roz brought up the subject of the cat. Within minutes the atmosphere changed, becoming thick with suspicion.

'But you must have let him out, Greg. I'm sorry. I know this is all very unpleasant but try to understand that he's our pet and we miss him very much.'

'You don't have to tell me. I'm a member of the Fancy too, you know. But I only opened the door once when some guy came to ask the way somewhere. And when I got back downstairs Madgers was still in his basket.'

The diminutive angered Roz as much as the lie. 'Don't call him Madgers. His name's Madgewick.'

'OK then, Madgewick. And he was still in the kitchen when I left.'

'Greg, how can you tell such lies? There was no way he could have got out of this house if you'd left him shut in the kitchen.'

'I beg your pardon. I'm sure I've got all sorts of mimsy little faults but I do not tell lies.'

Roz could not stop herself: 'I don't suppose you drink either?'

'I don't quite see the relevance of that rather spiteful

sneer at this precise moment in time but no, as a matter of fact, I don't drink.'

'It'll be Madgewick then who's been seeing off the whisky at such a high rate of knots.'

'I've no idea who it is but it certainly isn't me. Perhaps you've been seeing it off, as you so elegantly put it, yourself.'

'You rude sod!'

Greg flared his rocking-horse nostrils then drew on his rubber gloves with great finesse and started putting the breakfast dishes into the sink. 'I'll ask the agency to send someone else tomorrow, Madam.'

'Please do.' Roz left the room, taking her coffee cup in a shaking hand. 'Someone teetotal for preference.'

As she closed the door she heard him murmur: 'Stuck-up bitch.'

She stayed in her study for the next two hours, pretending to work until she heard the front door slam. Then she came downstairs and opened the bottle of Gewürztraminer.

Leo listened to her carefully edited version of this exchange. 'I know it's a bit of a mystery but I do think it's over-reacting to get rid of him. You don't know who we'll get next time. He was friendly and efficient even if he did pinch the booze.'

Although Roz now agreed with everything Leo was saying she kept stubbornly silent. They ate the casserole, hardly speaking. It was cooked in a packet mix. Roz had lost interest in food. It was almost as if she were pregnant. She felt slightly sick all the time, not with new life but with apprehension. She noticed that Leo did not have wine with his meal, which was most unusual. Probably encouraging her to drink less. She found a gibe hovering provokingly on the tip of her tongue. She clamped her lips together, gripping the bottom one with her teeth. A stream of abusive phrases ran and chattered through her mind. She selected the mildest of these and spoke.

'You're just like Job, aren't you?' She laughed falsely as people without courage do when they're being insulting; pretending she wasn't really serious. 'Stolidly sitting there. Wife threatened with death or worse. World falling round our ears. Children afraid and unhappy. Their pet vanished. What does it take to rouse you, Leo? Famine? Plague? The bomb? I can just see you sitting there when it goes off with your head in a fucking paper bag!'

'Stop it Roz.' Leo reached out and gripped her wrists. '*Now*.'

'I know why you don't care. You'd like to see the back of me, wouldn't you? Been screwing some nubile little nurse up at the hospital? Won't be long before I'm forty. Time to trade me in for a newer model.'

Leo pushed back his chair. It made a terrible grating noise on the stone floor. 'I'm absolutely sick of this. I'm exhausted. I've done three extremely difficult operations today. I know that one of my patients, in spite of everything I've been able to do, is going to die. She's younger than you are. You're turning into a self-pitying shrew. Now for Christ's sake shut up!'

'Oh your work – your noble work. I'd forgotten how important that was.' Roz listened aghast as the voice, thick with sarcasm, drove on. 'Of course you work all your anger off there, don't you? No wonder you remain so calm at home. What's it like to be able to slice into defenceless people? Hack them about? I'll bet you love it really, don't you? Come on, be honest. You're no better than this bloody pervert who's been threatening me. Except with you it's legal.'

Just as Roz's voice belonged to another person so now she seemed to be standing outside the scene watching, as if it were projected on to a screen. Everything was happening in slow motion and black and white. The man towered, tall and threatening. There were no background details, he just appeared, thrusting and angular, from nowhere. Slowly he extended his arm then pulled it right back as if preparing to strike. His clothes were all grey, his face white with coal-black eyes and dark welts of tiredness beneath them. The contrast was both crude and intense. He looked like a tragedian in a silent film. The woman had also risen. She too looked grey, with a mass of Medusa-like hair falling over her shoulders. She opened her mouth twice and yelled 'Butcher!' Roz heard her very clearly and thought, she is going mad. Then the man's arm began very slowly to fall down towards the woman's head. Far from shrinking she seemed to push her face forward greedily, grimacing up at him, daring the blow into existence. Roz cried: 'No, no,' and tried to step between the two figures. Then the telephone rang. Immediately normality returned. And colour. Leo's arm dropped to his side. Roz lowered her head to her breast, all anger gone, consumed with misery. Leo left the room and she ran after him. She stood at the door of the sitting room and listened.

'Yes but she's not well. This is Mr Gilmour.' A few moments later he said: 'Where exactly is that?' and wrote something down. Then: 'Yes, but I'm not sure when. I'll ring you back.' He wrote something else then hung up.

'What is it? What's happened?'

'That was the police.' He crossed to the chesterfield. 'It seems they've got him.'

'Him?' Roz frowned. 'Who?'

'For God's sake – who d'you think? The man who's been doing all this.'

'Oh.' She pulled out the nearest dining chair and sat down. She waited for relief, joy, happiness. 'Are you sure?'

'Of course I'm sure. He's confessed. They're holding him at Wapping Police Station.'

Roz took Leo's unresponsive hand as they walked over the glistening cobblestones. Narrow towering blocks of flats, cathedrals of gracious living, reared up between them and the river. Warehouse conversions: the splendid arched windows showing Tiffany lampshades or delicate chandeliers. A metal catwalk stretching overhead was painted ODDBINS and a huge custard-cream and bright-blue building hummed with the faint throb of machinery. A board outside read Metropolitan Police Boat Yard.

Then there was a gap between the buildings and she could see the river, ribbed with silver bars of moonlight. It was slapping against sunken piles of metal and stone walls. Against the skyline three motionless cranes posed like the prehistoric skeletons of giant birds. Next came a pub, The Town of Ramsgate.

'Perhaps we could have a drink afterwards, Leo?'

'Quite honestly all I want to do afterwards is get a good night's sleep. And then, I hope, see our life return to normal.'

Another patch of gentrification. A small green was snugly encircled on two sides by elegant Edwardian houses beautifully kept. A Porsche was parked outside one, next to a zapped-up customised Cortina. In the darkness the garden hedges looked midnight blue. A boat went by, a string of lights reflected in the water, its wash breaking up the moon's reflection. At the end of the green directly over the river were some stone benches.

'Can we stop for a minute?'

'What for? It's absolutely freezing.'

'Just for a minute.'

Leo made a sound – part sigh, part 'tsk!' – managing to imply both resignation at the vagaries of women in general and irritation at the behaviour of his wife in particular. But he stopped.

They looked down at the water. Close to, in artificial lamplight, it looked scummy. Plastic bottles, old tins and chunks of softened wood drifted by. A buoy bobbed drunkenly about.

'You don't have to do this, you know.'

'You heard what they said, Leo. He won't make a statement till he's talked to me.'

'He's confessed. That's enough for them to charge him.'

But she wanted to see him. Once the first shock had passed she had experienced so many emotions that now she had no idea how she felt. There seemed to be in her head a residue of all of them: relief, anger, excitement, anticipation and fear. They had all rushed forward in turn and now combined to make a battering-ram against her heart. She actually felt an intense pain in her chest which was affecting her breathing. But over all this, even stronger than fear was the most powerful curiosity. She *must* see him. This man who had, with such breathtaking and indifferent malice, so affected her life.

On the drive over she had pictured him a thousand times in a thousand different ways: young, middle-aged, old, fat, thin, bald, hirsute, tall, short. And what of her reaction? She had imagined herself (with vast effort) being understanding; and (with much less effort) having to be restrained from physically attacking him. Leo had tried to persuade her to wait until the next day, believing a night's rest would enable her to cope with the situation more calmly, but she had become almost frenzied at the suggestion and had tried to leave to drive to the station on her own. It was then he had got in a neighbour to sit with the children.

Roz tried to breathe more slowly and carefully. To calm down. After a moment she stood up. The sudden movement startled a gull standing nearby and it flew up, almost in their faces, emitting a harsh squawk.

The entrance to the station was at the side of the building and reached by a flight of stone steps. Inside it was warm, almost steamy. A sergeant behind the desk knew immediately who they were.

'Where . . . where is he?'

'In the interview room, Mrs Gilmour. Would you like a cup of tea before you go in? It's a cold night.'

'No. Thank you.'

'Perhaps afterwards then?'

'That would be very nice. What is his name?'

'Wouldn't give it. He's an odd one all right.'

Roz felt she should know his name. What should she call

him otherwise? Then the incongruity of her concern over a point of etiquette struck her and she almost smiled. A young constable with a notebook held the door open and she walked through. The interview room was at the end of a short corridor. He stood to one side and opened the door so that she could go first.

Immediately fear vanished and amazement took its place. A small man seated behind a Formica table rose courteously to his feet. Her first impression was that he was covered from head to foot with feathers. Her second more precise. He wore a flying helmet on which a variety of feathers had been glued in such a manner that they curved inwards, making fronds around the circle of his face; then a leather jacket, considerably too large for him, which had been painted, quite skilfully, with more feathers in brilliant colours. His trousers were of some yellow plastic material bumpily patterned and very tight, giving the illusion he was balanced on thin, horny legs. Neat little black shoes were decorated with a claw design. Even the skin on his face had a goosefleshy, newly plucked, faintly bluish appearance, like a chicken on a slab. Bright, beady, round eyes glittered. He beamed and started to walk towards her.

'Mrs Gilmour. We meet at last.'

Quickly the constable stepped between them.

Roz said: 'It's all right. He's harmless.' Torrents of disappointment broke over her, washing all other emotions away, leaving a great and deadening flatness. Her voice sounded as heavy as lead. 'He's a regular on my programme. I recognise his voice. It's nothing like the tape. He's not the man you want.'

When she came back from the interview room Leo had

been furiously angry. He had railed at the police for not obtaining the tape from Southampton Row and checking it against their prisoner. The police remained unruffled, saying the need to obtain a statement was paramount. He banked down his anger on the way home; it showed only in the over-controlled manner of his driving, but when they had gone to bed she had felt it pulsing behind every movement of his hands and body. For the first time she could not wait for their lovemaking to be over.

Afterwards she had got up, put on a dressing gown and gone to see the children. Kathy slept deeply, flushed face buried in the pillow, her thumb still resting on her bottom lip. Guy's duvet had slipped to the floor and he was lying awkwardly, one striped arm beneath his chest. Pins and needles in the morning. Gently she lifted him, straightened his arm and replaced the duvet. He murmured in his sleep but did not wake. She felt her love for them, rock-firm and eternal, securely in her heart. That at least would not change. That was something she could hold on to. Everything else seemed fluid, shifting and running towards and away from her in an alarming manner. Things she had thought unalterable were being transformed as she stood helplessly by. She tried to understand Leo's irritation and lack of sympathy; tried to believe that it was only because he did not think she was in any real danger that he seemed not to care. That he was just tired.

More and more Duffy was on her mind. She had even, an hour ago, seen his face above her own instead of Leo's. She tried to rationalise her feelings. He had been kind and sensitive where Leo had been almost indifferent. That was all it was. All she was experiencing now was gratitude;

affectionate gratitude. Yet even as she came to this conclusion her memories of their meeting at The Gay Hussar returned with a fresh and vivid impetus. She saw the light, golden hairs on the backs of his hands; saw his eyes change and darken as he had brought his face towards hers in the doorway and she correctly identified the dangerous and disturbing feeling. And it wasn't gratitude.

She wished it were daytime and the children were awake. She wanted to lift them up, to hold them close, to make a barrier against the outside world. Or perhaps a shield.

Fenn had worked out how he could not only walk openly up to Roz's front door but be welcomed in with open arms. He would wear a policeman's uniform. When this idea first struck him he had been impressed by the beauty of it; the simplicity. He had not thought hiring a policeman's uniform would be either difficult or complicated. But it had proved to be both.

He had looked up Theatrical Costumiers in the Yellow Pages and made a list. He had gone first to Morris Angel of Shaftesbury Avenue. There he had been told that, as a member of the general public, he certainly could not hire a policeman's uniform. He must belong to a bona fide theatrical company, any order would be checked by telephone with that company and, when collecting, he would have to produce proof that he was working for the said company. A letter on headed paper or similar documentation.

Travelling back to Islington he had pondered on and around this problem. He was reluctant to abandon the idea. He had to be alone with Roz when the time came, without interruption. He wasn't going to do it in some furtive, amateurish way hanging around in the cold and dark of the street. Waiting for her to park then grabbing her and afterwards running away. Where was the joy in that? It would be over before she realised it had started. And fumbling about when she was fully clothed he just might not finish the job. Now she was on her guard he could think of no other way that she would willingly let him in. There didn't seem to be any alternative to hiring a uniform. If he wasn't such a loner, if he'd ever run with the wrong sort of people, no doubt there'd be no problem. You could get your hands on anything if you were bent. But he'd always worked by himself. He thought of television and film companies and wondered how they got their costumes. Surely they didn't hire. People like the BBC for instance must have big departments of their own. But that didn't help him. There was no way he could get a costume from them any more than from the hire companies. The train drew into the Angel.

He was walking along Essex Road when he came to The Sun and Seventeen Cantons. Like almost every building in the street he had passed it every other day and seen it without seeing it, as it were. There was always a large board outside with chalked information. A jazz group, poetry reading, lunch-time theatre. Today it was the latter and the large chalked letters THEATRE stopped him in his tracks. He went inside, ordered a half and was given a glass of warmish, soapy tan liquid.

Now he was in the pub he wasn't sure what to do. At the end of the saloon bar was a tatty black curtain and a girl with a lot of long dark hair sitting at a rickety card table.

Fenn approached, nodding at the curtain. 'This the theatre?'

'Start in five minutes. Three pounds if you're not eating.'

Bugger that for a lark, he thought and went back to the bar, getting a large plateful of shepherd's pie and some very soft chips. He balanced this with a plastic knife and fork and his half. The girl lifted the curtain so that he could pass through. The inner room had one long table with a bench of equal length and three old round wooden ones on cast-iron legs. There were about half a dozen people sitting around. Noise and jolly guffaws from the bar made the atmosphere even more bleak than the setting warranted. There was a rostrum stage backed by more tatty black curtains. Fenn started to eat.

He knew nothing of the theatre and had never been to one. If asked what such a visit was like he would have described an array of limousines disgorging celebrities, a red plush and gold auditorium, spotlit gaudily dressed stars. Images culled from photographs of premieres or displays of stills outside the Palladium. The word fringe meant something over the eyebrows or round the furniture. So that when one of the people sitting at a table – a bloke in a T-shirt and jeans – stood up and started describing a fire at his grandfather's place, Fenn didn't know what to make of it. He felt very embarrassed (the guy was only a couple of feet away) and didn't know where to look. Then a girl came through the curtains with a banner with red ribbons hanging from it which read THE FIRE AT SIGNOR FERNANZE'S HOUSE. She came in and out at intervals over the next half-hour with different banners while this bloke spouted on. Fenn stopped listening and ate his food.

He wondered if or how he could turn this situation to

account. Could this crappy lot be called a theatre company? Would they be regarded as what the girl in Morris Angel's had called 'legitimate'? How could he find out? He wished he could remember something, anything from his conversation with the actor who'd helped him get his photographs done. Only listening to people until you'd got the information you wanted and then switching off saved a lot of time; on the other hand he now saw there could be advantages in listening and just storing stuff up. You never knew when it might come in useful.

They were both on the stage now, the girl was singing about the parched ground and the shrivelled fruit of the olive tree's womb. Suddenly in the middle of a line, almost it seemed to Fenn in the middle of a note, she stopped and they both bowed in unison, very deeply. The audience, such as it was, clapped a lot and they both jumped down from the rostrum with mock-shy, it's-just-us-after-all smiles, and started to mingle.

Fenn scraped up the last of his shepherd's pie and moved alongside. Both the cast said: 'Hi'; though without much interest. It seemed the members of the audience were all friends of the actors. They were talking about the olive growers of Tuscany in the early twenties and how, inexplicably, they had been neglected by poets and dramatists alike. Fenn tried to peel off a girl on the edge of the group.

'Any . . . um . . . chance of a job with the company? I'm –' a half-forgotten phrase rose to the surface – 'resting at the moment.'

'Aren't we all, darling. You'd have to ask Garsteen.'

'Garsteen?'

She nodded at the drapes. 'He's on lights. Or in the office. Same difference. You know there's no money? It's just a showcase.'

'Oh yeah . . . sure . . . naturally.'

He jumped on to the rostrum and pushed aside the curtain. There was a space about six feet square on one side of the stage. A chair, a table, a phone, a lighting board. And a huge man in a tartan shirt and jeans the size of a horse blanket, with a black beard spread over his chest.

'Garsteen?'

'Right.'

'I've just seen the . . . um . . . show. Wondered if there was anything going.' He had spotted, next to the phone, a stack of paper. A shiny black sun with stiff little rays on a white background, headed 'The Sun Theatre Company'.

'Sari.' He had a strong American accent. How come these guys managed to live over here, thought Fenn? Sponging off the state no doubt. 'We just cast play to play. The next's a Tennessee Williams two-hander, both parts female. Then a Sam Shepherd which I've just finished seeing people for.'

Fenn got up. 'Mind if I keep in touch?'

'Do that.' He was flicking various switches.

'I don't have your number. Could I –' He reached out. Garsteen grabbed his hand.

'Wahay . . . that stuff costs a zillion bucks a sheet. Strictly for letters to managements and agents . . .' He scribbled something on the back of an old envelope. 'Here.'

Fenn took the envelope. 'Will you be here tonight?'

'No show. We're strictly lunch time. Rehearsals though, around eight.'

'Fine.' He crumpled the paper into a ball, went back to the bar and bought a tomato juice. He kept his back to the entrance curtain but watched through the mirror. Bit by bit they all trickled out. His only worry was that one or more of the group would stay in the bar till the pub closed. Sure enough Blackbeard and one of the girls got on to the wine and toasted-sandwich circuit but left after about half an hour with her arm a quarter of the way round his vast waist. There were only a couple of people left; the barman flitted back and forth around a partition to the Public.

Choosing his time Fenn slipped behind the curtain then behind the stage. He snatched a couple of sheets of headed paper and folded them in half. Then he got his list of costume firms from his jacket pocket and sat down on the hardbacked chair. He pulled the phone towards him. He drew a line through Morris Angel and dialled the next number, a firm in Chiswick, then one in Covent Garden. Neither could help. The third in Holland Park asked his measurements, told him to hang on, then came back and said yes they thought they could fit him out. What was the company? He gave the name. They asked if he could bring authorisation and he was about to reply when he heard someone jump on the rostrum and the curtain was twitched aside. It was the barman.

'Thought you lot had all gone.'

'Sorry – I had to make some calls for Garsteen.'

'We're locking up now.' He didn't leave but stood, holding the curtain aside, waiting.

'I'm afraid the pub's closing,' said Fenn into the phone. 'All right if I come straight round?'

'Yes. We're open till five. Turn right when you come out

at Holland Park into Clarendon Road. Fairly Court's a cul-de-sac five minutes' walk along the left.'

They measured him for the uniform and found one that fitted almost exactly. The girl looked at his neatly written order then said:

'We have to check back with the company, you know.'

'Oh sure. I know the drill. Should by now. But I'm afraid we're only lunch time. Rehearsing tonight at eight. The number's on the letter. That's why I need the clothes.'

'There'll be no one here at eight. We'll check tomorrow lunch time.' She packed the hat and uniform into the bag, then hesitated. 'If your dress rehearsal's tonight haven't you left it a bit late? Hiring a costume?'

Inspired he said: 'Morris Angel let us down.'

It was as if just mentioning the famous name gave his errand authenticity. Her face cleared and she smiled.

'There you are, you see. The biggest aren't always the best.' She handed him the bag. 'Good luck.'

'What?'

'For your first night.'

Travelling back to Islington clutching his bag he felt jubilant. His earlier fears now seemed chimerical, entirely unworthy of him. He had behaved like a frightened boy seeing omens in this incident or that, believing that agencies outside himself could influence his destiny. He was ashamed of this backsliding and vowed to be more true to himself. It was not as if he had long to wait.

Sonia said: 'I want to report someone. For threatening behaviour.'

'This service is emergency only. Have you contacted your nearest police station?'

'No. I . . .' She hesitated. It was as if the impersonal voice had jolted her emotions and thoughts, shaken them up so they were forming a different pattern. New ideas and possibilities were jostling for position in her mind. No need to be hasty. She put down the phone. Then she put on the kettle and made some real coffee in a jug. She lit the gas fire, washed her face and hands and poured out the coffee through a strainer. It was very strong. She added milk and a little brown sugar and sat by the fire warming her hands on the cup.

For ten minutes or so she did nothing but savour her new position. For the first time in her life she was ahead of the game. And how close she had been to throwing in the towel. Where would be the advantage in that? He wouldn't even know who'd shopped him. And she would be back to square one. No. Fate had given her the upper hand and it was up to her to wield it cleverly. She was no longer 'in love', whatever that stupid phrase meant, and this, combined with the knowledge that she had so recently acquired, made her position practically invulnerable. She had got him exactly where she wanted him. How she would use this power she didn't quite know. Perhaps she would still make him marry her. Once she had a home and a child he could do as he liked. She knew him now; she would be going into it with her eyes wide open and absolutely no illusions. Not a bad basis for a partnership. The ferment in her mind started to settle.

She got up quickly. She now had such a strong sense of direction that it was almost as if she were being propelled by some outside agency. She couldn't wait for him to phone but got out her address book and flicked through the pages. He had never, although she had hinted often enough, given her his address. No matter. He'd give it to her now all right when he heard what she had to say. As she dialled the number she had the most vivid picture of him picking up the receiver and, for a second, a very faint echo of the old enchantment reverberated in her mind. Yes. They might well get married. It wouldn't be like it used to be but then, nothing ever was. A foreign voice answered.

'Is Fenn there?'

'I dunno. I'll shout.'

'No – wait. I think I'll come round instead. Only I'm not ringing from home so I don't have my address book. Could you . . . ?'

'Fourteen Lucy Place – off Packington Street. You want I should check he's in?'

'No, thank you. I'd like to give him a surprise.'

'Suit yourself.'

Sonia replaced the receiver and reached for the A to Z. The nearest station seemed to be the Angel. Her clothes felt crumpled and dirty, her face naked and her hair a mess. She was hunting through her wardrobe for something pretty to wear before she realised that smart clothes and make-up were no longer relevant. She was not going courting. She was going to war.

The meeting with the Birdman plunged Roz into a deep mood of fatalism which she could not seem to displace. Although she tried all sorts of little dodges to trick herself into a more positive frame of mind none of them worked for long.

Still she managed to cope. The next day a pleasant, middle-aged woman replied to her ad. for domestic help and was engaged. Roz answered her post, borrowing a dicta-typist from the pool. The Birdman did not take part in her Tuesday programme. Somehow she doubted she'd ever hear from him again.

Leo, convinced that everything was now running smoothly, had reverted to what Roz supposed to be his former self. She watched him rustling *The Times*, eating his dinner, playing with the children – but always from the viewpoint of a comparative stranger. He seemed to have hardly any connection with her at all. She wondered if this meant she had ceased to love him and, if it did, what a poor thing her love must have been to have foundered so easily at the first big hurdle in their lives. She had made some attempt to discuss this strange lack of feeling with Leo without being too specific. He had been comforting in a casual sort of way, saying it was a defence mechanism, purely temporary and brought into use by the body after a time of strain and shock to protect itself. She thought this was feasible and prayed that it was true.

She was attempting to avoid Duffy and, when this was impossible, trying to make sure a third party was present. If he sensed the reason behind these manoeuvres he said nothing but once, in Toby's office, she had caught him looking at her intently. He had given her a brilliant smile and she felt again that strange contraction in her stomach. The day after the incident at Wapping they were both in the canteen with Louise.

'Sonia's taking her time about coming back.'

Roz pushed cold baked beans around her plate. 'I rang this morning. There was no reply.'

'That's not like her.' Louise reached across, her raised eyebrows asking permission, and took Roz's beans. She started to spoon them in. 'She's the sort who'd come to work if she was dying.'

'Don't say things like that!'

'Sorry.' Louise stopped spooning for a moment and looked abashed. 'Didn't think.'

Why should she think? Roz believed Louise to be fond of her, but from the way the girl discussed the threats she might have been talking about a nightly drama series on television. Roz wondered if she was being unreasonable. Human beings could feel more than one emotion at the same time, after all. Why shouldn't Louise care about her well-being and enjoy the drama simultaneously?

Duffy said: 'I think you should ring up again when we get back to the office.'

Roz got up, not looking at him: 'I'll do it now. There's a pay phone by the lift.'

'That's ten pence!' Louise sounded horrified. 'I've almost finished. We'll be back downstairs in a jiff.'

'I'd rather not wait.' Roz took her address book from her bag. Louise was right. If Sonia was well enough to go out she would have come to work. As she picked up the receiver her sense of unease grew. There was no reply. Fifteen minutes later she returned to her office, made some coffee and tried again with the same result.

'No luck?'

She hadn't heard the door open. He sauntered over to

216

her desk and perched on the corner in the same way that he always did. It was just the effect on her that was different. Roz picked up the first papers that came to hand and crossed to the filing cabinet.

'They look like letters awaiting signature to me.'

'What?' She looked at them. 'Oh.'

'What on earth's the matter?'

'Nothing.'

'You're leaping like a salmon every time I come within five miles of you.'

She took a deep breath, turned to face him and lied boldly. 'I think this business with the Birdman has upset me. You know – thinking it was all over and then it wasn't.'

'Was he really peculiar?'

'Barmy. He had yellow plastic legs.'

'How wonderful.' Duffy laughed, his teeth very white against his tanned skin. 'I wish I'd been there.'

Oh so do I thought Roz, remembering the comfortless drive there and back and the sad union that followed. So do I.

She looked suddenly so distressed that his smile faded. 'I'd like to get my hands on this bastard. He'd wish he'd never been born.' Then, thinking to help her by changing the subject, he added: 'It's all very puzzling about Sonia. Either she's too ill to come to the phone or she's recovered and is acting very oddly.'

'I know. I just can't understand it.'

'Shouldn't we do something?'

'Well . . . like what?'

'A bit of checking up, I'd have thought. Where does she live?'

'Barons Court.'

'And what time do you pick up your kids?'

'Three-forty-five. But—'

'Tons of time.' He was picking up the internal phone and dialling. 'If anyone asks I'm over at Upton Park interviewing Billy Bonds.' He hung up. 'We'll drive to her flat and then I'll take you to . . . ?'

'Primrose Hill.'

'Come on then . . .' He was halfway to the door. 'What's the problem?'

'I . . . I don't think this is a good idea.'

'Can you think of a better one?'

She shook her head. The thought of being sealed up in a car, a few inches away from him, made her feel dizzy.

'Something might be seriously up, Roz.'

'I know.' He was right. And she could give no reason for refusing to go except the right one. Might as well light the blue touch paper she thought, as tell him the truth. She refused his offer to help with her coat and picked up her bag.

'We mustn't be late for the children.' She spoke very briskly, sounding like a teacher facing a particularly awkward class.

'No Ma'am.' He touched a blond forelock. 'Anything you say, Ma'am.'

In the car, in spite of his proximity, she felt better. It was good to be actually doing something. She kept her eyes on the road even when talking to him. The traffic was appalling. Although Duffy changed lanes frequently and skilfully the journey seemed endless. They finally got off the Cromwell Road with its orchestra of blaring horns and overwhelming stink of exhaust fumes.

'Rather a charmless area,' Duffy murmured, turning into Edith Road.

'It's that house. The one with the peeling columns.'

'Darling, they've all got peeling columns.' That wasn't true. One or two were quite smart. 'You mean the one that's the colour of decomposing liver?' When Roz nodded he parked as near to the house as he could. 'We shouldn't be a minute. Do you want to stay in the car and argue in case of traffic wardens?'

'No.' Roz was already getting out. 'She might be ill, in which case she won't want you barging in.'

'Charmed I'm sure. Nice to be wanted.' They climbed the steps. 'Oh lord – it's one of these.' There were about a dozen different bells and adjacent cards, in every sort of script and ink colour. 'That means we can't get in unless someone opens the front door.'

'I don't think so. I watched her go in and she just pushed it open.'

A neatly typed card opposite the bell for flat seven read 'Sonia Marshall'. Duffy leaned against the once-white, blistered door and they stepped into a hall. The floor and stairs facing were fitted with stained coconut matting. There was an aroma compiled of many smells. The freshest of these seemed to be curry but behind the curry was a great backlog of other smells: stale cabbage, fish, burned grills, mildewed washing, mouldy cheese. The sad residue of hundreds of lonely bed-sitter existences. It was very dark. Duffy pressed a light switch; the sort that worked on a timer.

'God. Fancy coming home to this every night.'

'And the weekends. What must the weekends be like?'

CAROLINE GRAHAM

Apart from faint sounds of reggae the whole place was quiet. They passed two bathrooms with lino, old-fashioned baths on claw feet and monstrous, rusted gas geysers. In one of the bathrooms were a lavatory and a gas ring.

'Gosh,' said Duffy, 'that's a real time-saver. You can fry your kipper while washing your feet while answering the call of Nature.'

'Whoever owns this must be pulling in around a thousand a week. You'd think he'd spend something on a can of paint.'

'Don't be naïve, Roz. That's not the name of the game.'

The door of number seven was as seedy and anonymous as all the others. Duffy knocked and Roz called: 'Sonia? It's Roz. Are you all right?' She pushed. The door remained unresponsive. 'Now what?'

'See if anyone knows anything.' Duffy crossed the landing and knocked on the other four doors, getting no reply. He ran up the top flight of stairs and did the same. Roz knocked again, pointlessly, on Sonia's door, then they walked to the floor below. They traced the reggae sound to number three.

An African opened the door. He had dreadlocks, a flowing crimson robe and, around his neck on a cord of plaited hair, a small drum. A strong, sweet smell came with him as he swayed on to the landing. Roz asked if he knew anything of Sonia's whereabouts. He stared at her.

'She live above me. I know she ain't there cause when she is there – man – the vibrations.'

'What do you mean?' Roz could not imagine Sonia leaping about or causing a disturbance of any kind.

220

'Bacchanalia, man. What do you think I mean?' Then, when she still looked puzzled: 'Ess ee ex.'

'Oh.' Roz could imagine Sonia at the centre of orgiastic scenes even less. She felt herself blush like a schoolgirl. 'When did you last see . . . I mean hear them?'

'Last night, last week, last year . . . whass time, man? You hung up on the clock face, baby?'

'Please . . . it's very important–'

'Roz,' Duffy cut in, turning her away. The door closed. 'He's on the ganja. You'll get nothing there.'

'But there isn't anyone else.' Roz moved reluctantly away. 'Maybe I should come back in the evening? When people who are out at work now are home.'

'I dunno.' Duffy's tone was not encouraging. 'They're so bloody desolate, these places. Half the time people in one section of the eggbox never speak to the people in the next section. It's worth a try, I suppose.'

As they started down the stairs he added: 'When I've dropped you I'll go back to the studio and have a word with Personnel. They'll have next of kin on her file – probably her parents. She might have gone home for a rest. I'll check up. Ring you later.'

'That's a good idea. You seem to be doing everything. I'm worse than useless.'

'I wouldn't say that. After all – careful!'

Roz's heel caught in the torn matting. As she pitched forward Duffy caught her in his arms. At the same moment the time switch clicked and the light went out. He held her for a moment, then let out his breath in a long exhalation. He buried his face in her hair.

'Ohhh God . . . I've dreamed of this . . . you'll never

know how many times.' His arms tightened. 'Don't push me away, Roz. *Please* don't push me away.'

It was worse, better, more marvellous, more terrible than she could ever have imagined. She had been right to be afraid. As she responded, parting her lips beneath his, he slipped his hands inside her coat, caressed her, pressing her closer and closer to him. She locked her arms around his neck. She felt light and boneless, her body fitting so wonderfully against his they might have been welded together. The kiss lasted for ever. She never wanted it to end. Then someone on the floor below switched on the light. They drew apart, Duffy exultant, excited; Roz dazed.

'Excuse *me*.' A stout woman laden with shopping was climbing the stairs. They drew apart to let her pass and the charge between them snapped. Roz felt the turmoil ebb and her blood begin to quieten. When Duffy stepped forward again she put up a hand to ward him off.

'Don't, Duffy. I . . . I can't handle this. Not at the moment. Not with everything else.'

'But you want me, don't you Roz?'

'I don't know . . . I don't know what I want . . .'

He didn't persist but the brilliant blue flame in his eyes stayed bright. She saw his new confidence and found herself resenting it and being excited by it in equal measure.

But how true were her feelings? The situation was so extreme. The threat to her life seemed to heighten everything. She felt as if she were the central character in a melodrama. All shades of grey had disappeared. Her response to Duffy's kiss had been volcanic, her disappointment in Leo bitter as wormwood. She seemed to be lurching from one emotional state to another with no breathing space in between.

She remembered suddenly a moment, seemingly years ago, when she had sat in her study, quietly content, congratulating herself on the harmonious order of her life. The poignancy of the recollection almost moved her to tears. She turned her face away from him.

'We'd better collect the children.'

The new daily had selected some food from the freezer and left it, thawing, in the kitchen. Sole and prawns in a cream sauce inside a scalloped pastry shell. Broccoli spears, mousseline potatoes. Orange mousse. Roz added a piece of double Gloucester. As it was Friday the children were staying up later than usual and would eat with them.

She laid the table as if in a dream. All emotions roused by Duffy's embrace had now faded, leaving her feeling languid and faintly queasy. She put out two wine glasses and tumblers for the children, filling them with lethally coloured strawberry squash. Leo arrived a little early, gave her a brief kiss and opened a bottle of Meursault.

'Better today darling?'

'Yes. Fine thanks.'

'How did the show go?'

'How does it ever go? A laugh a minute.'

'Sorry.' He shot her a quick glance, surprised at the evenness of her tone. 'Here. Have some lovely plonk.'

It *was* lovely. Crisp, even a bit flinty at first but with a wonderfully warm, golden aftertaste. She studied Leo and noticed that he looked rather tired. This caused her no concern. She wondered how he would reply if she put down her glass and said: 'I don't care about you any more'; or 'a couple of hours ago I kissed a man. If we'd been in a room on our own I would have gone to bed with him.'

Leo always sounded so professional now when he talked to her. Perhaps he would just reply: 'Now now. That's enough of all that,' and take her temperature. She found that she didn't really mind this attitude, she could cope more than adequately with the role of patient. It was the role of wife that was proving impossible.

Halfway through the meal the telephone rang. Roz pushed back her chair.

'I'll get it. Probably about Sonia. Someone was checking for me with Personnel.'

'No.' Leo pushed back his chair. 'Children, stay here. Let me answer it, Roz.'

She followed him up to the sitting room. 'It's all right . . . the number's been changed.'

'I'd still rather take it myself.'

Roz, although a few feet away, could hear the pips. Leo said nothing. Whoever it was started talking straight away. Leo listened for a moment then put down the receiver. Roz watched his face.

'What did he say?'

'It was a wrong number.'

'For God's sake, Leo! Stop treating me like a child. It's so bloody insulting.'

'I'm only trying to protect you.'

'It's too late to protect me.'

Leo shrugged. Starting back to the kitchen he said: 'It was the usual muck. Surely you don't want all the gory details.' When they were again seated at the table he added:

224

'I suppose if we hear it often enough it'll eventually become meaningless. Things do, you know.'

Roz fiddled with her orange mousse and wondered if he was right. But how often was often enough? Could she bear to play the tape over and over again until the words meant nothing? And would that exorcise or even just charm the malign energy she had heard throbbing behind every syllable?

Of course the man had got her new number. She realised she was not even surprised, then told herself to keep her thoughts within reason. She was on the point of allowing him the status of some all-knowing, all-powerful magus. He just knew someone who worked at British Telecom or, more likely, worked there himself. He would be some acned, weedy little clerk with access to ex-directory numbers. For all she knew he did this all the time, to all sorts of people. The police had as good as suggested this. Had asked if she'd checked with other well-known names. For all she knew there was a spate of it going on. She imagined ringing up Esther or Terry or Danny Baker and hearing them say: 'Oh *him*. He's been around since William the Conqueror. We've all had him.' But of course, if they didn't say that, things would seem that much worse.

Guy was discussing the latest money-making scheme of his friend Mervyn's father.

'. . . pavement yachting is going to be the next big thing. Mervyn says I could get one wholesale but I have to decide right away.'

Leo said: 'Eat up your mousse, Roz. Don't let a little shit like that take your appetite away.'

A delighted, self-righteous sucking sound from Kathy.

'We're not allowed to say "shit" at school, Daddy.'

'Of course you're not. That's what education's all about.'

'What d'you mean,' said Guy, 'that's what education's all about?'

'Apposition. The right word in the right place at the right time.'

'I don't see how logarithms fit into that theory actually, Dad.'

'You will Oscar, you will.'

Leo spoke automatically. His thoughts were entirely on the diatribe that he had just been listening to. He found it hard to understand, considering how he spent his days, why it was that he felt so violently sick after listening to a detailed description of how Madgewick reacted during his lengthy, drawn-out demise.

Chapter Seven

When the phone rang the next morning Roz was alone. She stood listening to the clamour. Answer me. Answer me. She told herself that whoever it was would ring again if it was important, then Mrs Phillips could pick it up and take a message. Roz had promised Leo – and it was not a promise hard to give – that she would not answer the phone again under any circumstances. She had never been so aware of the tyranny of the thing. She touched the phone. It vibrated gently under her hand. She knew his voice so well by now. One syllable and she could hang up. She didn't have to listen. She picked it up.

'Hello darling. How are you today?'

'Oh.' A rush of nervous excitement mixed with relief. 'It's you.'

'Of course. I must see you, Roz.'

'Listen Duffy. What I said yesterday . . . about not being able to cope with all this at the moment. It was quite true. I'm not being coy.'

'That's not why I want to see you. Well – it is but there's something else. It's terribly important. I think I've got a lead on your loony.'

227

'How? Oh – and did you find out about Sonia?'

'Yes . . . no . . . tell you when I get there.'

'Where? You're not coming *here*?'

He couldn't help but be pleased at the panic in her voice. 'Why not? We'll be chaperoned won't we? Isn't your Mrs Thingy coming in?'

Roz checked the grandfather clock. Mrs Phillips was due in fifteen minutes, long before Duffy would arrive. 'All right. Will you have had breakfast?'

'Just a Teachers on toast.'

'I'll make some more coffee.'

When her daily help arrived Roz ran out to the bakery and got some fresh brioches. She laid the table in the sitting room: butter, black cherry jam and fruit, and refilled the cafetière. Then she stood by the window and waited.

She was expecting to see his black Peugeot 106, then realised it would be impossible to park near her front door. It was a bitter-cold, brilliantly sunny day. Fronds of cotoneaster loaded with scarlet berries tapped incessantly against the window, propelled by the wind. Duffy ran up the steps at precisely five minutes past ten. He was wearing his outdoor broadcast kit: green parka, khaki cords, fur hat with ear-muffs, sheepskin gloves. He took her hands, looked at her intently for a moment, then let them go.

'Where's this famous coffee then?'

'I've laid the table in the sitting room.'

'Smashing. Lead the way.' He looked around the long, elegant room appreciatively, then followed her to the table. 'I hope you've got something hot in the oven, as all those stand-up comedians say.'

'Two Freudian slips in one sentence. You are doing well for only ten o'clock.'

We both seem to have hit on the same note, Roz thought. Friendly, jokey, not too close. She was grateful for his compliance but nothing could unmake the kiss, and when they sat at the table she placed herself a little further away than she would normally have done and knew that he had noticed. She was glad of the sounds downstairs; the clatter of pots and pans. When she drew up a chair her foot momentarily touched his and she willed herself to behave as if it was unimportant and not to snatch her foot away.

'What did they say in Personnel?'

'What indeed? I told Doris we were worried and that we'd called at the flat and asked what we should do next. She checked Sonia's file – her parents live in Rugby by the way – and rang them. They hadn't heard from her for over a week but last time they did she was in high spirits and talking of getting married to someone name of Fenn.'

'Getting married!'

'Quite. Not a mention of it in the office, I told Doris – never mind invitations flowing and a whip-round for a silver chafing dish. I said did she think a visit to the police and the missing persons routine, but she thought that was a bit heavy at this stage. She thought Sonia had probably just cleared off with her fella for a day or two. I said that was totally out of character and she said nobody ever acted out of character. When they seemed to they were just showing us an aspect of their character we hadn't seen before.'

'That sounds reasonable.'

'Nonsense. She's got it off that *Reader's Digest* psychology course they send Personnel on.'

'I mean it sounds reasonable to wait a bit longer before going to the police.'

'Wait. I haven't told you the rest. I was on the midnight shift last night. Hanging around in the reporters' room after the eleven o'clock headlines with nothing to do but wait for the twelve o'clock headlines and I thought, let's sit down, Duffield, like they always do in the Penguin Crime Classics with the green covers, and write a list. Everything we know about this weirdo, everything that's relevant so far, everything we know about Sonia—'

'But Sonia has nothing to do—'

'Let me finish, lovey. Sonia had never spoken of a boyfriend before the last couple of weeks?'

'No. I'd always assumed she didn't have one.' Roz realised how condescending that sounded. 'But of course she may have done.'

Duffy shook his head. 'I don't think so. She's not the sort to keep it quiet.'

'She kept the wedding quiet.'

'It may not have been settled. She hadn't known him five minutes. Now, think. Did you give Sonia your new home number?'

Roz didn't need to think. 'Yes.' She sat very still; slowly incidents began to interlock, a pattern to emerge. A pattern she rejected immediately. 'You must be wrong. I know she didn't like me but I can't see her doing something like that.'

'But she didn't know. Don't you see? It's because she didn't know that she passed out in the office when she heard his voice on the tape. He probably just went through her bag when she wasn't looking. Got hold of her address book.'

'If he knew Sonia that might explain how he knew his

230

way around the building. Where my office was and everything. She must have shown him round at some time.'

'She'd have had to sign him in at reception. There'll be a record. That *must* be how it is Roz. There's no other explanation.'

Roz felt the floor solid beneath her feet. The empty coffee bowl still warm to the touch, a curl of butter dissolving on a piece of still warm brioche. Reality. And this . . . Fenn was just as bound by reality as any of these humble things. No magician, no occult powers, no all-seeing eye. Just an unwitting accomplice: poor, gullible Sonia.

'You do see that, don't you Roz?'

'Yes.' She nodded. 'I'm sure you're right.' It was as if the linking of Fenn with Sonia had made him less frightening. She was so pathetic that some of her pathos seemed to rub off on to him.

'But what do we do now? I mean until we find Sonia we can't find Fenn. And in any case since she heard the tape and now knows that he's just been using her she may have chucked him. She was incredibly upset.'

'She'll still know how to trace him. Where he lives. Once she comes back we'll talk to her.'

'What if she won't tell us?'

'Then we'll get the police to talk to her.'

Roz said: 'Don't you think we should contact them right away?'

Duffy shook his head. 'No point. Not until Sonia re-emerges. They can't do any more than we can.'

'I suppose that's true.' Roz mopped up the last of her coffee with the brioche, reached for an apple and glanced at Duffy. 'I don't like that look on your face.'

'That's funny. I love the look on your face.'

'Stop it, Duffy.'

'Sorry. What do you mean anyway?'

'You might just as well be carrying a magnifying glass, wearing a deerstalker and playing a violin.'

'You overestimate my digital capacities, angel.'

'I'm serious. Don't go sleuthing around after a scoop. This man's obviously very disturbed. You don't know what he might do.'

'She really cares, folks.' Then, catching Roz's eye he added: 'What's your news?'

'Nothing much. He rang here last night. Leo took the call. Said it was the usual muck.'

'Don't you see the difference this makes, lovey? We've discovered things about him. You're in a quite different position now. Almost on the offensive.'

'I suppose I am.' It was all very new but already Roz felt a little better. Not exactly confident, until he was apprehended she would never be that, but she felt less hopeless. There was now something she could do, could come to grips with. 'I think it might be better if neither of us spoke to Sonia when she comes back. If we leave it to Toby or someone in—'

She broke off, the colour draining from her face. She felt pressing against the border of her consciousness a further appalling connection. Something that must be pushed away at all costs. 'Oh no . . .'

Duffy reached across the table and gripped her hand. 'What on earth's wrong?' She did not reply. 'Roz . . .' He got up and came round the table. 'Tell me. What is it?'

'I've got to make a phone call. I'm right. I know I'm right

– it's too much of a coincidence.' He watched her dial with trembling fingers. 'It wasn't Greg's fault.' She started to cry. 'Oh Christ Duffy . . . what am I going to do . . . ?'

'Darling don't . . . don't cry. Tell me what it is and perhaps I can do something.'

'They're a bit peculiar about giving out their workers' numbers. They always think you're trying to book them on the quiet without paying the fee, but surely if I explain – Hello?'

Duffy watched her taut, ashen face. Heard the words tumbling out, saw her eventually write down a number and hang up without a word of thanks. She dialled again.

'. . . He was an actor . . . the agency sent him when I wanted a temp . . . I accused him of getting drunk and letting Madgewick out . . . we had a row and he flounced off. I've got to – Hello? Greg? It's Roz Gilmour. Listen – I was mistaken about you. About letting out the cat. I just wanted—'

'It's pointless you asking me to come back, dear heart. I'm off to Liverpool rep. tomorrow. Dagger-carrying in *The Duchess of Malfi*.'

'That's not why I—'

'The Barbican audition was an absolute fiasco. I went totally to pieces. The proximity to all that greatness, I suppose. Mind you—'

'Greg. *Please*, this is terribly important.'

'Oh. Off you go then.'

'This man who is threatening me. He's . . . he's got our cat.' Duffy moved across and stood next to her.

'Nasty. But I don't see how I come into this. It all sounds too sordid for words.'

'The day he disappeared. When you say you left him in his basket.'

'And so I did, dear. No say about it.'

'Yes. I know. Didn't you tell me someone came to the door asking the way?'

'That's right.'

'What actually happened? Did he just ask and then go away?'

'Not precisely, Roz.' A pause, then his voice changed.

'Oh dear. This is what comes of trying to be helpful.'

'It's all right. Just tell me.'

'He asked the way to Chalk Farm. I said I was a stranger in these parts but I remembered seeing an A to Z on your dresser and told him I'd pop down and fetch it. So I did.'

'Leaving the front door open?'

'I'm afraid so.' An even longer pause. 'My God! You don't think he was in the house all the time I was working?'

'He must have been. There was no forced entry. And when I came home the cat had gone. And a generous amount of whisky.'

'Ohhh.' There was much relish and excitement in his voice. 'I feel cold all over.'

'Don't blame yourself.' Roz knew she sounded grudging. He had known about the threats and should, she felt, have been a lot more careful. 'Please tell me everything you can remember about his appearance, Greg. Every single thing. It's very important.'

Duffy watched her pen flying over the paper. The guy seemed to remember an awful lot. Then he saw her shoulders were shaking. When she hung up and turned to face him her face was drenched with tears.

'. . . people were so cruel to Madgewick Duffy . . . before we got him. He was lying in a dustbin, just thrown away to die. Oh God – I can't bear it if he's being hurt . . . I can't . . . we've got to do something . . .'

He hurried to her, instinctively taking her in his arms. 'Don't cry, my lovely.' He found himself lying to comfort her. 'He'll be OK. Cats – they're full of tricks. Probably making his way home right now.'

'Do you really think so?' Her expression was pitiful.

He couldn't help himself and bent his head to kiss her tears away.

'Shall I clear now, Mrs Gilmour?'

They drew apart. Roz said: 'Yes . . . thank you.' After Mrs Phillips had gone Duffy led her to the table.

'Come and sit down, love. Give me your notes. Come on . . . you'll feel better once we're doing something.' She sat with him, trying to blink back fresh tears. 'I must say your Greg seemed to remember an awful lot.'

'Yes. He's gay you see, and this man was apparently –' her mouth twisted on the words '– quite beautiful. Even allowing for a certain amount of romantic exaggeration I think we've got a fairly accurate description.'

'Let's have a look then. How does he compare with Lou's plumber? No moustache.'

'That could have been false.' She took a deep breath, sniffing back tears. He passed her a large, khaki handkerchief, rumpled but clean. She mopped her face, blew her nose.

'Build and height?'

'Slim, quite tall.' Roz looked at her pad. 'Very slender, just under six feet. Hair almost copper but mixed with gold.'

'Plumber wore a cap. Probably because his hair was so distinctive.'

Roz continued: 'Very straight nose, pale skin, compelling eyes. Almost tawny like a lion's.'

'Oh for heaven's sake. No doubt he had a glittering mesmeric stare as well. The trouble is, Roz, we don't know how much of this is fact and how much Greg embroidered once he knew who the man was.'

'I think if we drop the more dramatic of the adjectives we've still got a lot left. And a detailed description of his clothes, rather expensive and elegant by the way, which surprises me although I can't quite say why.'

'What's that?' Duffy peered at her writing. 'Deliciously what . . . ?'

'Deliciously full about the crotch.'

'Good grief. Still I suppose it's a point worth remembering.' He paused hopefully. 'Sorry.'

'Don't you see what a difference this makes? We now know almost exactly what the person we're after looks like.'

'Obviously it will be helpful to the police but as far as us looking . . . Roz, there are over four million people out there. We wouldn't know where to start.'

'But we do.' Roz gripped his hand so hard he winced. The tension in her stung his skin, like electricity. 'Listen. I remember this very clearly because the absolute incongruity of it struck me at the time. It was when Sonia gave me that incredibly expensive scent to try and I said her boyfriend must be a tycoon, something like that, and she said (Duffy thought the back of his hand would snap): ' "Oh no . . . as a matter of fact he lives over a chip shop in Islington." '

They stared at each other for a long moment, then Duffy said: 'I think you are breaking my bones.'

'Oh.' Roz released him. 'I'm sorry. Could we go now?'

'Wait a moment—'

'I *can't*. We've got to—'

'Just to plan, that's all. Islington's a big place. He could mean Kings Cross, the Angel, Highbury. Some people think the Balls Pond Road's in Islington. We've got to be systematic. Carve it into sections, otherwise we'll just be doubling back and repeating ourselves.'

'We'll take half each.'

'No.'

'But think of the time we'll save. It'll take twice as long going round together.' When he said nothing she went on defensively: 'You can't stop me,' then felt ashamed. He had immediately agreed to help yet it would have been quite understandable if he hadn't. The traffic hassle, the legwork, the parking problems, the cold unpleasant weather. And then she realised why he didn't want her going round on her own and was doubly grateful. 'I'll go and get the map.'

'I think,' he said as they pored over the pages, 'we should take first the area which everyone knows to be Islington, and only move out on to the fringe if that fails.'

She nodded. 'All right.'

'Have you got the Yellow Pages? There might be some chippies listed in there.'

'Not for North One.'

Duffy's finger traced a line. 'The traffic's one-way in a lot of these roads, which might cause problems. It won't take us long to get there. Down Mornington Crescent, right down Pancras Road and out at Kings Cross. You'll have to look out of both sides of the car at once. I'll look whenever we get into a crawl. I'll stop every time I see a place and as near to it as I can. OK?'

'More than OK. And thank you, Duffy.' She looked at him seriously. 'You are a lovely man.'

'No I'm not.' He grinned. 'I'm after a scoop. Imagine Toby turning duck-pond green with envy. It'd be worth all the legwork just for that.'

As they left the house Roz said: 'I've a feeling she'll be there with him, you know. Sonia.'

'We'll see.' The passenger seat of his car was full of junk. Old copies of the *Sporting Times*, a couple of Dick Francis novels, a paperback of aphorisms, a bag which had once held boiled sweets, and half a slab of fruit and nut. Duffy scooped up the lot and threw them into the back on top of a grubby tartan travelling rug and his Uher.

'Elegance is my middle name.'

'It's certainly not your first name.'

They pulled out into Camden High Street and almost immediately fetched up behind a vast green and yellow Habitat van. It took fifteen minutes before they reached Mornington Crescent.

'We'll never get there.' Whilst she had been talking in the sitting room, looking at the route, planning the trip, Roz's mind had been fully occupied but now, crawling along in the traffic, there was nothing to hold back the forming of terrible mind pictures. Madgewick being hurt, Madgewick dead. She stared hard at Marks and Spencer's, reading the window display: 'Ninety-seven per cent of our goods are British made'; committing the pictures of perfect food to memory. Then she thought of the dinner that evening and went slowly over every detail of preparation. She was just sprinkling toasted nuts over the cold lemon soufflé when Duffy said:

'Right. Start looking.'

They were passing the magnificent, soaring rose-red folly of St Pancras. A minute later Roz shouted: 'There! There!'

'For God's sake!' Duffy glanced in the direction of her arm which had shot directly across the lower part of his face. 'If you're going to do that another twenty times within the next few hours, by tea time I'm going to be a nervous wreck.'

'Sorry. Where can you pull in?'

'Nowhere. There are solicitors' offices above –' he glanced again out of the window – 'Alf's Fish Chips Eels Mash All Hot.'

'Oh.' She sank back into her seat.

'You'll find that quite a lot around here, I think. It'll make things easier in a way.'

Within the next half-hour, having traversed about ten streets, one accidentally twice, they had found five fish and chip shops. One was under a poolroom, one under another solicitor's office and one under a loan shark's, discreetly lettered in gold: 'Ledbury Financial Advancement Company'. The other two looked possibles. One was in Donelly Street just off the Caledonian Road. They parked illegally close by, got out and looked around for a warden. No sign.

'Come on,' Duffy said, 'we'll only be five minutes, if that.'

The windows above the shop had snowy net curtains and a fern in a burnished brass pot. Next to the shop entrance a wooden door stood open, leading to a flight of uncarpeted stairs. There was no bell or card. They climbed up, came to a second door and knocked. They stood for what seemed to Roz like half an hour. There were sounds within the room. Duffy knocked again.

' 'Ang on, 'ang on.' A shuffling sound came closer and a very old man opened the door. The view beyond was astonishingly neat and clean, as was the old man himself. 'What d'you want?'

'Er . . . we're looking for a young man.'

'No young men 'ere. Or young women either, more's the pity.' A sound between a whoop and a wheeze strangled at birth might have been a laugh. He added, with the swingeing irrelevance to which children and the elderly are prone: 'I'm eighty-four next birthday.'

'All we know about him,' said Roz, 'is that he lives over a chip shop in Islington.'

'I live over a chip shop in Islington.'

'Well – thank you very much.' Roz started to turn away.

'Look after meself. Sparkling, everything is. Do you want to have a look round?' He opened the door wider.

Duffy said: 'It's very kind of you but I'm afraid we can't stay. I'm illegally parked.'

'They want to put me in a home so you have to keep up to snuff. The minute you get a bit dishevelled about the place they're on to you.'

Roz said reassuringly: 'Everything looks lovely.'

'You from the Council?'

'No.'

'Well, please yourself.' And he closed the door.

As they went back down the stairs Roz said: 'Poor old man.'

'Not at all. I hope I'm in that sort of shape, or any sort of shape, when I'm eighty-four. Quick!'

The warden had about four cars to go. They got in and pulled away just in time. The second possible, although it had looked from the street like a private dwelling, was actually used by a nearby stationer for storage. Duffy neatly blocked off a section of the map with his pencil.

'Right. Section two. Start at the Angel – then up the Essex Road to St Peter's Street, right?' When she didn't reply he added: 'Don't look like that, lovey. We've only just started.'

Roz was staring at the page. 'It's just that there's so much of it. All these streets . . .'

'Go on. We've done a quarter already and its not even twelve o'clock. Look – there we are. Number one. Sea-Fresh Daily.'

'That's a fishmonger's.' But a moment later she saw: 'Pisces and Pizzas' and the hunt was on again.

By two p.m., calf muscles throbbing, they were standing underneath a sign promising 'Only the Best Fish n' Chips'. The faces which had in the last couple of hours appeared in various doorways were, in Roz's memory, starting to blend together. There had been young men, half a dozen, all shapes, sizes and shades, none within a thousand miles of what even their own mothers would call beautiful. A couple of elderly ladies, one spruce, one so dishrevelled it was hard to believe she could ever be knitted-up again. A middle-aged lady called Lana in a black net blouse and leather mini who offered Duffy (he arrived at the door a few steps ahead) French lessons, and an elderly couple who had stood at the door, stock still, apparently interlocked for mutual

241

support. They were still rooted there, frowning with worry and suspicion, when Roz and Duffy left.

They had found a one-hour parking zone nearby and now Duffy checked his watch. 'We've got nearly twenty minutes. Are you hungry?'

'Starving.'

'Well there's the Sun and Seventeen Cantons over the road or the Best Fish n' Chips.'

'Oh fish n' chips please. I'm never very happy about pub food. All those warmed-through Sweeney Todd pies.'

The main lunch-hour business had passed and they found a clean empty table by the window. Duffy went to the counter and came back with two golden wings of skate, crisp chips, spongy soft white bread, butter and a pot of freshly made dark brown tea. Roz ate up everything on her plate. There were even minute plastic boxes of sauce tartare with peel-back silver-paper lids. The skate smelt and tasted as if it had been swimming in the sea half an hour before. But as soon as she had finished her second cup of tea Roz felt the comfort that the meal had afforded draining away.

She said: 'What if Sonia was lying? About where he lived?'

'Why on earth should she lie in the direction of North One? If she'd said Belgrave Square there might have been some point.'

'I suppose you're right. On the other—'

'Hey! It's quarter past!' Roz grabbed her bag. They got up and hurried into and down the street, buttoning their coats as they went. They were five minutes overdue. There was a ticket on the windscreen.

'Bloody hell. They don't hang around in Islington, do they?'

'You must let me pay for it, Duffy. After all you're doing all this for me. And there's the lunch and everything.'

'Lunch goes on expenses. And you're certainly not paying for the ticket.'

'Halves then.'

'Oh, not the heavy feminist bit Roz, please.' Suddenly he sounded bad-tempered, almost peevish.

'Don't be so horrid. I'm just trying to be fair.'

He took the ticket out of the polythene wrapper, tore it across and gave her a piece. 'Halves it is then.'

She took it rather uncertainly and they got into the car. She decided, with a chill feeling that she recognised as embryonic despair, that he too thought their quest fruitless. But his next words gave the lie to this belief.

'We are idiots. We should have gone first to the Council offices. There must be a register of businesses there. And shops and restaurants. It would have saved half this buggering about.' He still sounded bad-tempered but in a positive, slightly aggressive way.

'Shall we do that now?'

'It's a bit late if you have to be at the school at three-forty-five. We'll finish our square on the map so we know where we are, then we'll start fresh in the morning.'

'I've got a programme.'

'Straight after, then. Can't your kids go out to tea or something?'

He made them sound nothing more than an irritating nuisance, Roz thought. She got irritated in return and spoke sharply: 'I'll try. It's a bit short notice.'

'Look – there's a Greek place. They do kebabs as well. Fresh from the sea if the neon sign's anything to go by.'

He was obviously making an effort to recapture the close, friendly feelings they had experienced earlier. Roz smiled, reading out the sign over the shop next door. 'Doreece. Good-As-New.'

'I'll bet she is,' murmured Duffy as he got out. There was an outside iron staircase to the flat above, leading to a shabby maroon door. They could hear the dim clatter of machinery. About to knock he saw it was slightly open, and pushed instead. They found themselves on a short landing facing a second door. On it was pinned a film poster showing a car chase and a full-bosomed Indian beauty with flowers in her hair and a slumbrous pout. Duffy knocked.

A squat middle-aged woman in black opened the door wide, then straightaway closed it to a chink. Roz had seen in that moment three or four girls crouched over sewing machines. The tiny room foamed with materials in dazzling colours; jam-packed into every corner.

'What d'you want? I am only making a dress for a friend. Not doing business.' Duffy put his question but after saying: 'We don't rent rooms,' she let loose a flood of Gujarati, some of which was tossed over her shoulder, when the machines started chattering again. Then she slammed the door.

'Today's been quite an education one way and another,' murmured Roz as they got back into the Peugeot. 'I've never seen a sweat shop before.'

Duffy drove for a few more minutes, then turned into the last street on his ruled square. Packington Street. He drove slowly, frequently looking out of the window.

'Nothing . . . well Roz . . . I think that has to be it for

today. I'll come out myself in the morning if you like. Get a list from the offices.'

'Wait! There's a turning at the end.'

Duffy nodded at a street sign. 'It's a cul-de-sac. Hardly likely to be anything there.'

'I think we should try, though. Then we'll have covered every single place in your square.'

She could see him deciding to humour her. 'All right, Rosamunda. If you want to check the dead end then the dead end you shall check.'

He swung the car to the right and drove into Lucy Place. They were in an enclosed, cobbled yard, two sides of which were taken up with the back entrances of a garment factory, three storeys high, whose windows, some of which were cracked or covered with cardboard, were thick with grime. In contrast the four little shops on the opposite side looked very smart. There was a typing and duplicating agency painted in shiny red and white with a large glass frontage through which the machines could be seen working. A window cleaner was going over the glass with a T-shaped pusher, sliding rivulets of water this way and that. His cart and ladder were parked near the entrance.

Next to the agency was Lamb's: 'Everything for Baby and Toddler'. This was green and daffodil-yellow and had a lot of showy children's clothes and plastic toys in the window. Then came a modest art shop with some framed maps and a display of oils and brushes and last of all, beneath a fascia of palm trees on a blue metallic background with leaping silver fish, was the Oasis Fish Bar.

After a moment Duffy spoke. 'Oh dear. Woman's intuition triumphs again over man's lack of faith.' He

glanced upwards. 'Flats above all the shops too. Congrat-
ulations.' He started to open the door. 'Come on . . . what's
the matter?'

Roz was staring through the windscreen up at the neatly
curtained sash window above the fish bar. It was almost like
something out of a child's drawing or a doll's house. So
symmetrically hung the neat side curtains' folds, so still they
might have been painted on to the glass. The net curtain,
neither white, grey nor beige but an unpleasant mixture of
all three, was precisely positioned halfway up the window
and was equally motionless. It looked like a dead eye. A
dead eye in a dead end. She couldn't stop looking at it. She
heard Duffy say something else, then his hand appeared,
disappeared and appeared again in front of her eyes. Her
brain registered the movement while her eyes saw only the
window. She saw it even through Duffy's flesh and bone.
She would have given anything to reverse time. To be living
five minutes before when she did not know the window
existed. She shut her eyes. It made no difference. The
window thrust itself to the forefront of her imaginings. She
turned her head aside and looked at Duffy.

'What on earth's wrong?'

She couldn't think of anything to say that made
sense. 'By the pricking of my thumbs . . .'? He would
think her stupid and melodramatic. She didn't want to
get out of the car. Whatever happened she would go
no nearer to the window than she was now. 'You go, Duffy.
I don't feel too good. Probably gulping down the fish
and chips.'

'Rubbish. Honestly Roz. You're as transparent as a
child.' All his bad temper had vanished. He reached out and

246

took her hand. 'You're not ill, you're frightened. What makes you think this is the place?'

She shook her head. She felt unable to speak. It was as if words – releasing into the air audible fashionings of what were, after all, only apprehensions – would give them some dreadful authenticity. Perhaps if she said nothing they could yet prove to be groundless.

'Look, love. We have spent all day looking for this place.'

'Yes, I know. I just didn't realise . . . what it would be like . . .'

'Will you be all right in the car?'

'Yes.'

She watched him walk away over the cobbles and disappear into the shop. She tried to slow down her breathing. To make it even and peaceful. Hard to believe it was a winter's day outside, the air in the car seemed so close. Almost stifling. She released her seat belt, pushed down her door lock, then reached over and did the same on the driver's side. It was foolish to feel even the slightest bit afraid. She was securely locked in a car in an open square overlooked by buildings full of hard-working people, none of whom meant her any harm.

Duffy was a long time. She glanced at his digital stick-on clock. They'd only just make it to collect the children. She closed her eyes and concentrated on her breathing. Counting the breath. One . . . two . . . three . . . It was definitely having a tranquillising effect. The pounding of her heart settled a little. She was breathing out on the count of seven when someone rapped on the driver's side of the glass. Breath suddenly stopped in her throat, she stared, wide-eyed, at the young male face, a few inches from her own. He was wearing a cap so she could not see the colour of his hair. Like the plumber. Just like the plumber.

As she stared he pushed his face closer, making a broad negroid nose on the glass, spreading his lips in a rubbery, pantomime smile. She shaped the words: 'Go away.' No vocal back-up appeared. He went into a hugely exaggerated mock-Jewish shrug and walked away to the centre of the courtyard. There he flung his arms wide and addressed the walls: 'Go avay? She vants I should go avay.'

She took advantage of his retreat to wrench open the door and dash across the courtyard. His voice pursued her.

'You're blockin' the bleedin' exit, darlin'. How the 'ell am I supposed to get me cart through that bleedin' peep 'ole?'

She was safe in the shop. If Duffy was surprised at the speed with which she catapulted through the door he said nothing. The shop was empty, not with the recently vacated air of a lively snack bar but really empty. Equipment clean and closed away, bright fizzy Fanta in neat inviolate groups of three. A poster for a bazouki concert. A Space Invader. Behind the bar was a curtain, brightly coloured plastic strips hanging motionless.

'I've been banging on the counter with no result.'

'They're obviously not open for business. I wonder why the door's unlocked?'

Duffy rapped on the counter hard, using his knuckles. Overhead a small dragging sound. Roz gripped his arm.

'That's coming from the room! The room we saw from outside.'

'Not necessarily. It's not always easy to locate sounds.

Anyway – what if it is?' She couldn't answer that. She dare not. 'It's probably Mr . . .' he squinted at the name plaque above the plastic fronds, 'Christoforou.'

Christoforou. The name reminded her of something. A film. She was in a cinema – it had been the Hampstead Everyman – on the screen was a shape both elongated and hunched, throwing a monstrous shadow; a leprous white bald head, snake's eyes and etiolated fingers with a life of their own, like a nest of young serpents, tipped with very long curved talons poised to rip and tear. The vampire Nosferatu.

'I'm sick of this place. Let's go. We know it's here. We can come back tomorrow.'

But at that moment, with a slithering, slapping sound, the plastic ribbons parted and Mr Christoforou came in. He looked sleepy (he was tucking his shirt into his trousers) and bad-tempered.

'What the hell you want?'

'I'm sorry but the door was open.'

'That's for the Space man. He comes to repair. You can see the shop's closed.'

'It's very important. We're looking for a young—'

Roz's voice cut in with an assurance which had passed beyond belief and into knowledge. 'Is Fenn here?'

She sensed Duffy's surprise. Mr Christoforou said: 'No. Haven't seen him for a couple of days.'

So there it was. Roz and Duffy clutched each other's hands. They felt like swimmers, who, kicking and floundering for hours out of their depth in an alien sea, now felt firm sand beneath their feet. For a moment neither of them knew what to say. Then Roz spoke. Her new-found confidence had routed fear entirely.

249

'Do you mind if we go up and check?'

Mr Christoforou hesitated then, as if moved by the intensity of her regard and the suppressed emotion generated by both of them, shrugged and held up the counter flap. 'You're wasting your time. Getting me out of bed for nothing.' He disappeared through a door in the hall, calling over his shoulder: 'Door on the right at the top of the stairs.'

They climbed the stairs and stood in front of the door. Roz stayed Duffy's arm as he was about to knock. 'No. Let me.' She waited a moment. With the cessation of fear had come pleasure bordering on triumph. Ridiculous childish phrases came into her mind; she could have called out: 'Gotcha!' The balance of power had shifted with a vengeance. She knocked, deliberately making it peremptory. Behind the door was silence.

'We're getting terribly pushed for time, love. If you want to collect your kids by quarter to four we'll have to go. We've been successful. All we've got to do now is report this to the police. Better have a word with Zorba before we go, otherwise he might say something. We don't want the little bastard coming back, then scarpering before we can nab him.'

They could hear shouting in the square outside. Roz said: 'There's someone in there. I know there is.'

'Well, they're not answering honeybun, so I don't see what else we can do.' He tried the handle. The door was locked. 'What the hell's going on down there?'

'I expect it's the window cleaner. He can't get his stuff out because of the car.'

'Come on. That's two good reasons for calling it a day.'

She followed him reluctantly down the stairs, looking backwards as if afraid the door would vanish. The only link with her pursuer. No. She didn't have to think like that any more. Now she was the pursuer. The second they emerged into the square the window cleaner strode over to them. Oddly enough now that he was red-faced and shouting with anger she did not feel at all afraid of him. He said to Duffy:

'Is that your fucking car?'

'Yes. Sorry—'

'I've got three fucking jobs to do in Packington Street. I'm running fifteen minutes late as it is. Maybe you don't have to earn a fucking living.'

'Wait a minute.' Roz opened her handbag. 'Please . . .' She got out her wallet. The window cleaner collapsed like a pricked balloon. You could almost see the ire hissing out of his ears and nostrils.

'Nah, nah. 'Salright. Just shift the gear, lady. Not to worry.'

She held out a ten pound note. 'I want to hire your ladder, please. For about five minutes.'

'Ah well. That's different.' He took the note. 'If it's business.' He went away and returned with the ladder. 'It's expanding. Can trap your fingers if you're not used to it.' Giving her a curious glance: 'You say where you want it and I'll put her up for you.'

'Outside the fish and chip shop. Up to that window above.'

She heard Duffy sigh, his impatience returning. 'You never give up, do you?'

The window cleaner erected his ladder, the base grating on the cobbles with a tooth-peeling metallic rasp. Two girls came to the window of the duplicating shop and took an interest.

'What's it abaht then? Are you detectives trying to catch him in flagrarnty? 'Ere – ' he grabbed Roz's arm '– you're not climbing up in them 'eels are you? My insurance won't cover you breaking your neck.'

'He's right. Don't be daft, Roz.' She had three-inch heels on snuff suede boots. 'Let me.' Duffy got on to the bottom rung. 'And as soon as we leave here the first thing we'd better find is a phone because we're never going to get to Primrose Hill in time.' He started to ascend.

Roz stood at the base of the ladder, watching. He stepped slowly and carefully, his gloved hands gripping the shining aluminium. She could see the scuffed backs to his brogues then, a moment later the soles, so deeply sculpted they seemed to be stuck all over with chunks of chocolate. Gravel and larger stones were embedded, and grass. His anorak ballooned suddenly in the wind. He was at the halfway mark.

Roz was absolutely convinced that Fenn was hiding in there. She pictured him perhaps cowering behind a chair or scrambling under the bed. She said aloud, through cold lips: 'See how you like it.' She recognised her pleasure, so intense it was almost sadistic, with some surprise. And yet why not? After all he had put her through she would have to be a saint not to enjoy seeing him get a taste of the same medicine. He would have heard them going down the stairs and must have thought they'd given up and gone away. Well – he'd have to think again. Duffy's face was rising to sill level now. She waited for his cry of affirmation.

But something was wrong. No cry came. Not a sound.

She saw the chestnut leather of his gloves tauten and gleam as his hands fiercely gripped the ladder. Then, just as suddenly, slacken. His body seemed to sway away from the ladder and at the same time half twist in the air so his face dipped into view upside down; a small black circle for a mouth inside a larger circle, cheesy and greenish-white, a cut-out substitute for a face.

Roz screamed. The man with her shouted: 'Christ.' Then: ' 'ang on mate.' He started to climb. Roz gripped the base of the ladder. Staring up at Duffy's appalling countenance she knew what he must have seen. Only death could make a man look so, and an ugly, violent death at that. Her heart sang a jubilato at her enemy's destruction.

'He's dead,' it sang. '*He's dead!*'

Chapter Eight

Roz reached up to help the window cleaner who had one hand against the small of Duffy's back, trying to push him closer to the ladder for support. For a couple of seconds the three of them clung there like a trio of incompetent acrobats. She heard Duffy murmur, in an old man's voice: 'It's all right . . . I'm OK.' Then, one at a time, the three of them stumbled to the ground. Roz held Duffy's arm. He looked into her glowing face, felt the unnatural strength of her body. She had the air of a gladiator.

'Oh Roz . . .' He shook his head and couldn't speak.

'You don't half look rough, mate. Go in the caff and sit down. You got no 'ead for heights you wanna keep off ladders.'

'I saw a pay phone in the hall. Has one of you got some change?' Duffy sounded as if he was just learning to speak. Every word came out weighted with forethought; each with the same amount of emphasis.

'Yes. I've got some. Will you be all right?' Roz moved away.

'I'll stay wiv 'im dear.' The tenner had obviously oiled a bottomless well of troubled water. 'No sweat.'

'After you've rung the school ring the police.'

'The police? Shouldn't I get an ambulance? If he's killed himself.'

'He hasn't killed himself.'

'But –'

'Please. I can't . . .' He shook his head, but looking away as if she was about to strike him. '. . . Just do it Roz.'

Beneath the benevolent gaze of the Caribbean lady she dialled 999 and asked for the police. In the seconds before they answered it struck her that she had no idea how she would reply if they asked her to give any details. It was Duffy who should have been making the call. She could see him through the still-stirring reeds of plastic, sitting by the open door with his elbows on the table, his head in his hands. The window cleaner was already acting like a minor character in a bad TV series, sometimes standing in the doorway to show anyone who happened to be watching that he had a part in the drama, sometimes gripping the shoulders of Duffy's anorak with a strained expression of manly concern.

When a voice answered Roz said: 'There's been an accident. Someone has died.' They did not ask for details, just the address which she gave, adding that it was a cul-desac off Packington Street. Next she found two ten-pence pieces and rang the school. It was already ten minutes after the final period. She spoke to Kathy's teacher. Guy had not yet arrived. She was immediately sympathetic and agreed to take both the children home with her to Fortune Green. Roz thanked her and was just saying goodbye when Mr Christoforou came into the hall. He was now wearing a rather soiled white nylon jacket over his shirt and trousers and had obviously woken himself up by dunking his head in a basin of water. His plumply brown face was still damp and his thick moustache and dark curls were glistening.

'What the hell you do with my phone? Clear away.' His English may have been slightly dodgy but the glare he gave Roz was clear enough. The legendary Greek friendliness obviously didn't travel. Roz was about to explain when a Rover police car entered the courtyard, parking directly outside the Oasis. Two uniformed officers got out and entered the shop. One, a sergeant, seemed to be in his late thirties, the other looked like a sixth-form schoolboy. Roz passed through the curtain followed by Mr Christoforou. The older policeman glanced at them all briefly then said to Duffy:

'I understand there's been an accident.'

'In the room on the left at the top of the stairs.'

'You haven't touched anything?'

'The room's locked. I saw through the window.'

The sergeant said to Mr Christoforou: 'Are you the owner of the premises?' Then, when he nodded: 'Do you have a key?'

'No. That bastard lost his so I lent him mine to get another cut. Of course he never bother.'

The sergeant closed the shop door and slid the bolt. 'I must ask you all to stay here for the moment please.' He left the shop, manoeuvring neatly between the tables then running up the stairs with a surprisingly light tread considering his bulk. The young constable followed. The people left behind heard the rattle of a doorknob, a gathering pause then a very loud crash.

Mr Christoforou shot out of the room and up the stairs.

He started shouting at the police. He began on an hysterically high note and went up from there; a deep, soothing rumble from the sergeant underscored the tremolo and the duet was punctuated by ever more forceful crashes of shoulder on wood. Then the lock splintered and, at the same moment, the voices ceased.

Roz recalled afterwards how quickly the two silences, that of the listeners – apprehensive and curious – and of the observers – thick with revelation – met and mingled, as if the horror curled down the stairs and into the room and they breathed it in like smoke. It lasted for only a few seconds, then they heard someone being sick.

Footsteps on the stairs. Mr Christoforou came through the curtains and fell into the nearest chair. Upstairs the retching continued, then a lavatory chain was pulled, Roz supposed by the young constable. She had never seen anyone with a brown skin go white before. The Greek was the colour of a chalky orange. He said:

'He must be mad . . . mother of Christ . . . he must be raving . . .'

Roz was worried by the present tense. She leaned across and touched Duffy's arm. He was lining up the cruet, a vinegar bottle and a red plastic tomato in a neat line. No matter how careful he was they were never quite straight. The bulge of the red tomato always protruded further than the curve of the vinegar bottle and when he lined it up at the front it stuck out at the back. He edged up the vinegar bottle an eighth of an inch, frowned and gently removed Roz's hand. He wouldn't look at her. They heard someone moving in the hall, a phone being lifted. The sergeant spoke, then it was replaced. He came into the room.

'A senior police officer will be here very soon and will want to speak to all of you.' He turned to Mr Christoforou. 'Do you have a room that he can use?'

'This is nothing to do with me, mate,' the window cleaner cut in, 'all I did was hire out me bleedin' ladder. I've got three more jobs to do in Packington Street. All the time I'm 'angin' abaht 'ere I'm losin' money.' But there was only a token resentment in his voice. His eyes said he wouldn't have missed any of this for the world.

'There's only the lounge. Is very clean.'

'Does it have just the one door?'

'That's right. Very private.'

'Let's have a look.'

The two men walked away. Roz thought of the policeman upstairs, perhaps half a dozen years older than Guy, guarding the body. Poor little sod. Still, he didn't have to look. He could pull the door to and stand on the landing. The remains weren't going to run away. She wished Duffy would say something. She didn't know what was wrong with him. Then she thought that he might be embarrassed by her jubilation. Perhaps even a little ashamed of her. It might be wise in any case to damp it down a little if she was going to talk to the police. Not that she'd had anything to do with the death, but still . . .

They were sitting around like actors waiting for their cue. Aware of each other's physical presence yet totally engrossed in their inner world, anticipating the scene to come. Roz wondered if the men on this case would liaise with Camden Town where she had first reported the telephone threats. They probably did it all by computer. She let herself experience the luxury of feeling safe. Something she had taken for granted all her life and would never take for granted again. The feeling had such a keen edge that its sharpness exhilarated her. She felt almost high. Two more cars drew up outside, only one marked POLICE.

Several men got out and one policewoman. Only two of the men were in uniform. They and the WPC stayed outside. The rest of the party crossed towards the shop. The sergeant hurried in from the back room and unbolted the door.

'Good afternoon, Sir.'

The small knot of people loosened. A tall, grey-haired man with a lantern jaw and a wide, narrow-lipped mouth stood out. He wore a black and white tweed overcoat and a soft, dark hat which he now removed.

'Sergeant. What have we got?'

They followed the sergeant through the curtain. Roz just heard his reply: 'A blade artist, Sir,' before they climbed the stairs.

Police Constable Farley heard them coming. A bunch of clumping, authoritative footsteps. He straightened up, moving to the very centre of the doorway in a demonstrably guarding position. He hoped his face wasn't covered in sweat. He had dried it only moments before but every time he envisioned the scene in the room (and he saw nothing else) it broke out again. Perhaps he would have to stay on the door. He prayed he wouldn't have to go back inside. If he did he would keep his eyes away from the bed. After all there'd be no need for him to handle or touch the body. Unless he had to help take it away. His gorge kicked like a wild thing and he fought for control. He'd seen photographs in training. Handled dummies. He'd known

259

CAROLINE GRAHAM

what the Force was all about. He hadn't expected to spend his life helping old ladies across the road. But the real thing wasn't like photographs. It had a terrible colour and smell. It didn't just lie still so that you could study it but leapt out from its setting, welding itself to your eyeballs, burning into your brain.

His sergeant, who had entered first, had said: 'Bloody hell.' As a piece of literal description it could not have been bettered.

Chief Inspector Pharaoh watched the young policeman lift the splintered door and move it aside. He noticed the greenish gills and eyes firmly fixed on the floor and wondered if he had looked like that thirty-five years ago. He stepped into the room. A butcher's shop would have seemed anaemic by comparison. The pathologist pushed past him and crossed to the bed. He handled the girl as gently as if she could still feel.

Pharaoh walked round the room. It was austere to say the least. Not in a restful way, as if the occupant had deliberately shed decoration and appealing artefacts for aesthetic or emotional reasons but seedily austere: a room half furnished by a mean landlord. By the door was a shelf of indescribably filthy books. The room was neat, only the bed, the heart of the storm, was in turmoil. One of the walls was covered with photographs. Many of the faces were adorned with rust coloured splotches, as if the sitters had been mysteriously ravaged by the plague. The wall behind the bed was also splotched with red, so heavily that, in some places, the original paper could not be seen at all.

Pharaoh looked at his watch. The scene-of-crime officers should be here soon. From the window he could see his men

260

outside roping off the shop front and pavement. People were already coming out of the factory opposite to gawp. He turned his attention to the bed.

Hard to tell how old she was or if she had been pretty. Her nose had been neatly sliced down the middle and pressed back, showing the springy cartilage and flesh. She was naked and lying on her back, her legs very slightly apart. The bedclothes were tangled and knotted together, splashed darkly with blood. She looked like a martyr from an Italian sixteenth-century religious painting, meekly dead of a thousand cuts. The pathologist moved one of her thighs and indicated to Pharaoh a dangling sliver of soft tissue.

'Look at this, Alan. There's more enjoyment here than anything else. You'd better shift on this one.'

'Not nice.' If Chief Inspector Pharaoh resented the implied stricture his voice did not show it. 'How long has she been dead?'

'Hard to be too precise. The PM will narrow it down. The room's cold now and there doesn't seem to be a fire. On the other hand it's over the shop and when that's open the warmth's bound to affect the temperature in here. I'd say around forty-eight hours.'

Pharaoh nodded. The scene-of-crime men arrived, donned gloves and started to work; taking samples, labelling, filing away; a thorough documentation of the room. When he left they were peeling off, with a sharp instrument, strips of the rusty wallpaper.

Downstairs the sergeant came forward. 'Mr Christopher has offered us his lounge, Sir.'

'He the owner?'

'That's right Sir.'

'I'll see him first. And ask PC Bazely to come in, would you?' He winced slightly on entering Mr Christoforou's lounge, marking the contrast between its vulgar over-stuffed opulence and the stark charnel house upstairs. He pulled out an armchair, trembling with golden fringe, to face the settee, and put a low onyx coffee table between the two. When Police Constable Bazely entered he indicated the cocktail bar where there was a high stool. The constable sat, resting his notebook on the surface of the bar. Chief Inspector Pharaoh nodded to the sergeant who was hover-ing in the doorway. He left, returning with Mr Christoforou who entered his own sitting room as uncertainly as if it was a minefield. He perched on the arm of the settee. Chief Inspector Pharaoh sat in the chair. After a few basic prelim-inary questions confirming Mr Christoforou's background and position as owner of the premises he said:

'How long have you been renting out the room upstairs?'

'About three years.' He added defensively; 'Is no good making it nice. People are pigs. You know?'

'And the last tenant?'

'He comes . . . three months or so.'

'Does he have a job.'

'No idea. He pay the rent. That's all I worry about.'

'When did you last see him?'

'The day before yesterday. Night time. Usually I don't see him come and go. There's a fire escape. A door on the landing, iron steps to the back and another door out of the yard to an alley. But I go to the hall to get more chips.'

A stroke of luck. Pharaoh had seen the chips, great blue polythene sacks of them, stashed against the wall by the pay phone. 'What time was this?'

The Greek shrugged. 'We'd been open maybe an hour. About eight . . . Half gone eight . . . We due to open again soon. How my customers going to climb over all these rope?'

'I'm afraid you won't be able to open tonight.'

'Not open! Is not my fault a girl get killed upstairs. What happen to all my business? The police going to pay?'

'It will probably increase a hundredfold once this gets into the papers. Human nature being what it is.'

Mr Christoforou simmered down. 'A hundred eh?' He nodded. 'Maybe if we show them the room we up the prices?'

Pharaoh said: 'Did you see the murdered girl arrive?'

'Yes. She rang the phone first. Said she wanted to give him a surprise. Then she arrived—'

'Wait. Tell me everything you remember of the telephone conversation.' He listened then said: 'So she didn't have his address?'

'Said she hadn't got her book.'

'She didn't say where she was travelling from?'

'No.'

'Did you let her in?'

'Yes. She came to the shop. We'd just opened. People don't know the back way unless you explain.'

'And you knew your tenant . . . ?'

'Fenn.'

'. . . Was in then?'

'Sure. I hear him open the door on the landing . . .'

'The room's directly over the shop. Did you hear nothing? No sign of a struggle?'

'Not really. There's people talking in the shop. Lot of

263

clatter. Radio on. Is pretty noisy. Maybe I hear a bit of bouncing –' he gave a greasy wink and tapped a nostril with his forefinger – 'know wad I mean?'

Well, the PM would show if he had had her first. This really was proving extremely nasty. 'Will you please describe him as accurately as you can.'

When Mr Christoforou had finished Pharaoh thanked him. When he left the sergeant reappeared in the doorway. The chief inspector asked to see next the man who had discovered the body.

Duffy was looking pale and shocked. He gave his name and address and occupation then described the events that had led to the discovery.

'And you think this girl is Mrs Gilmour's secretary?'

'It's the most likely thing. Once he realised she had discovered what he was doing . . . It seems a bit mad – I mean the worst you could have got him for was making threats – but then perhaps he is. Mad I mean.' Pharaoh nodded. 'You've got to protect Mrs Gilmour,' Duffy added urgently. 'We all thought he was some harmless nut making unpleasant but empty threats. But this . . .' his voice trailed off helplessly.

'Would you be prepared to identify the body, Mr Duffield?'

Duffy looked sick and fearful. The sight he had glimpsed through the bedroom window would stay with him for the rest of his life. The thought of actually entering the room, of taking a closer look, filled him with nausea.

'We can't compel you to, of course. Her parents—'

'Christ, don't ask her parents!' The thought of a middle-aged couple, supporting each other, looking down at what remained of their daughter was more than Duffy could bear. He got up. 'All right. Is she . . . it . . . still here?'

'Yes.' Pharaoh led the way upstairs. A young constable was standing in the doorway; the door was leaning up against the landing wall. The room seemed full of men all doing things with deft, quiet assurance. In spite of the coldness of the day the air was warm with a rich, metallic odour that Duffy's stomach recognised as blood. The pathologist looked across at them.

'Just about done here.' He moved away from the bed. Alan Pharaoh stood aside.

Duffy walked across the room then turned his head with difficulty as if someone was pushing it around against his will, to look at what lay there. Pharaoh watched his face, waxen pale, fill with incredulity and horror. Now, once having looked, it was as if he could not look away. He stared and stared, sweat rolling down his face. He whispered:

'. . . I don't know . . . you can't tell . . . yes . . . I suppose so . . . Oh God . . .' He turned and ran, pushing the young constable violently aside. Downstairs in the sitting room he confirmed that the body he had seen was that of Sonia Marshall.

Next Chief Inspector Pharaoh interviewed the window cleaner. The novelty of being part of a murder investigation was now wearing off and he had reverted to his previous complaining attitude. Having confirmed the accidental nature of his involvement, the inspector got him to sign a statement and let him go.

The sergeant entered. 'Mr Christopher is making coffee, Sir.'

'Good. That'll be welcome. I'll see Mrs Gilmour now.'

'Sixty pence black or eighty with milk and sugar.'

'What? Oh – black.' When the coffee came it was like mud. You could stand your spoon up in the silt at the bottom.

The sergeant said: 'I think it's foreign, Sir.'

The inspector looked across at Mrs Gilmour and received his first surprise. Although she was obviously making some effort to control her expression he got a strong feeling that she was consumed with pleasure, almost with elation. If what Duffield had told him was true not only did there seem to be no reason for this but the reverse should have been the case. A man who had threatened her life had killed and disappeared and was on the loose, somewhere in London presumably. He assumed she understood the situation correctly but to make things quite clear opened the interview by saying:

'Mr Duffield has identified the dead girl as your secretary Sonia Marshall.'

A long pause, then: '. . . Girl . . . ?' It was a frog-like croak. He watched her face carefully. Saw it transformed. No. She had not known the true situation. 'I don't understand.'

'You knew a murder had taken place here, surely?'

'Of course . . . no . . . That is . . . I knew there was someone dead upstairs. I thought he'd killed himself.'

'I'm afraid not. We wouldn't have all this,' his gesture encompassed the policeman with his notepad, the sergeant, the room above, 'in the case of a straightforward suicide.'

'Of course not. I'm sorry. You must think me very stupid.'

'Not at all. We all snatch at the chance to believe what we very much want to believe. No doubt Mr Duffield found it hard to disillusion you.'

'But he should have done.'

'Yes indeed.' She looked quite broken. He felt as if he had trodden on a butterfly. 'I'd like you to tell me if you would what you know of this man, starting from the very first time he contacted you.' She stared at him. 'Take your time.'

Eventually she said, slurring her words as if exhausted: 'But I've been through all this. At Camden Town.'

'I know. And I'll be getting all the records and statements from there and Southampton Row, but I'd like to hear you go over it again.'

So she went over it again. How they had worked out his connection with Sonia. How they had tracked him down. She seemed to be speaking for hours. More coffee arrived, muddier and nastier than the last if that were possible, with a bill in the saucer. There seemed to be no sounds in the world but the drone of her voice and the soft rustle of the policeman's flipped-over pages. At last she was finished.

The inspector said: 'I must ask you and Mr Duffield to come to the station, read over your statements and sign them.'

'I'm tired.'

'I'm sorry.' He didn't sound sorry. 'It won't take long. Someone will escort you home. Will your husband be there?'

'I suppose so.' She had not given Leo a thought since they had got to the Oasis. She looked at her watch. It was gone seven o'clock. He would have arrived home to an

CAROLINE GRAHAM

empty house. No children. No message. Surely he would ring Kathy's teacher to check if she had collected the children? She wondered if he would remember that, since Mrs Holland had taken over the PTA, her home number was in their joint address book.

'What time does your husband leave in the morning?'

'Eight-thirty . . . quarter to nine . . .'

'We will have an armed man in the house by then. And a policewoman.'

'. . . Oh . . . if you think that's necessary.' She gazed at him blindly, looking almost puzzled. For one heartless moment he wished he could drag her upstairs and force her to look at the body. Then he realised that her seeming indifference was nothing more than an inability to take it all in. And who could blame her?

'Mrs Gilmour, until we catch this man you should not be alone. Either in the house or travelling to and from work.' He said, less forcefully: 'I don't think you quite realise the danger of your position. I doubt if this man is sane. He's certainly obsessed with you. And he's not going to give up.'

'Yes. I've always known that, really. Right from the beginning when everyone else was saying he was a harmless nutter. I was never able to believe it.'

She got up stiffly. He walked with her to the door. The sergeant met them, saying: 'Your husband's here, Mrs Gilmour.'

She stopped in the doorway. Duffy was sitting at one of the tables, deep in conversation with a much older man. A middle-aged man with a deathly, grey face and stooped shoulders. When he saw her he got heavily to his feet.

'Leo?' She hurried, almost ran to the table. He put his

268

arms around her and pressed her fiercely to his chest. He stared down at her face and touched her hair. They stood together for a long moment. There was a movement behind them and Roz sensed rather than saw Duffy rise and walk away. He didn't look back but spoke to the sergeant by the door then left the shop and got into one of the police cars which then moved off into the night.

'You must come away . . . darling you must come away. I'll take you to my mother's. We'll go tonight . . . now.'

'Leo, wait. Are the children all right?'

'What?' He looked intensely puzzled, as if she had spoken in a foreign language.

'The children.'

'Oh . . . yes . . . Mrs Holland's keeping them until tomorrow. She told me where you were.' He said, for the third time: 'You must come away.'

Over his shoulder, in the light from the courtyard lamp, she could see cars parked behind the roped-off area outside the shop. People had collected behind the rope and were staring in at the brilliantly lit room. She felt as if she were on a film set. Chief Inspector Pharaoh approached them.

'Mr Gilmour?' When Leo nodded he continued: 'Your wife has to come to the station to sign a statement. You'll have an escort home. Someone will go in and check the place before you enter. Is your house secure?'

'I think so. All the windows have locks. We've got a mortice and chain on the front door. Two bolts on the back.'

Roz listened, thinking this is just how someone would talk if they were sleepwalking.

'Do you have a firearm of any description?'

269

Leo looked blankly surprised. 'Of course not.'

The inspector continued briskly: 'In the morning an officer will come to the house accompanied by a policewoman. He will be armed. Please do not leave until he arrives.'

'You needn't bother. I'm taking my wife away. And the children. None of them are coming back until this lunatic's caught.'

Now Leo's voice took on a fierce colour. He was holding her less tightly and Roz turned in his arms, looking at the inspector and back at her husband. In spite of the aggressive tone in which Leo spoke and the force in his arms she could sense the fear, leaping through him like a forest fire. It released in her own heart a great protective tenderness. She, the one at risk, was the one to comfort. She felt strength rise in her as she stared at his ravaged face.

'I see.' The inspector's voice was not unsympathetic. 'I quite understand that would be your immediate reaction but I hope, perhaps after discussing it with your wife, you will change your mind.'

'She's not staying here staked out like a sacrificial goat just so he can make an attempt and your man may or may not get him in time.'

Leo was shouting now and Roz felt, mixing in with the feelings of tenderness, the beginnings of anger. She felt she must make a move or speak or her sense of self, gradually eroded over the past two weeks, would splinter away into nothing.

She knew Leo's motivations were honourable: love and concern for her wellbeing. She felt she should be glad of this. After all there were people in the world about whom no one cared if they lived or died. She should be grateful she was loved. But why should this give the lover rights of domination? The right to treat her as incapable? She spoke up, her voice firm:

'I don't want to argue here. It's like being in a goldfish bowl.' She walked away, without asking the chief inspector's permission, back to the sitting room. She said: 'We have no idea where this man is, do we? Just somewhere out there.'

'That's true. But we have a very detailed description from Mr Christoforou and we hope to get an Identikit drawing done and show this to him. Then it will be circulated. As a suspect in a murder case, police everywhere will be looking out for him.'

Leo said: 'He could be miles away by now.'

Pharaoh replied: 'I don't think so.' He glanced across at Roz, hesitated then said: 'The unpleasant fact must be faced that wherever your wife is he is not going to be far away.'

'You're wrong about that. I don't even intend telling you where I'm taking her.'

They were doing it again: men colluding. Even when they were arguing they were colluding.

She said: 'I'm not going anywhere.'

'You'll do –' Leo stopped. The others looked at him. He knew they had mentally finished the sentence. He stood helplessly looking at Roz. How could you suddenly say to an intelligent, capable woman with whom you had lived for fifteen years, who had taken decisions affecting your and your children's lives without consulting you because that was the sort of relationship you had, to do as she was told? It was not instinct or even guile which made him speak next as he did. He spoke from the depths of his heart as if no one but his wife was present: 'Roz – if anything happened to you I couldn't bear to be alive.'

She came across to him immediately. She gripped his hands: 'Listen Leo. If I run now we're never going to have any peace. Yes – I think you should take the children away. He can get at me through them more powerfully than any other way. He may never think of it but we can't take the risk. But I'm staying here.' He started to speak but she carried straight on. 'Even if I go I can't stay away for ever. What if he isn't caught for a month? Six months? A year? Some murderers are never caught. Are we supposed to live apart – me hiding like an animal in a hole – for the rest of our lives? And do you think he's not capable of watching the house and following you when you come to visit us? Darling, I know how it is. If the situation were reversed I would feel the same.'

She slackened her grip, holding him more gently. She realised she spoke no more than the simple truth. The sight of his despair, his drawn ageing face stamped with love and fear, had shocked her own love back into life. She felt it now buoying her up: love for him, their children, their life together. How singularly precious they all were. Now it was her involvement with Duffy that seemed trivial, no more than an exaggeratedly romantic, slightly unreal interlude. She continued: 'I won't ask you to take it calmly – that would be fatuous – but the police have promised me protection and when he tries,' their hands locked instinctively together, 'they'll get him.'

'Oh God, you can't be sure of that, Roz.' Leo turned to the chief inspector. 'Can you guarantee that?'

'We can guarantee your wife will have protection, Mr Gilmour. Obviously we cannot guarantee her permanent safety.'

'You see!' Leo turned back to Roz. 'You don't mean anything to them. You'll just be another fatality. A statistic. We can sell the house. Move away—'

'Leo. Think about what you're saying. You'd break up the children's lives, part them from their friends, interrupt their schooling. Your own work would suffer. Think of your research. You're part of a team at St Thomas's. You're publishing now. You can't start from scratch anywhere else. I will not have our family lives blasted apart by one madman whom I've never even met. *I will not have it, Leo.*' Roz stood, almost panting, grimly aware that this sudden burst of energy had been fuelled by terrible mental scenes of Fenn's destruction. Where did such images come from to invade the mind of a woman from a quiet, loving, non-violent background? She thought, we are all capable of it, I am capable of it, of killing someone. She felt the knowledge altered her in some subtle way that she could not define. She continued, more quietly: 'I want to see him. I want to see what he looks like. To put a shape and face to all the filth that's been oozing into my life, spoiling our happiness, hurting my children.' She turned to Pharaoh. 'I'll come with you to sign a statement now.'

As they left the room Leo said: 'The press should have this by tomorrow. Once the public knows what he looks—'

The chief inspector interrupted: 'On the contrary. I shall ask for the media's cooperation in keeping this out of the news. He might just go to earth when he hears the body's discovered, maybe for months, and we'll never winkle him out.'

'That's what a rational man would do perhaps, but surely an obsessive—'

'You must let me handle this as I see fit, Mr Gilmour.'

Roz felt the tension between them, solid as a wall. Another minute and they'd be snapping like terriers. The shop was almost empty. Outside the police were trying to move people along who were determined to remain fixed. As Roz and Leo stepped into the fluorescently lit area a murmur of sound arose and people pressed forward.

'Isn't there a back way?' Leo asked.

Mr Christoforou shrugged. He was tearing up a little stack of unpaid bills. He tossed the pieces into the air. 'Sure – help yourself. Everybody else has.'

They retreated through the hall and found the back door, which opened on to a seedy back yard stinking of stale frying-oil and fish. There were old wooden boxes stacked, an oil drum, a lean-to that smelt even worse than the fish. An old-fashioned yellow street lamp in the alley behind shed a sulphurous glow, like limelight, over the scene. They started to pick their way towards the door which led to the alleyway. Flanking it were two overflowing dustbins. On top of one something moved. Roz stood still.

'Leo . . .' She moved closer. What she saw then finished her completely. Anger fled. Strength evaporated. Tears of relief, of weakness, of she knew not what rolled unchecked down her cheeks. '. . . Oh Leo . . . look . . .'

Squatting on a pile of rotting fish-heads and innards, a fringe of gleaming ivory backbone sticking out from each side of its mouth, was a large, oddly shaped and even more oddly coloured cat.

Fenn sat on the edge of his bed listening to the man behind the plywood partition on his left coughing and spitting, God knew where as there was no basin or pot in any of the cubicles. He had got the address of this decaying rat-hole from the back of a door in the Gents' at Dalston Junction. Young people arriving in London were urged to contact the organisation if they had nowhere to go, presumably to keep them away from bad company. It made you laugh.

He had been laughing on and off ever since he had left the Oasis. At one point, picturing Sonia's face the second she had realised he was about to give her a nose job, he nearly had hysterics and had to sit in the gutter until he could settle his shaking frame. Luckily this was London and one more person behaving a bit out of turn caused hardly a second look. Because he had to be careful. He had to complete his mission; once that was done he could laugh all he liked. As long and hard as he liked. Then there would really be something to celebrate.

Behind the partition to his right he could hear a rich, gurgling snore; regular but just out of step with the hawking and spitting. Not that either bothered him. It was nearly morning. He hadn't slept. He was like a firework on a long, slow fuse. He could feel hatred fizzing in his veins. Hatred, reduced in the crucible of his ambition to a single, molten force. His mind was unpolluted by concepts of good and evil. He could not remember when these ideas ever had any currency for him. The energy pounding in his body forced him to his feet, but in the plywood eggbox there was nowhere to go. He sat down again. He wasn't bothered about not sleeping; he'd come in here to get off the streets, not to rest. There would be no rest for him until it was all over. He felt under the iron bed for his uniform in its plastic bag. He knew it was there but he had to keep checking. Sonia hadn't been found yet or it would have been in all the papers, perhaps even on the news. Her destruction had been spectacular enough.

He had known the moment he had opened the door why she had come, just for a second their usual roles were reversed. They looked at each other, she knowing, pleased, wearing her tiny triumph like a battle pennant; he, thrown off balance, alarmed. But then he had smiled, opened the door wide and, by the time it had closed behind her, he had regained his equilibrium. Not that he had let it show. After her rather florid accusations making use of a lot of pious phrases, he had acted the worried lover to perfection. A little shame-faced (I hadn't really meant to let it go so far), fiercely loyal (I couldn't stand the way she treated you) and, finally, lustfully besotted. He had said:

'I wonder darling if I'll ever be able to see you' (deftly removing blouse) 'and not immediately want to take you in my arms' (ditto skirt) 'and cover you with kisses.'

She hadn't even attempted to be subtle. 'It just means we'll have to get married a bit sooner than we thought. A wife can't testify, you know . . .' She sealed her fate with an arch look.

'You don't know how often I've pictured you here . . .' he parted and gently rearranged her limbs, 'like this.'

'Silly boy.' How sweet his kisses were. He'd never kissed her like this before. 'You only had to invite me.'

'I couldn't, angel. It's so awful. I wanted you to think I was . . .' He left his hopes dangling wistfully in the air above her head.

Sonia's heart warmed and opened. After the tender embraces his first revealing, vulnerable remark. 'As if I'd care. It's you I love.'

A long, happy pause. Fenn tried to keep his mind on things. It was a novelty for him to try to please another person. A novelty for Sonia, too. The juxtaposition struck him as delicious. After all, the greater her pleasure the greater her fear when the tidal wave of realisation broke.

Well, that was how he had meant it to be. And he was getting on fine. Deeper and deeper and pacing it right, speeding up a fraction at a time. Dwelling on the final blow straight to the heart. The thought of doing it, of the force that would be needed, was incredibly stimulating. He thought he would do it just as she came.

Afterwards, after it had all gone wrong, he thought about the phrase, 'I don't know what came over me', that he had so often read in the papers. He had always regarded it as a right cop-out and, if true, as disgustingly weak. He had always known exactly what he was doing and could not imagine it otherwise. He despised people who were not a hundred per cent in control. And then it had happened to him.

He had placed the knife, to be handy, on the crappy bamboo cupboard next to the bed; whipping it out of the waistband of his jeans when Sonia, back turned, was peeling off her panties. This meant it was in his line of vision. Each time he withdrew it attracted his attention and, in his mind's eye, re-entered Sonia's body with him. It was as if there were three components in the sexual act instead of two. Then when he was nearly there he had, quite without volition, suddenly transferred all his weight to his right arm, snatched up the knife and slashed open her nose. It had been so quick that her shock and horror had given him a moment's grace. He rammed his fist in her mouth and finished quickly.

He didn't like to think of what had happened next. All the things his knife had done. So stupid; delaying his escape. If he had just changed then and left straightaway the oily Greek downstairs wouldn't have seen him. Not that he'd suspected anything or the girl would have been found by now. He made a great effort to change the direction of his thoughts. There was no point in dwelling on things that were over and done with.

He could hear milk crates rattling outside the building. Although it was still dark he guessed it was around seven. He would be able to get a scummy bowl of the grey muck they called porridge downstairs. He hoped nobody but the kitchen staff were around. He didn't want another dollop of what the people who ran this dump called counselling. The night he'd arrived some freak with a beard and a dopey smile and a manly handshake had tried to find out about his background. If he'd left home because of a row, if his parents would be worried, if he had any friends in London. As if he didn't have enough on his plate without coping with do-gooders.

But he was in luck. The kitchen was empty except for an Indian girl slurping out the gunge into stone bowls. He took one and sat in the furthest corner where, in spite of his resolve, he found his thoughts returning to his room in Lucy

Place. Once Sonia had been found even the mentally retarded pigs would be able to put two and two together. Of course the identification might take some time (he had left her handbag on the Tube) but there was no escaping the fact that every minute brought the discovery of Sonia's body closer. He should be getting a move on.

He left his gunge and went up a level to what they called the day room. It was painted a vile green colour with stupid drawings and letters pinned to the walls from grateful inmates. The transistor was chained to the table. So much for fostering the mutual trust the bearded geek had burbled about. Fenn found Capital and waited for the news summary which, at that hour of the morning, was not long in coming. Nothing about Sonia. He decided to go out and buy a paper, just to double-check. He took his carrier bag and left the building.

The nearest kiosk was outside Kings Cross. He helped himself to a *Sun* and went into the station refreshment rooms to get a bit of warmth. It was nice to be back in the land of the living, away from the down and outs. He bought a cup of tea and a sticky bun as well. That should take away the taste of the cement. There was a jolly hiss of steam from the urn, the first travellers were filling up the tables. He started at page one of his paper and went very carefully through every column inch. Nothing.

So he still had the advantage of surprise. Roz still wouldn't know if his threats were serious. She would be no more on her guard than usual. In fact, as he had not been in touch for a day or two, probably a bit less. And today was not a *Roundabout* day. Today she would be at home. He had discovered by watching the house that her husband (the widower to be) and his snotty kids left around eight-thirty and the char didn't come for another hour.

He would put his uniform on at the last minute. No point in taking unnecessary risks. Perhaps in the Gents' at Camden Town. All he had to do was wait until anyone who had been in there when he arrived had left. Then he'd be fine. Nothing remarkable about a copper emerging from a public toilet. Even the filth had to go some time. He would leave his carrier bag behind.

He had no thoughts beyond the actual death itself. No plans. Although his mind pictured her last torments in a hundred ways it could not seem to conjure up any scenes that might be enacted in the aftermath. So bound up was she in his life that it was almost as if when she ceased to exist, he ceased to exist.

He looked at the clock. Seven-thirty. Another ten minutes and he'd go. Camden Town was on the Northern line. He wouldn't even have to change.

She had not slept all night yet did not feel at all tired. She had lain, fitting snugly against the curve of Leo's back, in a strange state almost of suspended animation. She did not feel much at all, no fear or anger; it was almost as if the day would never come. Leo had woken around three and tried to persuade her to take a tablet but she refused. Now they were sitting over coffee looking at *The Times* and the *Guardian*.

'It looks as if the press have cooperated. There's nothing in either of these.'

'And nothing on the eight o'clock news.' Roz stroked Madgewick who, stretching out in all directions, extended his legs stiffly past her lap then drew them in and tucked them underneath his belly. He had received her cries of joy and hugs the previous evening in a very sanguine manner and had been positively cross when she had tried to remove a large fish head from his jaws before carrying him to the car. This morning he was having a sulk and refusing to purr although whether this was because of the sudden snatch from his galvanised cornucopia or because of their carelessness in allowing him to be stolen in the first place, there was no way of knowing.

'The children will be so pleased he's back. Did you tell Mrs Holland what time you'll be picking them up?'

'I said the police should be here by nine. She'll take them both to school and I'll pick them up there. She talked to the Head at St Christopher's so they'll know why Guy is absent.'

'You'll stay and have lunch with my mother won't you, Leo? Kent's a hell of a way – there and back without a rest.'

'Don't be daft, Roz. Of course I won't. I want to get back here to you. I still think they'd be all right on the train. They could travel with the guard. After all Guy's nearly thirteen. And their grandma could meet them at Deal.'

'No. We had all this out last night. I don't want them out of your sight until you leave them safely with her. They'll be anxious enough as it is having had to spend the night away from home without being shut up in a railway van with a stranger.'

He knew she was right. It was not that he didn't love his children, simply, as he realised now for perhaps the first time, that he loved his wife over and above everything else. He had never before tried to disentangle or weigh

281

separately his love for his family. There had been no need. The three people were almost welded into one in his mind: a domestic trinity. They were the foundation on which everything else was based. He was not anxiety prone and never tortured himself with visions of what his life would be like if something happened to them but now, since the discovery of Sonia's body and his subsequent dreadful conversation with Duffield, he was having to face that possibility.

He recognised the sense of everything Roz had said. It was only after the man had been captured that either of them would feel safe and if, by staying in circulation, she could help to bring this about, then that was obviously the logical thing to do. But fear knows no logic. He was fighting all the time the most terrible sense of foreboding. He wanted to behave like the hero in the most simplistic fiction. To snatch her up and carry her away, disappearing into a mythical sunset. He had an atavistic yearning to arm himself; to carry a club or a gun and to stand between her and danger. He was rather shocked at how near the surface these feelings were, gathering just under the skin of his daily life as he was reading *The Times*, eating civilised lunches with his colleagues, relaxing with Roz at the end of the day.

He knew the police would be near but they could not be so close as to be visible, otherwise the whole point of the exercise would be lost. If he was very quick she could be dead before they got to him. And the fact that he would not consider the risk of capture (obsessives rarely did) was in his favour. Also there was no way of knowing what weapon he would use. He might not use a knife again. He might have a sniper's rifle and be hidden somewhere just waiting to pick her off. He might hide for months and then, when they had half forgotten him, plant something in her car. He might – the doorbell rang.

'I'll go.' He got up, dabbing his mouth with a napkin. 'It'll be the police.'

Roz watched him go then got up and, tipping Madgewick on to the floor, started to clear a place at the table. Perhaps whoever it was would like some coffee, or was drinking on duty against the rules? Surely that was just alcohol. She heard Leo open the front door and got out a croissant from the bread crock. A moment later Leo was back in his outdoor coat. He stood hovering in the doorway, knowing what they had agreed, not wishing to go.

'I don't like leaving you.'

'Darling, I shall feel much better once I know you've collected the children and are on your way. And now I've got the flower of the Force to protect me.'

'More of a bud than a flower. What's it a sign of when policemen get younger and younger?'

'That we're getting older and older. Look at you,' she came to him and touched his sideboards gently as he took her in his arms, 'grey as a badger.'

They stood together for a moment. In spite of the physical closeness of their embrace it was curiously non-sexual. Leo felt almost as if he were holding a lost child yet could not have said if he were comforting the child or consoling himself. At last they drew apart, still holding hands.

'I've put the coffee on. They might want some.'

'It's just a he.'

'Oh. I thought a policewoman was coming as well.'

283

'I expect she'll turn up. Well . . .' He didn't move.

'Look. I'm going to go and get a clean coffee cup and saucer from the corner cupboard and when I turn round I want to see you gone. OK?'

He walked away, he never knew how, out of the kitchen, through the hall and into the street.

Roz heard the door bang and immediately experienced the first flickerings of doubt. Was it really necessary for Leo to take the children to Kent? Couldn't they just have stayed with friends locally? Even if he didn't stay for lunch it would be perhaps four o'clock before he was home. That seemed like for ever. Why had she been so insistent? It seemed to her now the height of folly. What was one policeman against a really determined killer? But there would be more men outside, surely. Marksmen, concealed in the street. She hoped they would send a policewoman. Some feminine company would be nice.

She felt a definite throb of tension, as if her nervous machinery had been resting overnight and was now, sluggishly, starting up again. Yes. Any company would definitely be nice. She called up the basement stairs: 'Hello?' There was no reply. She mounted a couple of steps. 'Would you like some coffee?' Still nothing. The machinery had a little more power behind it; gathered speed. She felt as if a small bird was caught, fluttering wildly, in the back of her throat. Silly to be afraid. She took a deep breath, swallowed the bird, walked up the rest of the stairs and into the hall.

Leo walked very slowly away from the house. He kept looking back at the tall, elegant windows hoping that perhaps Roz would hurry to the sitting room after he had left to wave. But of course today's parting was different. As it had been so hard to get him out of the house in the first place she wouldn't do anything that might draw his attention back. He crossed the road so that he could keep the house in sight for a few more moments. He felt wretchedly uneasy. Was it the youth of the policeman that bothered him? Also, now he came to think of it, the man hadn't been visibly armed. He heard again Roz saying: 'I thought a policewoman was coming as well?' Surely it was odd they hadn't arrived together?

His footsteps slowed. As they got to the corner of Gloucester Crescent and Inverness Street they stopped altogether. He stood on the edge of the pavement, next to a florist's van with an Interflora symbol on the side. In the driving seat sat a pretty girl in a nylon overall, next to her a tall, brawny man was talking intently. She nodded and listened, keeping her eyes on his face.

It was no good, Leo thought. He just couldn't go. Whatever it was that was pulling him back to the house was too strong to be resisted. He would take Roz with him to Kent, bring her back home and stay with her himself whatever the police said. 'And if he had a chance, the narrowest, thinnest chance to get his hands on the murdering bastard–

'Mr Gilmour!'

The burly man was clambering out of the van and staring at him. Leo frowned. He had seen the man before, and recently. Then he remembered. It was the sergeant who had accompanied Chief Inspector Pharaoh yesterday. He had been in uniform then of course, which was why it had taken a moment to recognise him. No doubt the pretty girl was a policewoman. He felt better now he had seen the reinforcements. But there was something wrong. The sergeant was gripping his arm.

'What are you doing out here, Mr Gilmour? You agreed not to leave your wife alone.'

'She's not alone. One of your men—'

Although Leo's understanding of what had happened and his great leap back towards the house were virtually simultaneous, still the sergeant was on to him, clinging like a great bear to his back and shoulders. The girl banged on the panel behind her seat then spoke urgently on her two-way radio. The back door of the van burst open. A man in a dark high-necked sweater, knitted cap and reefer jacket fell out and almost cleared the length of the vehicle in one movement. He and the sergeant hung on to Leo. For nearly two minutes the monstrous hump swayed backwards and forwards and down until he stood, like a horse at the end of a breaking, panting, his head drooping, his gaze on the pavement. Although the sergeant now released him the other man held firm. People were gathering, quite a few of them in the road, where they were blocking the traffic.

'Listen Mr Gilmour. If we'd let you go in there she'd have had no chance. The first sound would have been enough to set him off. As it is—'

'He's killed her, he's killed her.' Leo sagged, like a ventriloquist's dummy, in the policeman's arms.

'No he hasn't. I know these buggers. I saw that girl last night. They play games. Cat and mouse.' Leo groaned. 'If he thinks it's safe he'll spin the enjoyment out.'

'Christ.' He wept then: 'Roz . . . oh Roz . . .'

'Come and sit in here.' They bundled him into the van

next to the policewoman. Two Rovers drew up and parked behind them. Several men got out. Leo could see them in the wing mirror going up to the sergeant. They stood conferring, not seeming in any hurry. The marksman put his head through the window next to Leo. He was unshaven and had a bitter, pock-marked face. His breath stank of stale beer and cigarettes. Leo looked at him: a man he had never seen before in his life and on whose skill his future happiness and that of his children depended. He felt he should say something, plead with the man. Offer everything he owned, his life . . .

'What's the back approach to your house, Sir?'

'Hopeless. An open yard, there's no cover and you'd have to climb over from the garden backing on.'

Why wasn't it night time? The man could easily have got right up to the house then. Oh why had he ever left her?

'Any windows open?'

'I don't think so.' He saw Roz backed up against a wall, a blade at her throat. 'What are you waiting for!'

'Nothing now. They've been blocking the road at both ends. Got to keep people away from the house. A crowd outside's a real giveaway. Could I have your keys please, Mr Gilmour?'

'I let him in, you know,' Leo said as he handed them over. 'I opened the door and invited him in. I was as close to him as I am to you. I left him alone with her. I left my wife alone with a bloody madman with a knife. Did you know that?' The marksman walked away. He turned to the policewoman, gripping her arm. 'Did *you* know that?' His face was a mask of anguish, begging for reassurance, begging her not to judge.

'Barrett's one of the very best, Mr Gilmour. The man won't get away.'

'I'm sure he won't.' Leo leaned back and closed his eyes. All he could see were rivers of blood.

He had his back to her as she entered the hall but turned when he heard her footsteps, taking off his hat and stepping towards her.

'I wondered if you'd like . . .' The words tapered off, a dying fall. The winter light streamed through the stained glass, mottling his face with livid patches of scarlet and indigo, touching the bronze aureole of his hair with fire so that he looked like some dreadful medieval symbol of plague and pestilence and death.

'Hello Roz.' Triumph consumed him. She could almost smell it. 'I'm here, you see. Like I promised.'

They stood facing each other with perhaps six feet between them. At first she wasn't able to speak but just stood staring at him. All through the night images of him and of their confrontation had presented themselves. Despite Greg's description she had pictured him always as a bit seedy, in black leather punkish clothes with a pasty, vicious little face: small-time, fuelled by a dangerous, high-octane mixture of envy, hatred and stupidity. But he was tall, slender with broad shoulders beneath the policeman's jacket. His concentration on her was total. He had stalked her and now he had trapped her he waited, confident of his reward. His stillness was remarkable. He seemed to have all the time in the world.

So potent was the authority that emanated from him, she started herself to almost believe in the rightness of his claim.

Instead of terror and rage she felt an insidious lethargy, bordering on despair, sweep over her. Her posture was one of complete submission. His proximity acted like Novocaine, numbing all resistance. She felt almost relieved that it would soon be all over. She thought, what am I after all that such a fuss should be made? A transient bundle of atoms. A woman with a trivial radio show who has never finished the book she always meant to write. It seemed to her now that her death would hardly cause a ripple. The children would be sad for a while but they'd recover. They had a father and grandparents and friends. Leo would marry again. Someone young. Perhaps there'd be a new family. She would drop out of the world and the world would close up behind her and in a very short time it would be as if she had never existed at all. She tried to think of a reason for not surrendering to her own destruction but could think of none.

It had been a bad moment when her husband opened the door. He should by now have taken his poncey little kids in his poncey foreign car and left. But he'd only said: 'Ah – here you are. Come in,' then cleared off and left Fenn alone with her. The joy of it. What he'd go through afterwards. Might as well have stuffed an apple in her mouth and trussed her up while he was at it. In the couple of minutes he was downstairs saying goodbye Fenn had time to relish the irony. He wondered a little that they were so obviously expecting the police but reasoned that after all his jolly tapes and phone calls it wasn't all that surprising. She was probably making a statement of some sort. Perhaps even asking for police protection. He could have burst his gut at that one. There was no sign of the kids.

It struck him that in an odd way he felt grateful to her. Without her he would never have known how clever he could be. Before he had known her his life, he now saw, had been a mess. A chaotic muddle of unfocused lusts and envy; but once his quest had been revealed clarity and order came, and true meaning. They were equal now. Rich and famous; the words which had once brought bile into his mouth were now revealed for what they were truly worth. She was rich and famous and it had gained her nothing. Now she was not even his equal; she was his victim.

She looked very beautiful; her hair was loose, tumbling over her bowed shoulders. She wore a dress of soft apricot stuff that clung to her lovely figure. He would have her first and Christ it would be exciting, not like Sonia who was willing and stupid and wanted him. But he would make this one want him as well and if he couldn't . . . well, he felt himself stir with anticipation . . . that might be even better. He started to speak. His tone was gentle enough but there was nothing gentle about his words. He described himself, what was happening to his body, and then he started to describe hers. How he had pictured it in his room, then how he saw it now and what he would be doing. At one exciting point in his recital (he was describing one of his more complicated little tricks) she straightened up and pressed her hands over her ears and the movement thrust her breasts out tautly against her dress. This deliberate attempt to lead him on caused Fenn a slight disappointment. She was just like all the rest then when it came to the push (nicely witty), longing for it.

And then two things happened. He stepped forward which was a mistake. He saw straight away that the action had broken the hypnotic hold he had over her. And, behind him, the letter-box flap moved.

Roz, looking over his shoulder, saw this and could not stop her reaction showing on her face. Excitement, hope and then anger at her foolishness. By her inability to conceal her feelings she had given away the only advantage that whoever it was out there had. The advantage of surprise. But she had reckoned without Fenn's overwhelming vanity.

'What sort of fool do you take me for, Roz? That's the oldest trick in the galaxy. You look over my shoulder, register surprise, I turn round, you make a run for it or jump me. Do you think I never go to the movies?' He felt the speech went some way towards re-establishing his superiority. Nobody made a monkey out of him.

Roz stood quite still, as alert now as she had been stupefied seconds before. The knowledge that help was at hand had been enough to reactivate a passionate longing for survival. And with the knowledge came fear. She had so much to lose. Now that he had stepped away from the stained glass he had lost the extraordinary quality the livid colouring had given him. But if he looked more ordinary he also looked more dangerous. She looked into his eyes, yellow goatish mad eyes, and her fear doubled, tripled, leapt ahead.

Then he suddenly shouted: 'Hoopla!' and flung up his hand in a messianic gesture. She followed the movement, seeing a flash of light, a silver gleam. She looked past him again. Now in the centre of the letter box was the round metal O of a gun barrel. He licked his lips and the spittle shone like snail slime.

CAROLINE GRAHAM

'What do you think of her?' He held up the knife, presenting it for Roz's admiration. 'Slides in like butter. Truly.' He said the last word as if she had demurred. As if he was a salesman selling a kitchen gadget and she had expressed a small measure of uncertainty.

'Is that what you killed Sonia with?' The words were out before she could stop them. She felt the atmosphere change, intensify. He frowned, then looked cunning. Any trace of handsomeness disappeared. The spittle dribbling from his mouth became fluffy, foam-like.

'You don't know about Sonia.'

'No. That's right.' She took a step back and, as if this was the signal he had been waiting for, he sprang. Roz screamed and screamed again. His breath was like a furnace on her face. He pressed his mouth to hers not in a kiss but as an assault, a smashing of bone on bone. They struggled and the sounds were like some terrible dark mating ritual. Sounds of breath being pumped out, grunts and cries. She saw there was no hope unless she could put some distance between them. She knew nothing of guns but felt the closeness of her attacker must stop the marksman firing. Surely there was a chance the bullet might pass through him and into her. They were in a direct line from the box. If only she could get him to stay where he was while she moved away.

She became aware from the loathsome pressure of his body that he wanted her, then, with a flash of terror, that the knife was touching her throat. He moved it slowly down the apricot wool, which parted like tissue paper. She felt the point gently prick her navel. She stopped struggling and stayed stock still. The merest movement might push it in. He looked down at what the opening of her dress revealed.

'Very nice.'

'Please,' she must think of something, there must be something. 'You're so close . . .'

'Not as close as I'm going to be.'

'I mean . . . I can't see you properly. You're . . .' She gagged on the words. 'You're so handsome. If you stand a little away . . . just for a moment . . . then I can see you better.'

It wasn't going to work. She had pleased him, he was almost smirking, but that was all.

'I've undressed you, darling . . .' The knife tenderly dimpled her soft flesh. 'Aren't you going to do the same for me?'

Terror had made her sick, now she thought she was going to faint. Oh God, she prayed, please don't let me faint. The knife pressed again. She raised trembling fingers to the buttons of his jacket.

'Just the zip sweetheart . . . just the zip . . .'

She touched him, struggling to hold back the vomit in her throat and said: 'I never thought you'd be satisfied with such an easy victory. I always rather admired your cleverness . . . the way you got into the house . . . getting all your messages across.' At the limit of her endurance she had found the means to reach him. The lust in his eyes became mixed with displeasure.

'What do you mean – an easy victory?'

'Well . . . you haven't even given me a run for it. After all, where can I go? I'd never get to the door . . . or to the phone. Even the fox gets a chance. Anyway . . . wouldn't you like that, Fenn? Be honest . . . a chase . . . upstairs . . . downstairs . . . ?'

'And in my lady's chamber? Yes . . . I'd like that. My lady's chamber. Maybe that's where I'll catch up with you? Maybe I could do it on the bed . . . or in the bed?'

He had let her go. She steeled herself not to move as her dress fell apart. His eyes studied her.

'Are you going to give me a start?'

'I don't know.' He gave her a gruesome teasing parody of a lover's look. 'Not too much of one. Don't want you opening a window and jumping out do we? Cheating my baby.' And he laid the knife against his lips.

'Will . . . will you count to ten?'

'Five, sweetheart . . . I'll count to five . . .'

She felt behind her for the first stair with her heel and stepped back.

'One.'

She had to hold his gaze. Whatever happened he must not look round. She wanted to turn and run but dare not.

'Two.'

He couldn't stop staring. He had never, not in all his books and magazines or in his most thrilling fantasies, seen such heavenly breasts. So full and ripe and golden; her skin was as warm as the colour of her dress. He wished now he'd cut just a little lower. Still – there was plenty of time. He had never had anyone like her before. And of course the reverse was true. She'd probably no idea what it could be really like. Perhaps once she knew she'd be as bad as Sonia. Never able to leave him alone. But of course there would only be the one time. Or would there? He was getting confused.

'Three. You're not getting anywhere, little fox. I shall be jumping on you in a minute . . .'

She could feel each groove of the stair carpet pressing into the soles of her feet, see the bloom of her fingerprints on the polished banister. The world had shrunk to this. She was aware of feeling tremendously alive; of her heartbeat and pulses, brain circuits and coursing, warm blood. If she stepped diagonally back next time she would no longer be in the line of fire.

'Four.'

An explosion filled the hall. The noise was terrifying. Like a bomb. The sound crashed round and round the walls, reverberating, echoing until Roz thought her head would burst. A smashing, splintering sound and the glass of the hall door fell in.

Fenn climbed the stairs towards her, a red rose blossoming on his chest. He was shouting filthy, dreadful things. She backed away. His face and eyes were dead but he came on. There was another shot and a second rose appeared, lower than the first, the petals opened voluptuously, slowly until the two roses joined. He dropped the knife and opened his arms wide.

He whispered: 'Five' but his breath was cold, with only the memory of life in it. Then he fell away, gracefully and without concern, into the hall below.

Headline hopes you have enjoyed *The Envy of the Stranger*, and invites you to sample the beginning of *The Killings at Badger's Drift*, the first Midsomer Murders novel featuring Detective Chief Inspector Thomas Barnaby.

Prologue

She had been walking in the woods just before teatime when she saw them. Walking very quietly although that had not been her intention. It was just that the spongy underlay of leaf mould and rotting vegetation muffled every footfall. The trees, tall and packed close together, also seemed to absorb sound. In one or two places the sun pierced through the closely entwined branches, sending dazzling shafts of hard white light into the darkness below.

Miss Simpson stepped in and out of these shining beams peering at the ground. She was looking for the spurred coral root orchid. She and her friend Lucy Bellringer had discovered the first nearly fifty years ago when they were young women. Seven years had passed before it had surfaced again and then it had been Lucy who had spotted it, diving off into the undergrowth with a hoot of triumph.

Their mock feud had developed from that day. Each summer they set out, sometimes separately, sometimes together, eager to find another specimen. Hopes high, eyes sharp and notebooks and pencils at the ready they stalked the dim beechwoods. Whoever spotted the plant first gave the loser, presumably as some sort of consolation prize, a spectacularly high tea. The orchid flowered rarely and, due to an elaborate system of underground rhizomes, not always in the same place twice. Over the last five years the two friends had started looking earlier and earlier. Each was aware the other was doing so; neither ever mentioned it.

Really, thought Miss Simpson, parting a clump of bluebells gently with her stick, another couple of years at this rate and we'll be coming out when the snow's on the ground.

But if there was any justice in the world (and Miss Simpson firmly believed that there was) then 1987 was her turn. Lucy had won in 1969 and 1978, but this year . . .

She tightened her almost colourless lips. She wore her old leghorn hat with the bee veil pushed back, a faded Horrockses cotton dress, wrinkled white lisle stockings and rather baggy green-stained tennis shoes. She was holding a magnifying glass and a sharp stick with a red ribbon tied to it. She had covered almost a third of the wood, which was a small one, and was now working her way deep into the heart. Ten years could easily pass between blooms but it had been a wet cold winter and a very damp spring, both propitious signs. And there was something about today . . .

She stood still, breathing deeply. It had rained a little the evening before and this had released an added richness into the warm, moist air – a pungent scent of flowers and verdant leaves with an undernote of sweet decay.

She approached the bole of a vast oak. Scabby parasols of fungus clung to the trunk and around the base was a thick clump of hellebores. She circled the base of the tree, staring intently at the ground.

And there it was. Almost hidden beneath flakes of leaf mould, brown and soft as chocolate shavings. She moved the crumbs gently aside; a few disturbed insects scuttered out of the way. It gleamed in the half light as if lit from within. It was a curious plant: very pretty, the petals springing away from the lemon calyx like butterfly wings, delicately spotted and pale fawny yellow but quite without any trace of green. There were no leaves and even the stem was a dark, mottled pink. She crouched on her thin haunches and pushed the stick into the ground. The ribbon hung limp in the still air. She leaned closer, pince-nez slipping down her large bony nose. Tenderly she counted the blooms. There were six. Lucy's had only had four. A double triumph!

She rose to her feet full of excitement. She hugged herself; she could have danced on the spot. Nuts to you Lucy Bellringer, she thought. Nuts and double nuts. But she did not allow the feelings of triumph to linger. The important thing now was the tea. She had made notes last time when Lucy had been out of the room refreshing the pot and, whilst not wishing to appear ostentatious, was determined to double the choice of sandwiches, have four varieties of cake and finish off with a home-made strawberry water ice. There was a large bowl of them, ripe to bursting, in the larder. She stood lost in blissful anticipation. She saw the inlaid Queen Anne table covered with her great aunt Rebecca's embroidered lace cloth, piled high with delicacies.

Date and banana bread, Sally Lunn black with fruit, frangipane tarts, spiced parkin and almond biscuits, lemon curd and fresh cream sponge, ginger and orange jumbles.

And, before the ice, toasted fingers with anchovies and Leicester cheese . . .

There was a noise. One always had the illusion, she thought, that the heart of a wood was silent. Not at all. But there were noises so indigenous to their surroundings that they emphasized the silence rather than disturbing it – the movements of small animals, the rustle of leaves and, overall, the lavish ululation of birdsong. But this was an alien noise. Miss Simpson stood very still and listened.

It sounded like jerky, laboured breathing and, for a moment, she thought that a large animal had been caught in a trap, but then the breathing was punctuated by strange little cries and moans which were definitely human.

She hesitated. So dense was the foliage that it was hard to know from which direction the sounds came. They seemed to be bouncing around the encircling greenery like a ball. She stepped over a swathe of ferns and listened again. Yes – definitely in that direction. She moved forward on tiptoe as if knowing in advance that what she was about to discover should have remained forever secret.

She was very close now to the source of the disturbance. Between herself and the noise was a tight lattice of branches and leaves. She stood stock still behind this screen then, very carefully, parted two of the branches and peered through. She only just stopped a sound of horrified amazement passing her lips.

Miss Simpson was a maiden lady. Her education had in many respects been sketchy. As a child she had had a governess who turned puce and stammered all through their 'nature' lessons. She had touched, glancingly, on the birds and the bees and left the human condition severely alone.

But Miss Simpson believed deeply that only a truly cultivated mind could offer the stimulus and consolation necessary to a long and happy life and she had, in her time, gazed unflinchingly at great works of art in Italy, France and Vienna. So she knew immediately what was happening in front of her. The tangle of naked arms and legs (there seemed in real life to be far more than four of each) were gleaming with a pearly sheen just like the glow on the limbs of Cupid and Psyche. The man had the woman's hair knotted around his fingers and was savagely pulling back her head as he covered her shoulders and breasts with kisses. So it was that Miss Simpson saw her face first. That was shock enough. But when the woman pushed her lover away and, laughing, scrambled on top of him, well . . .

Miss Simpson blinked, and blinked again. Who would ever have thought it? She eased the parted twigs back together and, holding her breath, gently let them go. Then she stood for several minutes wondering what to do next. Her mind was a mass of conflicting thoughts and emotions. She felt shock, intense embarrassment, disgust and a very faint flicker, instantly and resolutely suppressed, of excitement. She felt as if someone had handed her a ticking bomb. Having, by force of circumstance and natural inclination neatly sidestepped all the mess and muddle of selection, courtship, marriage and the resulting clash of arms, Miss Simpson felt singularly ill equipped to handle it.

A prim irritation started snagging the edge of her mind. A 'tsk' almost escaped her lips. In the middle of a wood of all places. When they each had a perfectly good home to go to. They had spoiled what should have been a really wonderful day.

Now she somehow had to get away as silently as she had approached. She studied the ground thoughtfully. She must avoid snapping even a twig. And the sooner she moved the better. For all she knew they might almost have come to . . . well . . . whatever point it was people came to.

And then the woman shouted. A strange terrible cry, and a bird flew up from the thicket right into Miss Simpson's face. She cried out in her turn and, full of shame and horror at the thought of discovery, turned and started to run. Seconds later she tripped over a tree root. She crashed heavily to the ground but panic drove out any feeling of pain. She scrambled to her feet and ran on. Behind her she heard a lumbering, crashing sound and realized they must have jumped up and torn the branches aside to see what was happening. They would recognize her. They must. She was only a few yards away. Surely, naked, they wouldn't pursue?

Her eighty-year-old legs responded to demands that hadn't been made on them for years. Flying up behind her at odd angles like freckled sticks, they carried her, in an incredibly short space of time, to the edge of the wood. There she rested against a tree, listening and panting, her hand on her flat, agonized chest, for almost five minutes. Then she walked slowly home.

Later that evening she sat on the window seat looking out over the darkening garden. She pushed the casement wide, breathing in the fragrance from nicotiana and night-scented stocks planted directly beneath the window. At the end of the lawn was the faint white blur, almost blue in the dusk, of the beehives.

Since her arrival home almost three hours ago she had

sat thus, unable to eat, becoming more and more aware of the pain in her shin, and less and less certain of what to do next.

Everything was changed now. They knew that she knew. Nothing could alter that. Would that it could. She would have given anything to put the clock back to yesterday. It was her own vanity that had got her into this mess. Wanting to crow over her friend; wanting to win. Serve her right. She sighed. All this castigation didn't solve a thing.

She wondered if they would come and see her, and turned cold at the thought. She imagined the awful, three-cornered conversation. The hideous embarrassment. Or perhaps they wouldn't be embarrassed? To be able to frolic about in the open like that argued a certain brazen confidence. Perhaps she should take the initiative and approach them. Assure them of her continuing silence. Miss Simpson's fastidious soul was repelled by the idea. It would look as if she was forcing further intimacies that they may well not want. How strange it was, she thought, to be suddenly handed a startling new piece of information about two people one thought one knew well. It seemed to colour, almost cancel out, all her previous knowledge of them.

She shifted slightly, clenching her teeth against the pain from her bruised leg. She recalled wistfully the moment she had discovered the orchid and how much fun it would have been making the celebration tea. She could never tell Lucy now. Everything seemed grubby and spoiled. She eased herself off the window seat, went through the kitchen and entered the perfumed stillness of the garden. A few feet away her favourite rose, a Papa Meilland, was about to flower. Last year the buds had been struck by mildew but this year all seemed well and several dark, glowing scrolls hinted at the glories to come. One looked as if it would be fully open by the next morning.

She sighed again and returned to the kitchen to make her cocoa. She unhooked a spotless pan from one of the beams and measured out the milk. She had never felt more keenly the truth of the saying 'a trouble shared is a trouble halved'. But she had lived in a small village long enough to know that what she had discovered could safely be discussed with no one – not even dear Lucy, who was not a gossip but who had absolutely no idea of concealment. Nor the people one would normally have regarded as natural confidants such as her own solicitor (now on holiday in the Algarve) and, of course, the vicar. He was a terrible gossip, especially after the Wine Circle's monthly get-together.

She took an iridescent fluted cup and saucer (she had never been able to adapt to the modern fashion for hefty mugs), put in a heaped teaspoon of cocoa, added a little sugar and a sprinkling of cinnamon. She could tell her nephew living safely in Australia, but that would mean writing it all down and the very thought made her feel slightly sick. The milk foamed up to the saucepan's rim and she poured it into the cup, stirring all the time.

Sitting in her winged chair Miss Simpson sipped a little of the cocoa. If no individual was to be trusted surely there were organizations one could talk to at times like this? Never friendless in her life, she cast around in her memory for the name of a society which helped those who were. She was sure there had been a poster in the offices where she had gone to argue about deductions from her pension. A man holding a telephone and listening. And a name which had struck her at the time as faintly biblical. Inquiries would know. Thank goodness everything was automatic now: nothing would have got past Mrs Beadle on the old post office board.

The girl knew immediately what she meant and connected her to the Samaritans. The voice at the other end was most comforting. A little young, perhaps, but kind and sounding genuinely interested. And, most important, assuring her of complete confidentiality. However, Miss Simpson, having given her name, had hardly begun to explain the situation when she was interrupted by a sound. She stopped speaking and listened. There it was again.

Someone was tapping, softly but persistently, at the back door.

A Ghost in the Machine

Caroline Graham

THE SEVENTH NOVEL IN CAROLINE GRAHAM'S BESTSELLING SERIES STARRING DETECTIVE CHIEF INSPECTOR BARNABY.

Mallory Lawson and his wife Kate can't wait to make the move from London to the village of Forbes Abbot – life will be so much gentler and simpler. Or will it?

Forbes Abbot, for all its old-fashioned charm, is not the close-knit community it seems, and little differences and squabbles can become violent – even murderous. Detective Chief Inspector Barnaby has encountered many intriguing cases in his years on the force, but the case of the ghost in the machine is one to test even the most experienced of detectives.

Acclaim for Caroline Graham's Novels:

'Lots of excellent character sketches . . . and the dialogue is lively and convincing' *Independent*

'Read her and you'll be astonished . . . very sexy, very hip and very funny' *Scotsman*

'Characterisation first rate, plotting likewise . . . Written with enormous relish. A very superior whodunnit' *Literary Review*

'Waspishly funny tale of murder . . . solved by the appealing Chief Inspector Barnaby' *Telegraph*

'Simply the best detective writer since Agatha Christie' *The Sunday Times*

978 0 7553 4221 1

headline

The Killings at Badger's Drift

Caroline Graham

THE FIRST NOVEL IN CAROLINE GRAHAM'S BEST-SELLING SERIES STARRING DETECTIVE CHIEF INSPECTOR BARNABY.

Badger's Drift is, to all appearances, pretty, quiet and peaceful: the perfect English village. But dark currents run under the surface.

When well-liked villager and spinster Miss Emily Simpson steps out for a gentle stroll in the woods one day, she has no idea she won't be coming back. But she happens to glimpse something amongst the trees, something she was never meant to see, and that means she must be silenced.

Most assume that Miss Simpson's death was natural, but nonetheless, Detective Chief Inspector Barnaby is brought in to investigate. Sure enough, as he begins to scratch away at the surface of village life, a web of affairs, rivalries and scandals comes to light. And when a second, horrific killing takes place, Barnaby realises Badger's Drift is harbouring a murderer to be reckoned with . . .

Acclaim for Caroline Graham's novels:

'The classic English detective story brought right up to date' *Sunday Telegraph*

'The best-written crime novel I've read in ages' Susan Green, *Good Housekeeping*

'An ingenious plot and excellent characters . . . Well written, witty and elegantly plotted' *Guardian*

'Simply the best detective writer since Agatha Christie' *The Sunday Times*

978 0 7553 4215 0

headline

Now you can buy any of these other bestselling
books by **Caroline Graham** from your
bookshop or *direct from the publisher*.

FREE P&P AND UK DELIVERY
(Overseas and Ireland £3.50 per book)

The Killings at Badger's Drift	£7.99
Death of a Hollow Man	£7.99
Death in Disguise	£7.99
Written in Blood	£7.99
Faithful unto Death	£7.99
A Place of Safety	£7.99
A Ghost in the Machine	£7.99
Murder at Madingley Grange	£7.99

TO ORDER SIMPLY CALL THIS NUMBER

01235 400 414

or visit our website: www.headline.co.uk

Prices and availability subject to change without notice.